MISS RATTAN'S LESSON

'I promise I shan't scream!'

'A woman birched on the bare cannot make such a promise.'

He took her silk stockings and bundled them into a ball, which he pressed to his lips and nose for a moment before pressing it firmly against her mouth. 'A hand-spanking will warm you up, so I'll start with a set of a couple of dozen. Then, when you're warmed up, a little rest – and then the birch.'

MISS RATTAN'S LESSON

Yolanda Celbridge

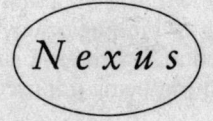

This book is a work of fiction.
In real life, make sure you practise safe sex.

First published in 1998 by
Nexus
Thames Wharf Studios
Rainville Road
London W6 9HT

Typeset by TW Typesetting, Plymouth, Devon

Printed and bound by
Cox & Wyman Ltd, Reading, Berks

ISBN 0 352 33275 1

Contents

1

A Maid's Imperfection

The young man cycled along the white clifftops, allowing the hard Channel wind to slow his pace as it blew his mane of ash-blond hair back from his forehead. An observer might have seen him work harder at the pedals than was necessary, as though to justify his slowness. He wore a black jacket, like a schoolboy's, and grey pinstriped trousers neatly clipped at the ankles, though the chalky Kentish sward held no threat of muddying him. His strong handsome face held the secret charm of a future master, but still shone with the boyish innocence of an eighteen-year-old; his blue eyes, full lips and high cheekbones were set in a stony stare that was determined yet melancholy. From time to time he stared at the blue-grey expanse of sea, eddied with white-capped waves, as though searching for the nearby coast of France, longing to swim there and escape whatever fate oppressed him.

Fields came right to the edge of the cliffs, and the farmers turned to look as he passed. Then, dutifully, he turned left up a rutted path that was the right of way between two fields. Expertly, he negotiated the ruts, as though he knew the path well. He cycled on for two miles, heading inland past coppices and hedgerows and signs of human habitation, until he came to a paved road where he turned right, again with every indication of familiarity. A further mile brought him to a high hedgerow with a gate. He stopped and dismounted, opened the gate and wheeled his cycle through, then carefully shut the gate behind him. Here he saw a vast expanse of tended lawn, flowerbeds awash with colour, orchards and ornamental ponds. This was no farm. It was Rattan Hall. The ride up its long winding driveway seemed the hardest part of his journey.

He parked his cycle as politely as possible against one of the two stone dragons which guarded the entrance steps, and ascended these with every sign of nervousness and a heavy heart. His breath was a sigh over the gentle breeze. He knocked on the door, the brass knocker with a dragon's head clanging hollowly through the huge mansion. After a little while, the door creaked open.

The young man started, as though the person who opened was not what he had expected. Before him stood a young woman, scarcely more than a girl, who was dressed in the latest fashion as a 'flapper': her dress of shining black silk in subtle contrast to her lustrous russet hair, cut short and bobbed, with two artful curls by the side of her full, rouged lips; sheer white silk stockings and black patent-leather shoes with pointed toes and very high heels. Her shoulders were bare, the creamy skin adorned with a choker of pearls in a single strand, and the dress clung to her very full figure by means of two thin straps, so flimsy that they seemed carelessly thrown on her as an afterthought, with no real strength to support the tight dress, as though it might blow away at any moment. The fashion of the moment was for the flat-chested, mannish look, and this tight sheath did its best to flatten the swell of her bosom; its best was not good enough. The hem of her dress was high, almost shockingly so, and well above her knees, showing an expanse of silk-sheathed thigh to which the young man's eyes could not help but stray. He blushed, knowing the young woman had instantly understood his gaze. She smiled affably, but with a hard glint in her green eyes.

'You'll be young Thomas Peake, then?' she said, in a voice as soft as a flute. 'Your aunt telephoned. It's short notice. But everything is in order.'

'Y-yes, miss,' stammered the male. 'I have a note – for Colonel Rattan.'

He extracted an envelope from his pocket, and the young lady ordered him to hand it over. Uncertainly, he obeyed.

'I wasn't expecting –' he began.

'Colonel Rattan is in town,' she said crisply, 'and the servants have the afternoon off, so I am all alone here for the moment. Such a feeling of power! Mistress of my own domain, for a little while at least. Power is so giddy-making, isn't it? I expect you felt that, when you were a prefect at Abingdon.'

'You seem to know a lot about me, miss,' he said.

She laughed, and his suspicion melted.

'It's my business to know about you,' she said mysteriously, 'otherwise the job won't be done right. Let's see . . .'

She tore open the envelope, read the note, and frowned.

'Well!' she said, 'you *have* been a naughty boy, haven't you, Thomas?'

She looked up and saw defiance in his face, then smiled.

'Sorry – a naughty *young man*,' she said. 'You're almost eighteen, aren't you? But that still doesn't give you the right to help yourself to your uncle's cigars, when the poor gentleman is halfway around the world surrounded by his sugar cane, earning your bread and butter for you.'

'I'll be joining him when I come down from Oxford, miss,' said the young man fiercely, 'and I'll earn my *own* bread and butter – and his! My uncle and aunt have treated me with such kindness: she is right to have me punished for my ingratitude, even though it was only one cigar. But if Colonel Rattan is away, I'll come again tomorrow.'

He turned to leave, but the woman put a hand on his shoulder and stayed him.

'Not so fast,' she said. 'I told you everything was in order. Your aunt explained on the telephone that you are sent here for your beatings when your uncle is away; that her poor arm hasn't the strength, and that anyway it's better for a young male to be beaten properly, by another who knows the drill. I've often listened when my papa thrashed you, and wondered what your squirming young bottom looked like under the rod ... Don't blush! You took it very well, and he canes strongly – I should know. So, young Peake, you haven't had a wasted journey, for I know the drill as well as any male ... And, from your aunt's note, it seems she requires you to be thrashed *most* soundly this time – as though you haven't been before!'

Thomas Peake gasped in surprise.

'Newton Abbot was quite a progressive girls' school,' she said mysteriously. 'They taught us self-sufficiency, and that, if a job is worth doing, it is worth doing well. So you and your aunt may be assured, young Mr Peake, that this job shall be done superlatively well. We have the whole of a lovely summer's afternoon in front of us, while I take my time in caning you. Hadn't you better come in? By the way, Thomas, I'm Susan. My friends call me Susie. *You* may call me Miss Rattan.'

'Yes, Miss Rattan,' said Thomas.

'I expect you are familiar with the dear old cottage,' she said airily, with vague gestures at paintings, tapestries, antique furniture and chandeliers, 'or, at any rate, the part where your business is transacted.'

Thomas said that he was normally beaten in Colonel Rattan's study.

'Well, I think it will be nicer to work in the drawing room, don't you?' said Miss Rattan cheerfully. 'It is

4

much bigger and less cluttered, so I can have a good run at you.'

She opened the door of the drawing room, with French windows open on to a rose garden whose scent filled the air. Vases of flowers stood all round the salon and, together with the floral patterns on couch and armchair, made it a haven of light and colour. Miss Rattan said that it was so much nicer and feminine than her father's stuffy old study, with all its smells of leather and books and pipe smoke, and that Thomas would have something pleasant to look on as he was beaten. He murmured that the salon had a lady's touch.

'Yes,' said Miss Rattan, 'a lady's touch is always most effective, isn't it?'

She rounded on him with a penetrating stare that left no doubt as to her meaning, and brought colour to his cheeks again. She laughed daintily.

'You *are* shy,' she said.

'It is just that . . . I have never been beaten by a lady before, miss,' he murmured.

'Then you have a lot to learn,' she said gravely. 'Let us sit on the sofa while you tell me something about yourself. For example, why are you wearing your school uniform? Term is over. And you are a big boy – you seem to have outgrown it somewhat.'

Thomas explained that his aunt thought it appropriate kit for a beating. 'It will take me down a peg, miss. And, yes, I have rather outgrown it. My aunt warned me not to split my trousers when I . . . when I bend over for you know what.'

'Well, I think you look rather sweet in it, so I shall have to find other ways of taking you down that peg, eh? Don't worry, you shall be in no danger of splitting your trousers. Bring me my cigarette box and lighter – it's over there – and my holder, please.'

Thomas obeyed, and Miss Rattan placed an oval cigarette in the silver holder, then cocked it in her mouth and waited with raised eyebrows until he realised what was required.

'I'm sorry, miss,' he blurted, and with trembling fingers produced flame. She swallowed aromatic blue smoke and exhaled gently over his face.

'Haven't you forgotten something?' she drawled, crossing her legs so that he could see the tops of her white stockings, the white garter belt and a gleam of forbidden silk at the lady's place between her thighs.

She made the motion of tipping ash.

'O . . . please excuse me, miss,' he stammered, and fetched an ashtray.

'My,' she said in amusement, 'they don't seem to teach you manners at Abingdon, do they? While you are on your feet, go to the pantry and make us tea. You can make tea, can't you? It is good for a boy – sorry,' she added with heavy irony, 'a young man – to learn a maid's skills occasionally. The tea things are all there. And while you are gone, I'll have a little think about just how I am going to arrange our business.'

Thomas left the room, returning after an interval with a silver tray and tea things, which he placed proudly on the small table before the sofa, only to be reprimanded and sent back for the custard creams.

'A good maid knows instinctively that a lady's tea is not complete without custard creams,' she said as he poured them both cups of tea.

When this was done, he was permitted to join her on the sofa. Miss Rattan helped herself to a biscuit from the proffered plate and, as she did so, lazily crossed her legs again, so slowly that the dazzling white gleam of her silken panties, stocking tops and garters was on full view for a lingering moment. She gazed at Thomas with a knowing and quizzical expression.

'So,' she said at length, wiping crumbs from her perfect lips, 'tell me something of yourself, young man. If I'm going to thrash you, I must know whom I am thrashing. It is a lady's way – we cannot do something properly unless we have a personal interest in the matter. You are going up to Oxford. That must be thrilling. I suppose you are awfully clever.'

'Not really,' said the young man. 'I won a scholarship to my college, but it is a tied scholarship, that is, reserved for the family of the benefactor, not an open one. It seems that I am the only eligible male this year. I'm not much of a scholar. But reading Mods and Greats – that is, Classics – you don't really need to be, just have a good memory.'

'I would not have thought a classical education much use on a sugar plantation,' said Miss Rattan. 'I'm not sure what sort of education a man needs in the West Indies.'

Rattan replied that his Papa thought a classical man could master anything, since his mind was disciplined.

'The body, too, needs discipline,' said Miss Rattan, sipping her tea, then crossing her legs once more and leaning slightly forward to smooth down her skirt – which had little need of smoothing – so that her pendulous breasts could be seen tucked in their silken sheath, without benefit of brassière or corselet.

Miraculously, the narrow dress did not spill out its precious contents. The young man breathed very deeply.

'I am no stranger to discipline, miss,' he said. 'I can . . . take it, as I think you well know.'

She smiled impishly.

'I know well that you shall *have* to take it,' she said, 'unless you want to finish your tea and pedal home squealing to your aunt that you couldn't stand a beating from a woman!'

Thomas shook his head, but watched her stretch her arms; their sinuous, graceful muscles spoke of the gymnasium and sports field. Close to her, he smelled her fragrance, a musky aroma of flowers and sweat that was not the scent from a bottle but her own pure

7

womanhood. By her expression, one could tell that she knew the power of her scent to be more terrifying than the harshest caning. The young man shivered. Her eyes inspected him with a most intimate attention, and she saw his body respond. Her smile widened in mischievous amusement.

'Does the thought of a beating excite you?' she murmured.

'Why, no, Miss Rattan!' he exclaimed, blushing the fieriest crimson. 'I am nervous. I hate being beaten, and just want it to be over with as quickly as possible.'

She made a tutting noise, and said that it would be an awful shame to spoil such a lovely sunny afternoon by hurrying things.

'I suppose at your school, canings were swift and joyless – whack, whip, ouch, and over?'

'Yes, miss, more or less – but I cannot see how a caning can be joyful.'

She paused, as if pondering his statement.

'You have been here a dozen times for a beating in the Colonel's study. Yet still you are naughty. Do boys learn nothing from their punishments, or are they too headstrong? And when you gave the cane as prefect, describe your feelings. Were they of revenge, for the canings you yourself had taken in earlier years?'

'No . . . I felt I was teaching a lesson. As a lesson had been taught to me.'

'And did you take pleasure in beating a boy's bottom? In seeing him squirm and shudder? Answer truthfully.'

'I was doing my duty, Miss Rattan.'

'You must not dissemble, or your punishment now shall be harsher for you. Did you not feel the slightest exultation at your power – the power of your rod over another's helpless bottom?'

'A little, perhaps.'

'So you *were* dissembling. Hmmm . . . now, how many strokes of the cane made a beating?'

'Six, usually, miss, in front of others, or four for a dorm caning. The Headmaster would sometimes give twelve, in private. I had that once, as a fourth-former. O, how it smarted! I can still remember it.'

'Yes, you spoke of your good memory. Why only four for a dorm caning?'

'Because that was taken only on thin pyjamas, and not on trousers, and pyjamas split more easily. Also, it was considerably more painful.'

'Well, there is no danger of that today, Peake. It'll be bare bum.'

'Miss?'

The young man gaped in horrified surprise.

'Bare bum. I cane only on the bare – girls *or* boys.'

He gasped and swallowed, evidently fighting to control his emotion.

'Never been caned on the bare before?'

He shook his head numbly.

'Afraid you can't take it?' she whispered.

'I can take it, miss,' he replied.

'Then let's to the business,' said Miss Rattan. 'I shall go upstairs to Daddy's study and choose some canes, so that we may agree on which we think best. While I am gone, I want you to shift the sofa a tiny bit that way – see? – and push the armchair forward, near the French windows. I'll take you bent over the chair: like that I'll have a good long run at you, and you can look out into the garden and breathe the scent of flowers while I'm thrashing you.'

He set himself to the task, and when it was completed, Miss Rattan reappeared, bearing two canes and dressed in a different costume. Now she wore a schoolgirl's white gym kit: nothing but a tight cotton blouse and a frilly pleated skirt that flounced upwards as she walked, revealing her shining silk knickers quite openly, and the mons that swelled firm and ripe under the tight clinging silk. Only on a second glance was it apparent that she

9

had removed her stockings, so creamy smooth were her bare legs. She wore ankle socks and tennis shoes with thick rubber soles.

'If you are in school uniform, I suppose it is proper for me to be a schoolgirl,' she said gaily. 'And my shoes and tennis skirt are more comfortable for running at you, and will give me a firmer delivery for the beating.'

She smiled grimly.

'Yes, boy, you can see my knickers,' she said. 'But you saw them before, didn't you, when you peeked.'

'I did not, miss!' he cried.

Miss Rattan wagged a crooked finger.

'Dissembling again,' she said. 'Don't lie, boy. A lady always knows when a gentleman has his eyes on her private places.'

'Well . . . I couldn't help it, miss,' he said miserably. 'You crossed your legs so . . .'

'So shamelessly? What if I did? A gentleman always knows to avert his gaze, no matter how shameless a lady may be in her own house. As to your thrashing, I've been thinking. "Most soundly" was what your aunt said, concerning your offence of stealing, and obviously leaving the details up to me. I think that six of the best – tight ones – should take care of that. But there are your other – I won't say offences, rather imperfections – since you have been in my house, and an imperfection is worse than a mere offence, as it involves thoughtlessness and lack of manners. You parked your wretched pushbike most insolently against one of my pet dragons; you failed to bring my ashtray, or offer me a light for my cigarette, or serve a proper tea; you have been peeping at my knickers – and my bosoms too, I shouldn't wonder – with a total disregard for decorum. I think all that merits a considerable extra chastisement, don't you?'

'I suppose so, miss,' said Thomas in glum submission.

'Of course, if you are frightened . . .'

He did not protest, but said quietly that he was not frightened, and would take it like a man. A new defiance sounded in his voice, but it was a determination to submit to his punishment.

'We were taught at Abingdon both that it is cowardice for a man to strike a lady, miss,' he said, 'and that only a cur refuses to submit to a lady's just anger.'

'Finely spoken, sir,' said Miss Rattan, 'but you are wrong in one small point. I shall chastise your naked flesh not in anger, but in kindness and correction, so that you may atone for your imperfection and feel better. Now, I think that for your sound beating, the ashplant will be suitable – she is light and springy, and I am sure you are accustomed to it from my Papa's arm. For your further imperfections, a sterner implement shall be required, and for this I propose the rattan – my own name, by just coincidence – which is four feet long, quite heavy and very severe indeed. Now a chastisement of this sort must not be rushed; the bottom to be laced needs to be warmed and accustomed to modest pain, before the serious pain is inflicted. A caning, you see, must be balanced, like a meal. So, I propose to warm you with a bare hand-spanking, say two dozen slaps – not much, you'll agree. The slaps will get harder, and then you may rest, and get accustomed to the smarting of your bottom. Then six with the ashplant, at one-minute intervals; a further rest, then another set of two dozen spanks; then the rattan.'

'It sounds awfully harsh, miss,' he said. 'But I shall take it. All that, and then six with the rattan . . . O!'

She wagged her crooked finger again.

'It shan't be six with the rattan, sir,' she whispered, 'it shall be a full dozen.'

He had not time enough to show his horrified astonishment as she briskly ordered him to take position.

'I'll want your bum quite high across the chair back,'

11

she said, 'so take everything off below your waist –
everything – then knot your shirt up quite high, under
your ribs. Then spread your thighs and bend over,
standing on tiptoes. If you are on tiptoe, you can't
wriggle so much to spread the pain, but I suppose you
know that already.'

He turned to strip, aware of her eyes keenly on his
middle as he removed his own panties; then, with back
turned, he knotted his shirt as she ordered and took
position over the chair back.

'My, you are well formed,' she cried, before pushing
the back of his neck roughly down into the cushions.
'You dangle quite – intriguingly. I think you know what
I mean. Don't be bashful! I'm no blushing novice.'

In the distance, a clock chimed half past two. She
began to walk slowly around the chair, humming to
herself and taking deep breaths.

'Isn't the garden wonderful?' she said.

He craned his neck, with his chin pressed to the chair,
and smelled the roses, watching as her skirts flounced
near his eyes, and the bulging panties moved in a sinuous
rhythm as though her full mound was a live creature
writhing in its silken prison. Her smell, deep with flowers
and sweat and earth, mingled with the rose scent, and he
breathed hard. Suddenly, without warning, he felt a
stinging slap on his left buttock and jerked with surprise.

'One,' she whispered, then followed it immediately
with a slap to his other fesse: 'Two.'

There was a pause, and then the third and fourth
slaps came; a further pause, then the next two.

'I always think it's best to take each fesse in turn,' she
said casually, 'don't you? The pain is more concen-
trated. And don't get a swollen head if I tell you it is
lovely the way your dangler, and your plums, jump as I
spank your bum. I hope that's not too uncomfortable;
it's hard for a girl to imagine. Are you smarting yet?'

'A little,' he admitted.

She murmured approval, and delivered six slaps in fierce succession, which made him clench his buttocks.

'O, yes,' she said, 'a little squirming now! And some nice red showing, earlier than I expected, in fact. That's the first dozen; the second dozen will be a little harder, and faster. So we'll just rest a moment, and then . . .'

He jumped as a flurry of blows fell on his naked bottom with an unrestrained fury that had him squirming, and brought a lump to his throat.

'Tricked you, didn't I?' she chuckled.

'O, miss, that wasn't . . .'

She put a cool finger to his lips.

'Never tell a lady she isn't fair. A lady isn't supposed to be fair. And don't cry out as I punish you. Never. You may squirm and flinch and clench your bum-cheeks – in fact I don't think you'll be able to stop – but never cry out. Or the punishment is increased. Most . . . severely.'

As she said this, she repeated the flurry of slaps to his trembling buttocks, until she pronounced the set over.

'There, a good two dozen! I say – your dangler seems to have disappeared! And your plums aren't swaying at my spanks, they are all tight, somehow . . . I say, Peake, isn't it lovely to spank or cane? To remind the squirming bare bum of its lowliness . . . And the funny thing is, when you take it yourself, it can make you feel *more* superior. Hurt much?'

'Gosh! Yes, miss.'

'Stand up, then, and rub your bum if you want.'

She picked up the ashplant cane, and brought it down with a noisy swish on the arm of the chair. The young man shuddered, gingerly rubbing his sore bottom, and said that he preferred not to stand. Miss Rattan laughed. The tip of the ashplant poked between Thomas's thighs, and tapped something hard and straining, then the tight, soft orbs beneath, causing him to moan.

13

'So that's where your dangler's gone! My, my. I don't think I've ever . . . Well! You must tell me the truth. Do you always get like this when you receive a beating?'

'Why, no, miss, I swear!' he cried. 'I told you – I have never been beaten by a lady before!'

'Hmm,' she said, allowing her cane to tickle up and down between his thighs. 'And when you were delivering a beating? To a boy in dorm, his bum tight against his pyjamas.'

'O, miss, it is shameful!'

'The truth, boy!'

The ashplant whistled again next to his body.

'Yes, miss,' he sobbed. 'Sometimes . . .'

'Very hard? To the full?'

'Yes.'

She reached out and stroked the inflamed skin of his spanked bottom and said with a gentle, cooing voice, 'I know what goes on, Thomas. Boys will be boys . . . like stealing cigars, eh? But now you are to be a man. You have never been beaten by a lady, but you must have kissed some, with those strong lips of yours . . .'

'A few, miss.'

'And anything more? Truth, please.'

She tapped between his legs again.

'O! No, miss! I know what you mean, but . . . nothing more.'

'You must have wanted to.'

'Yes.'

'So, the thirst burned within you. You quenched it . . . Games with yourself? To bring the juice from these fruits?'

She tapped the stiff plums; he nodded miserably, and she laughed.

'There is nothing wicked, Thomas. Naughtiness is not wicked. Why, ladies do it too, and our juices are sweeter.'

He jumped as she brought the cane hard across his naked buttocks.

14

'A set with the cane should cool you,' she said. 'Six, now, and don't squeal.'

The six strokes were delivered at intervals of one minute; his bottom clenched well before the expected cut. At the sixth stroke his legs jerked straight behind him and he stood trembling on tiptoe. Miss Rattan said that he could rest before his next spanking, which would warm his bum satisfactorily for the heavy cane.

'You'll want to sit,' she said. 'If you insist on this modesty – here, put this on.'

She handed him a black satin skirt with a white frilly apron, which she took from under a cushion on the sofa.

'The parlourmaid must have left it,' she said with an amused grin. 'Fancy – doing the housework, and putting herself at her ease, in her knickers! Daddy shall have to find out which one, and deal with her firmly. I wish I could be there, for I love to watch a maid be reminded of her place. The skirt has a rubber waist, and should fit you. Go on . . . no one else will see.'

Thomas stood, cupping his manhood, and awkwardly slipped into the maid's skirt. Miss Rattan whistled.

'You look almost pretty!' she exclaimed. 'But your bulge hasn't gone. If anything, it has got bigger. Walk around if you like, Thomas, and let the air cool you; I suggest you fan yourself with your pretty new skirt.'

He did so, gingerly and evidently embarrassed, the more so when she giggled.

'I'm sorry,' she said. 'It is just so funny, a male wearing a skirt – a male like you, and in that state . . . But it's awfully nice. Come, sit beside me and we'll talk. We have plenty of time before your next set.

'You know,' said Miss Rattan, 'it must be awfully exciting to own a whole island in the West Indies.'

'Not all of it!' laughed Thomas, pleased at her gaffe.

'Still, exciting to me,' she said, and sighed. 'I am not going to university, nor am I going to roam the world and have jobs and see lovely places. I am only a girl, you see, Daddy's darling, and I am going to be married. I am going to live in a huge sugarplum mansion in Newport, Rhode Island, overlooking the sea, and have a yacht and servants and jewels and be very rich. With Mr Harold F Parkhurst.'

Thomas looked at her, as though her tone discouraged congratulation.

'Mr Harold F Parkhurst is older than I am,' she continued very quietly. 'He is nearly forty years of age, but he has a wonderful athlete's body. He rows, he plays polo, he fences, he sails. He swept me off my feet. It was love at first sight. At Henley, or Cowes – I can't remember where. Mr Harold F Parkhurst is very big in the distilled liquor trade in North America, and Daddy, as you may know, is director of the Loch Mor whisky distillery. Daddy is also, as you may not know, rather broke – *sans le sou*. North America at the moment is a very tasty market for imported liquors. Mr Harold F Parkhurst spends a lot of time not in Newport, Rhode Island where, as he puts it, the swells live, but in Chicago and Brooklyn, where, apparently, they don't. I shall live in Newport, Rhode Island. He thinks me *classy*.'

'And what do you think of him, miss?' said Thomas.

'I think him very rich. I told you, it was love at first sight. Well, time for your second spanking, sir.'

Miss Rattan brightened as Thomas took off his maid's skirt and resumed his position for the spanking; she noted that he was still rather stiff. Before he had time to react in embarrassment, her hands fell, both at once, on to his bare bum.

'That only counts as one spank,' she said gleefully, and continued the spanking with unerring force and precision, at intervals of about fifteen seconds.

'How I love to spank the bare,' she said suddenly. 'And cane a naked croup, to watch my victim squirm and redden under my rod. You know that feeling of power, Thomas, as you caned the boys on their thin pyjamas, watching their bums tremble for you. It made you stiff then, just as your sense of my power is making you stiff now. Power is the only excitement, and if I am no more than a princess in a gilded cage, I am not sure how much I shall really have. Power is the only beautiful thing, Thomas, and above all things the power of a whip on naked flesh. Even the flowers, and the scents of an English garden, scourge our lustful senses. I shall be surrounded by things – possessions that men think beautiful. You shall have power, Thomas, you shall be master of your fields and the bodies of your servants. I do not think my husband will wish me to whip him. But I mean to. I must have that dominion.'

Thomas asked, gasping with pain, if she preferred spanking males or females, and she answered that both had their charms; that Newton Abbot truly was a progressive school, and that girls alone got up to all sorts of games. She described games of spanking and whipping, elaborate rituals of gags and masks, chains and bonds of leather, rope or even rubber; of confinement in stocks or pillory to be whipped on the naked back and buttocks, of love games between females every bit as ardent as those between male and female. Amid the smarting pain of his spanks, Thomas was spellbound, and answered her question that he was indeed excited by her strange, magical tales of restraint and punishment, but could not tell why.

After the two dozen, his bottom was crimson. Miss Rattan saw him look at himself in the window-pane and smiled in delight.

'I knew you looked pretty!' she cried. 'And now –' her tone suddenly became sombre '– you shall become the prettiest young man in Kent, for I shall flog your bare bum until she blushes like the sweetest rose. I shall teach you a lesson you shan't forget.'

17

'I have already learned so much from you, miss,' he murmured. 'You have . . . enlightened me.'

In position once more, Thomas breathed harshly as the woman's footfalls snapped towards him. Miss Rattan had gone to a distance of ten yards, and her run-up was a frightening warning of the pain to come. The first stroke of the rattan brought the only cry of agony from the semi-clad young man. It was a low growl, a moan deep in his throat that rose to a sobbing squeal.

'O, miss, how it hurts,' he said, his voice breaking. 'I don't think I can stand another eleven.'

'You must stand another twelve,' came her voice from the room's far end, 'for your squealing gets you the cut over.'

Thereafter he was silent. The only sounds in the room were the ticking of the clock, the thud of Miss Rattan's feet as she rushed to deliver her fearful cane strokes, and the young man's agonised dance of pain as each stroke made his legs buck rigid behind him.

'Take that,' she hissed, her voice suddenly cold with passion. 'Take that, you man. How I hate you. How I hate you all. Why are you still hard, taunting me with your power. My rod is the true power, the only power. Think of that when you are at Oxford with your fine friends, or lording over your plantations. It is a woman's rod of hatred and revenge that has crimsoned you and made you squirm like an eel. Power, sir, power is all, and lashes falling merciless and hard on a naked body are the truest power of all. There is nothing else.'

When the last stroke had fallen on his bare buttocks and the beating was over, Thomas panted, sobbing, that she had had her vengeance; that he was no longer hard. His thighs glistened, and on the floor between his legs was a white shining pool. Miss Rattan stooped and touched the liquid with her finger, tasted it, and smiled to herself, then told him he could rise, as his penalty had been paid. The clock struck four, and she said it was time for him to return to his aunt's house.

Grimacing as he donned his own clothing, the young man let slip a mumbled phrase which was scarcely discernible – shy, terrified but full of longing. He asked if he might presume to hope for an opportunity to take his own vengeance – just a little, the merest whisper! – on the lovely person of Miss Rattan. Or perhaps – undoubtedly! – this most insolent suggestion to her would merit his own further correction. She smiled coolly.

'No, sir,' she said, 'for much as I have enjoyed whipping your bare bum, my curiosity has been satisfied and I have seen enough of you. My ship sails from Southampton at midnight tonight, and I am to be married in America next week. So it is unlikely we shall ever meet again. And why should we? I dare say I shall find bottoms enough to whip in America. I leave you with this favour – you may henceforth call me Susie . . .'

'But, Miss Rattan – Susie . . .!'

'Go away!'

As the young man cycled from Rattan Hall, with every sign of extreme discomfort, the tears on his face were of pain; when he arrived home, the clifftop air had dried his tears, and his face was a mask of stone.

2

Birched on the Bare

The moon was waxing, which aided the unsteady progress of the two young men as they approached the college wall.

'I say, Peake, hold this bottle, will you, and give me a leg-up,' said the smaller of the two, a young man in a dishevelled velvet suit.

'I can't do both at the same time, Binky,' said Thomas Peake. 'You hold my bottle, I don't need a leg-up.'

'Then I'll be stuck,' grumbled Binky. 'Why do we have to climb in, like felons? This is the twentieth century, you would think someone at Oxford would notice.'

'A gentleman must suffer for his pleasures,' said Peake. 'And don't howl so loud, or you'll have Stan waiting for us with a two-shilling fine and a visit to the Dean. And count your blessings, for if a bulldog had caught us in a low townie pub it would be worse than that, up before the Proctors and probably a term's rustication. It is a good thing publicans respect their betters, and their shillings, and keep private rooms for gentlemen.'

'Blast Stan,' opined Binky. 'Blast the Dean. Blast Oxford. If I'm caught climbing in again, I'm done for. Come on, we'll climb together. Ouch! I think I've ripped my suit. Blast, blast and double blast.'

'That would be triple blast,' said Peake, as they clambered over the ivy-clad wall and into the college garden. 'At least your bottle's safe.'

As he sidestepped an outcrop of the brickwork, he saw a scrap of torn cloth snagged on it, and picked it up. It was a sliver of red silk, curiously perfumed. They peered across the bowls lawn and into the dark shrubbery. Only a few lights burned in the rooms of scholars working late.

'Coast clear, I think,' said Binky. 'Time to tiptoe.'

'Wait,' said Peake. 'There is something there.'

He pointed to the bushes.

'See? There is someone by the roses.'

'O, Lord!' moaned Binky. 'It is Stan. Quick, hide the bottles. I've an essay to finish for tomorrow morning and I shan't be able to write unless I stay squiffy.'

'Not so fast. I don't think it's Stan. He likes to catch you red-handed just as you're coming down the wall.'

'A burglar! Yes, I can see someone moving. Gosh! Some horrid sweaty townie with tattoos. Let's vanish, Peake.'

Peake pointed out that, to get to the garden gate, they had to pass the intruder's position. He ordered Binky not to funk, and to follow him boldly; the presence of the intruder at least told them that Stan the porter was not prowling.

As they approached the shrubbery, there was a distinct rustling, as if the intruder was trying to conceal himself further. Binky grabbed Peake's arm and put a finger to his lips, pointing towards the sanctuary of the gate, and the quadrangle beyond, but Peake was undeterred. He plunged into the shrubbery, towards the south wall, and just by the bricks he saw a dark figure crouching on the ground, as though to hide. The figure had its back to Peake; facing him was the rich curve of a bottom, swathed in black, with two well-muscled legs tucked tightly beneath the buttocks, yet unable to

21

conceal the strips of white flesh atop two embroidered stocking tops. The intruder was a female.

He reached out and clamped an ankle. Binky was hopping in frustration on the lawn behind. Peake looked down at the face of the intruder and gaped in astonishment. The intruder was clad all in black, and made no sound as he moved his grip to her wrist.

'It's all right, Binky,' said Peake. 'I don't think this one will make any trouble. I'll deal with it. Go ahead and finish your essay – I'll come for my bottle later.'

A thankful Binky scampered away into the dark college.

'No use trying to climb out over this wall,' said Peake. 'The best way is that one, where you came in. I like your disguise – but red knickers tend to give you away when you are scaling walls, and your skirt gets bunched up.'

'How do you know?' she said, quite calmly.

Peake reached into his pocket, withdrew the piece of silk, and gave it to her. She sighed. Then he plucked the woollen cap from her head and allowed long shining tresses to billow over her shoulders. They formed a shimmering vision: black jacket and skirt, black stockings and shoes, and raven hair, framing a strong pale face with rosebud lips. Her figure was slim and even elfin, yet the ripe swellings of her breasts and croup left no doubt as to her sex. She did not resist. Nor did she refuse to identify herself: Jane Reculver, a first-year at Somerville, reading Honours Moderations.

'Yes, I've seen you in lectures,' said Peake. 'I'm a fresher too, actually. Isn't it customary in these cases for you to squeal indignantly and demand I let go?'

Jane Reculver shrugged.

'I've been caught,' she said. 'It is fair that you should hold me. What are you going to do?'

'I take it that you were after our roses – our college has the most glorious rose garden in Oxford. But why?'

'It is for my chum, Edwina Cheshunt,' she said. 'Her

nineteenth birthday party. What are you going to do with me?'

'Report you, of course. It is a little late to rouse the Dean, but I can attend to that tomorrow. Then he will report you to your own Dean, and she will report you to the Proctors, and . . . well, I suppose you'll be fined or more likely rusticated. Girls aren't allowed in college at the best of times, unless chaperoned, and as for breaking in, dressed as a burglar, to *steal* . . .'

'Roses grow in the earth, and the earth belongs to all of us,' replied Jane Reculver softly. 'If anything, it belongs to the female more than the male. But it is a male world, with male laws, and a male holds me, so I must submit. Sir – surely there are ways by which I could make amends, yet avoid needless scandal and distress to others.'

Her eyes were wide in appeal, glittering like a kitten's.

'There might perhaps be another way to deal with the matter,' said Peake, frowning. 'You have broken the law, male or not, and must pay. You accept that, at least.'

'I do,' sighed the young woman.

'Then I shall think about it, Miss Reculver,' he said. 'If you will please meet me for tea tomorrow at the Randolph at four, I shall let you know my decision. Now, you had better leave the proper way – not through the front door, but the "official" climbing-in wall. I'll give you a leg-up.'

The young woman's lips creased in a half-mocking smile, and she gave him a deep and searching look with her lustrous brown eyes. Then she returned to the entry wall, and Peake told her to wait a few moments. He made crackling noises in the garden, and when he joined her by the wall, he held a bouquet of freshly plucked roses.

'Take these,' he said without smiling, 'for I could not see you go home empty-handed. If you are going to pay the price of mischief, it is right you should enjoy its fruits.'

He helped her climb over the wall; halfway up, she paused, and her skirt rode up to reveal the shiny red knickers he had surmised. They clung to her full bottom, and in the centre was a hole where she had torn them, through which was visible for an instant her wrinkled brown bud.

'I shall look forward to tea, sir,' she said gravely, and was gone.

Peake made his way to Binky's room to reclaim his bottle, and was pleased to see Binky had not yet opened it. They did so. His friend was agog for details and with the bravado of the unthreatened, described in blood-curdling detail what he would have done to the miscreant.

'O, poo, Binky,' said Peake, 'it was just some little town oik. I gave him a thrashing and sent him on his way. Punishment should do no more than fit the crime, you know.'

The next day, Peake arrived at the Randolph Hotel at ten minutes to four; Jane Reculver was there already, waiting for him in the vestibule and looking demure in a calf-length green dress, beret, and shoes, with white stockings and – rather fetchingly – a garishly mismatched college scarf wrapped around her neck. The effect was of a rather awkward schoolgirl. She smiled shyly as he approached, clutching her patent-leather handbag and affected surprise when he took her hand in greeting, although her grip was firm.

'Mr Thomas Peake,' she repeated slowly, looking him deep in the eyes upon his introduction.

In the tearoom, they found a table by the window, and he moved back her chair for her; she accepted the courtesy with a flutter of her eyelashes and allowed him to take her jacket, which she folded and placed demurely on her lap, with her handbag and scarf on top. She wore a lime-green silk blouse, quite close-fitting, which allowed the fullness of her breasts to be seen plainly, and it was plain, too, that she wore no undergarment: the outline of her very pert nipples stood stiffly beneath the silk, as though to belie the modesty of her appearance. Her perfume too was discreet, but expensive, as though she were only playing the part of a student, and belonged in grander surroundings.

Peake looked out on Cornmarket as the befrilled waitress served them their tea. Her narrow, boyish face looked down at her cup with faint amusement, as though it were a prop in a stage play. They drank.

'Reading Mods, eh?' said Peake. 'Not many girls –'

'A challenge,' she interrupted. 'You don't think me forward? Too . . . modern?'

'Not at all. Latin and Greek are scarcely modern.'

'And that is their beauty. They are of no practical use whatsoever, and so their study is the purest discipline.'

'There is substance, Miss Reculver,' Peake said. 'We should see poetry in our ancient texts, not the dry academic dust of our professors.'

'I envy you, Mr Peake, for you are male, and can see poetry. I see grammar, rules . . . discipline. The passion of young males constrained by hexameters, trochees and spondees, as a breast is constrained by armour plate, or a waist by corsetry. That discipline is true beauty to me.'

'A cake?' said Peake.

'Thank you,' she said gravely. 'I adore custard creams. So wicked. As you, Mr Peake, must think me. I thank you, by the way, for the roses, and so does Edwina. The question is –' she laughed nervously, and wiped a crumb from her chin '– how do you propose to make me pay for them?'

'I have given it some thought,' said Peake.

His face was expressionless, his voice flat. She smiled ruefully.

'I suppose you have devised some penalty that will be awfully embarrassing. Something to humiliate me, for the honour of your college. You males don't really like women at all, do you? I think you resent our presence at Oxford.'

Peake gave no hint of reaction.

'And sneaking into your garden at night ...' She blushed very faintly. 'I suppose I deserve ... whatever you have in mind.'

'What should I have in mind?' said Peake quietly. 'Do have another custard cream.'

'Thank you. You are very kind. It would be awful if you wanted to hurt me, but I will accept what you think just.'

'Perhaps you have some ideas – your lady's privilege, miss. After all, it was your suggestion that we avoid the ... usual procedures.'

She giggled, and her face reddened pleasingly.

'I'm very embarrassed,' she said. 'You'll think me awfully silly and girly.'

'I promise I shan't,' said Peake with the hint of a smile, which made her blush more. 'Do finish the custard creams, I can order some more if you like.'

'I must seem greedy! It is just that I am so nervous.'
She paused.

'You make me nervous, Mr Peake,' she said, with a crease to her rosebud lips.

'This silly idea of yours,' he murmured.

'When I was at boarding school, amongst girls, you know, we had our own rules, and a sort of disciplinary code, and ...' She took a deep breath. 'Well, you could give me a spanking. On my bottom.'

Jane Reculver looked at him with wide eyes and open mouth.

He said nothing, but met her gaze.

'I mean,' she blurted, 'you could spank me, and I wouldn't mind, really. That is, I would mind, that would

26

be the whole point, but I wouldn't mind your doing it . . .'

Peake put a finger to his lips to indicate that she should be silent, and stared at her with mild amusement.

'Yes, Jane,' he said, 'I could give you a spanking.'

She sighed, and breathed sharply, whistling with her teeth, then smiled.

'I hope you won't be too hard on me,' she murmured.

Peake added a spoonful of sugar to his tea, and stirred it slowly.

'There is the practical problem of where and when,' he said. 'It is, of course, out of the question to do it in your or my rooms. I have friends who live out of college, but it would be quite improper to ask for the use of their flat, and I am sure the same goes for you.'

'Not exactly,' she said demurely. 'But do go on.'

'I have in mind a secluded reach on the the upper River Cherwell,' he said. 'We could take a punt – they do them at Cherwell Boathouse as well as Magdalen – and go north, away from the city. After the Moorings public house, the land is flat and rather dull; very few sail that far.'

'I love punting,' said Jane. 'The lovely fresh air would ease the pain of your spanks! When would you like to do it?'

'There is no time like the present, I suppose,' said Peake. 'It won't be dark till well after nine, and that gives us plenty of time. I'll have to be back at college by midnight, unless I want to risk climbing in again, but we might have time for a bit of supper . . . afterwards.'

'You make it sound like a treat instead of a punishment!' she cried. 'Let's go.'

Peake left cash for the bill, and rose. As they went out into the bright sun of St Giles, towards the Banbury Road, he said softly, 'There is just one thing, Miss Reculver. It won't entirely be a treat: although justice must be tempered with kindness, justice there shall be, and I intend to spank you very firmly for your insolence, and teach you a lesson you shan't forget in a hurry. Oops! Mind that taxi. You do understand? If you want to change your mind . . .'

'Thank you – I didn't see it coming. The traffic is so careless! Yes, Mr Peake, I fully understand. My poor bottom is going to smart dreadfully, and I expect no less. I am used to it, and I can take it, though I'd prefer not to.'

'You understand that your spanking shall be on the bare.'

'I beg your pardon?'

'Bare bum. You'll have to lower your knickers and take it on the bare bottom.'

'O . . .' She blushed. 'That could present a problem, Mr Peake. You see, I am not wearing any knickers.'

The lowering sun was golden through the trees as Peake expertly poled the flat craft through the reeds. All around was the peace and solitude of a dreamed-of English countryside, the ducks and fish their only companions. Jane sat back in the punt, at her ease on cushions, and watched the young man's muscles ripple as he propelled them north. She nursed a small hamper, as well as Peake's shirt and jacket, for he was stripped to the waist, and sweating.

'It was so thoughtful of you to get some picnic things, Mr Peake,' she said.

'A little wine will do you good after your punishment, Jane,' he said. 'You'll be quite sore – very sore, in fact.'

'I don't doubt it,' she replied. 'You are so strong, and your muscles so fine and taut! I get the very shivers when I think of the spanking you'll give me.'

'Not long now,' he said, 'we are nearly at the place. In fact, I suggest you open the wine now, and we may take a glass before we begin.'

She did so. A few minutes later they came to a bend

28

in the river, where weeping willows overhung the water, brushing them as the punt glided towards the shallows. Beyond was a glade, with elms, birches and sycamores. Peake sat, and accepted a glass of wine.

'To your health, Jane,' he said.

She raised her glass and touched his.

'To my punishment,' she said. 'I feel curiously excited, even though I know it will be horrid. Here you are, a perfect gentleman, and yet in minutes I shall be a squalling little schoolgirl, bent over your knee and wriggling with my bare bum all red and sore from your spanking. How it makes me tremble! Yet wouldn't life be simpler if every impropriety could be punished thus? None of these Deans and Proctors and fines and rustications . . .'

'When you were a schoolgirl, Jane, did that happen a lot?' asked Peake.

She nodded.

'Spanking on the knickers?'

'On the bare, sir,' she whispered, a pretty flush suffusing her elfin features. 'It was a progressive school – Newton Abbot – but the punishments were traditional.'

'So that is why you are wearing none,' said Peake with a grim smile. 'You *knew* . . .'

'Well?' She grinned coquettishly. 'I often go bare, I love the cool air on my lady's place. But what if I did guess? A spanking! Why, that's noth –'

Her hand flew to her mouth.

'You were going to say "that's nothing"?' said Peake evenly. 'At Newton Abbot, were you acquainted with a lady called Miss Susan Rattan?'

'O! Don't mention that name! She was the Head Prefect in my junior year! O, that minx!'

'And she beat you, I am sure,' said Peake. 'Well, Jane, this puts a new slant on things. You have dissembled somewhat. I guess that your bottom is no stranger to stronger treatment, so that a mere spanking would be no atonement at all. For that little artifice, you have earned . . . an extra refinement. I mean the rod.'

'Caned on the bare, Mr Peake! O . . .' She stifled a sob.

He nodded towards the coppice.

'Come on, Jane,' he said pleasantly. 'It won't be the first time. We shall select some suitable twigs and make a switch for your poor bottom. Why, even I am beginning to feel sorry for it – the lacing it must take. But if you want to call it off, if you haven't the grit, just say so.'

In silence, she got out of the punt and went into the glade, where she began to select branches from the trees, pausing to inspect, then choosing or discarding with nimble fingers. Peake followed her in silence. She seemed to know what she was doing, and in a short time presented him with a garland of rods, mostly two or three feet in length, and the majority of them birch twigs.

'I hope this will be enough for my switch,' she said hesitantly. 'Please say it is.'

Peake scrutinised the flail. It contained nine rods, and he looked her in the eyes, then shook his head. It was not enough; she must find more. She obeyed, and returned straight to the noblest birch tree, where she fetched a flail of at least fifteen rods, so that her scourge was mostly of birch, with a colourful sprinkling of other woods. Amongst the rods clustered stems and leaves of green stinging nettles, and Jane explained that it was a Newton Abbot tradition: a 'Dartmoor bouquet'. Peake nodded his approval.

'So it seems I am to birch you, miss,' he said. 'You have taken the birch before.'

'Yes.'

'On the bare, I assume. Painful?'

'You cannot know how much it hurts!' she blurted.

30

'Then why . . . ?'

'I just don't want you to be cross with me, Mr Peake. I don't want you to think I have got off lightly. I want you to thrash my bare bum as it deserves, and hurt me so much that . . . that you will be cross with yourself.'

A mischievous smile played for an instant on her honeyed lips. He did not return the smile, but said she must bend over and lift her skirts well above her buttocks, then touch her toes and hold herself there. She shook her head sadly.

'That won't be enough. For a birching, I'll need to be tied. It's the only way. Otherwise I can't take it.'

She gestured at the birch tree itself.

'Fitting, don't you think? My arms will just stretch around the trunk . . . and my legs, too. You'll have to tie my wrists, of course, but I think it should be ankles as well. I know I'll squirm like the dickens. When I'm bound, you had better unfasten my skirt completely, I think, for it won't stay up. I know you are a gentleman, and won't peek at my lady's place.'

Jane kicked off her shoes, positioned herself obediently around the tree trunk, and stretched out her wrists for binding. Peake tore some thick bindweed creepers and tied her wrists tightly in a reef knot, forcing her breasts to press firmly against the trunk. All the while, she was mewling softly, almost in song, as though her punishment had already begun. He looked at her splayed stockinged legs, and lifted her skirt. The peaches of her taut bottom were smooth and creamy, as though no whip had ever graced them. White silk stockings were affixed to a lace garter belt, and he began to unfasten the suspenders.

'What are you doing?' she cried with a hint of alarm.

'I'm taking off your stockings. When I wrap your legs around the tree, I don't want them to get ripped.

'O . . . yes, thank you.'

Deftly, he took her long bare legs and lifted them a

31

foot above the ground, then whipped the bindweed round and round them until they pinioned her body to the tree. Then he took her blouse and lifted it up to bare her back, tucking it up on her shoulders.

'O, sir,' she murmured. 'Whatever are you doing . . .?'

He did not answer, but ripped some more bindweed and began to wind it tightly around her waist and back, pinioning her to the tree with a green corset.

'I can't move a muscle,' she breathed in awe. 'I am very afraid that you are a cruel man.'

'There is something else,' he said. 'I shall have to gag you, miss. I am going to thrash you very hard, and I cannot let you scream.'

'O! No! I promise I shan't scream!'

'A woman birched on the bare cannot make such a promise.'

He took her silk stockings and bundled them into a ball, which he pressed to his lips and nose for a moment. Then he filled her mouth with the stockings, wound the garter belt twice around her lips, to hold the gag in place, and fastened it at the back of her neck.

'There!' he said. 'I think we are ready. But in your confusion, Jane, you forgot something. You did not ascertain how many strokes you are to receive. Too bad – you are well gagged, and debate is impossible now. Well, I don't suppose a clean dozen with the birch, and one for luck, will be too horrid for you – although you'll smart for a while.'

Her reaction was sudden and violent. A frenzied squeal gurgled in her throat, and she shook her head violently from side to side.

'Mmm! Mmm! Mmm!'

Her trussed body shuddered in protest. Peake ignored her.

'A hand-spanking will warm you up, so I'll start with a set of a couple of dozen. You know as well as I that the first few strokes, or slaps, seem like real hell, and you don't think you can possibly take more. But when your bum warms to the rhythm, it is not so bad.'

He lifted both his arms and cracked his palms across her naked buttocks. She let out a low, despairing moan, but as he continued the spanking, she fell silent, although her fesses began to twitch and squirm a little as they reddened. By the end of the second dozen, her croup blushed, and her body trembled. When he stopped spanking, she sobbed quietly for a moment, and said, 'Mmmm' as though in relief.

'A little rest, and then the birch,' he said, picking up the flail and swishing it noisily against the tree bark. He stroked her bare fesses, and told her she was nicely warmed.

'A dozen with the birch shall be easy now,' he said, and she moaned again, but ruefully rather than in fear. 'So it won't be a dozen.'

He ran the tips of the birch across her buttocks and down her stretched furrow, where the tender wrinkled bud of her bumhole was just visible.

'Mmm?' she grunted, in question.

He lifted the birch high.

'It shall be twenty-five, Jane. We have plenty of time, and I'm going to whip you nice and slowly, at my leisure, until your bum is blushing like the sunset. Every one will smart worse than the last. Very tight – real stingers. And you'll feel the nettles tickle you. Don't worry, I'll have some dock leaves ready. I couldn't accept your promise not to scream out, Jane, but you may accept my promise that birching your naked bum will certainly not make me cross with myself.'

The first cut of the birch stroked her bare behind, and her buttocks jumped as her whole body shuddered at her pain. Yet Jane Reculver made not a sound. And throughout her birching, there was no noise from her other than an occasional muffled 'mmm' grunting deep in her breast, which could have been agony, or determination, or even a strange, grim satisfaction.

These grunts were loudest when Peake stroked her directly on her furrow, the tips of the birch touching her bumhole, or on the soft inside backs of her thighs, where his birch penetrated so skilfully as to ruffle the tangle of dark mink-hair that hung from her lady's place. At each stroke, she nodded her head up and down like a pigeon's in time with the almost balletic squirming of her buttocks.

'You take your thrashing well,' said Peake, as he paused to wipe his brow, but she did not acknowledge his compliment, save for an increased wriggling of her bottom, as though she were impatient for the beating to continue.

By the last stroke, her bottom was a mass of flaming crimson. When he released her from her bonds, she at once seized his proffered handful of dock leaves and, mindful of nothing else, turned and wiped her bottom quite frantically with the soothing greenery. She seemed careless of modesty, for her front was turned to her tormentor, displaying a mink of quite astonishing dimensions, a veritable jungle of dark curls that seemed to have covered her belly, fount and upper thighs like the flowering bindweed which trussed her. The insides of her thighs were glistening wet. Peake made no comment, but watched as she rolled up her stockings and took her skirt from him. When she was dressed, she took the scourge, then knelt quickly at his feet and kissed it. Her skirt clung to her firm thighs, showing a patch of moisture between them. She sprang to her feet with her face a mask of anguish that belied the softness of her words.

'I shan't forget that lesson in a hurry,' she whispered. 'You have known how to master me, so it would be fitting I call you master. May I have your permission to do so?'

'Of course,' said Peake.

In the boat homewards, she sipped wine and nibbled

Bath Oliver biscuits, lying on her belly with her chin propped in her hands, and gazed up at Peake with the pleading eyes of a whipped puppy. Ocasionally he accepted her glass. His attention was on the river.

'Master,' she said, 'may I speak?'

He nodded.

'You would do me honour by accepting an invitation to Edwina Cheshunt's birthday party, which is tomorrow. You would see what use your stolen roses have been put to. O, please – if I have been insolent in interrupting your thought, then I beg to be chastised for my insolence!'

Peake smiled.

'I'll come,' he said. 'But first, I'll chastise your insolence with a late supper at the Moorings.'

He gestured towards a low thatched inn, a short distance ahead. He roped the punt, and they entered the noisy tavern, where a group of horsemen and women in boots, jodhpurs and riding jackets were well flushed in drink. Conversation was difficult in the hubbub, so they stood silently at the bar – Jane begged permission not to sit – and drank ale, with bread, cheese and a hot pie. Jane looked up at Peake – at her master! – with adoring eyes, as though beseeching permission to take each bite or each sip. Suddenly Jane jumped as though she had been struck. Peake looked up – his companion *had* been struck! A tall, blonde female, in tight riding clothes that gloriously embellished the strong swelling of her figure, stood before Jane, flexing her riding crop and smiling with broad red lips.

'Janny!' she cried. 'What brings you here? A little punting? It's such good exercise.'

She glanced fleetingly, and with undisguised amusement, at Peake.

'And I can guess what exercise you've been up to,' she said mockingly. 'Splendid! A girl needs a little light relief. Can't stay. Must dash! Don't forget the party tomorrow, and make sure you're properly dressed. Do bring a friend, by all means.'

With that, she suddenly put her arms around Jane Reculver, and kissed her full and sucking on the lips, squeezing her in a long, hard embrace. Then, with a backward, mocking glance at Peake, she rejoined the departing riders. Jane was trembling and flushed in genuine confusion. Peake raised a questioning eyebrow.

Jane sighed. 'Master . . . that was my friend, Edwina Cheshunt.'

3

Pampered Bottoms

Jane was waiting under the clock at Carfax as Thomas Peake made his way up the High Street. He tipped his hat.

'O, master – Mr Peake – you are sweet! I don't deserve it.'

Peake laughed as she took his gift, and said it was only a box of chocolates.

'I would have brought flowers, but you might think I was teasing. And anyway, you have Edwina's roses.'

Jane clutched the ribboned bouquet of stolen pink roses from the college garden.

'Perhaps I should get a present for Edwina's birthday.'

'O! Don't worry about that. You don't know her – she might think you a forward male. I have taken care of her present. And anyway, Edwina doesn't accept presents from men. I don't mind if you tease me,' added Jane very seriously. 'I expect to be teased. But we are going to a party, the chocolates might melt . . . O! so confusing.'

She placed them in the deep pocket of her fur coat, a huge sable which covered her from neck to ankle and which seemed at odds with the warm evening. Her raven hair was covered in a floppy cashmere beret, from which hung two pigtails, braided with silk ribbons, like a schoolgirl's.

'It can be cold at night, up in Headington,' said Jane, smiling vaguely. 'That is where Edwina's house is.'

'She doesn't live in college?' said Peake.

'Not any more. Sent down . . . Failed her Prelims last year.'

He waved for a taxi, and when they were seated, she gave the address as Headington Towers. Jane sat folded in her coat as though for protection, not just from the imagined cold, as Peake tried to ascertain what Edwina actually did. It seemed that she did nothing much, was quite rich, and had stayed in Oxford because she was in with a rather gay set.

'She goes up to town a lot,' said Jane. 'I think failing Prelims was only an excuse to get rid of her; she thought of college as a sort of occasional dining club, really, and that she could come and go as she pleased. Don't mention getting sent down, though. It is a bit of a sore point.'

Peake said he could not imagine the strong woman he had seen in the Moorings having any sore points.

'Unlike you, Jane,' he said. 'Your bottom – it must still smart! You took your birching so bravely, and I am proud of you.'

The effect of his casual compliment was electrifying. Jane blushed deeply, took his gloved hand and began to stroke and press it in feverish excitement.

'O, thank you, master!' she cried. 'You mean it? Yes, it still smarts, but only a little. It has gone from crimson to a lovely purple with blackish bits. O, I have looked at my bare bum for hours, and shown my friends! They admired me so . . . You don't mind, do you?' she added anxiously.

Peake shrugged. 'Girls will be girls,' he said. 'And you may call me Thomas, if you like. I think we have achieved a sufficient degree of intimacy, don't you?'

'Intimacy . . .' she whispered, as though it were some new and exotic perfume. 'Master, I should feel ill at ease calling you by your first name.'

'Mr Peake, if you like, then,' he said, and she nodded gratefully.

'And, if I am improper, Mr Peake will attend to my wayward bottom,' she murmured, as though intoning a psalm.

Peake removed a Havana cigar from his humidor, and she lit it for him, cupping her hands to catch the bitten end which he spat out. Her smile of contentment was quite radiant. Before they reached the house, Peake ordered the taxi driver to stop at a dingy wine merchant, where he inspected the labels for a bottle of decent Burgundy.

'Men drink claret; women Burgundy,' he explained.

'But I think Edwina should prefer champagne,' said Jane.

He chose a bottle of demi-sec champagne, and they proceeded towards Headington Hill and the darkened suburbs, Peake explaining that he would feel awkward if he arrived empty-handed. The house was a large mansion, set back from the road, on the city's outskirts, and with grounds overlooking river and slumbering spires. It was something like Rattan Hall, with a high-spiked wall instead of hedgerow, and the house itself was in the spiky Oxford Gothic style, which gave it a rather menacing look. The forecourt was already well occupied as the taxi drew up. There were Mercedes, Rolls Royces and American cars, all conspicuously of the 'gay' set. Jane saw Peake's attention. She said she was sure in the West Indies that the fast set had their own yachts.

'What do you mean?' said Peake sharply. 'I never told you about my family and estate.'

'Why, master – Mr Peake – you must have mentioned it, otherwise how should I have known?'

He looked at her deeply, then nodded as though he believed her. The woman sighed in relief. As they climbed the steps to the front door, Peake said he was glad of his gift of wine, and that he had never before heard of a lady who refused gifts from men. Jane said gravely that wine was quite appropriate. She added nervously that she hoped Edwina would not be cross with her.

'For bringing wine?' said Peake drily. 'Or a male guest?'

'Not that,' she murmured. 'For . . . the other thing. *Timea Danaos et dona ferentes.* "Beware Greeks even when they bear gifts." Edwina does not accept gifts from men; she accepts *offerings.*'

Edwina did accept the offering, though not in person. The door was opened by a male in correct evening attire, like Peake's. Peake thought he recognised him from lectures: a second-year man at Trinity, or perhaps Univ. He seemed slightly embarrassed as he admitted them. They were invited to leave their coats at the cloakroom, where another male with slicked-down hair was in attendance, and Peake did so, but Jane refused. The slicked-down man nodded as though this was in order, and they entered the salon where the cocktail party was already very animated. Jane said that she loved a good 'cockers p' and Edwina's were the best.

Peake looked for their hostess amid the throng of peacock males, their evening dress embellished by red or purple cummerbunds and sashes, and the sea of sparkling women in little black dresses that revealed much flesh, or else sumptuous frocks, robes and ball gowns which did not. Dress was eclectic; Jane's sable coat attracted no more than a raised eyebrow or two. They made their way to Edwina, who was standing with a turquoise cigarette holder coquettishly poised, saying nothing, but listening with a sardonic smile to a gaggle of eager girls and men whose contrived nonchalance paid court to their hostess. She gave the impression of saying nothing because she did not need to.

Edwina wore a sweeping black dress of silk, with thin straps and a neckline which showed the amplitude of her milky full breasts; at her neck was a single velvet

40

strand which held a diamond. The conceit of her dress was that it fastened only in two places, held in each by a diamond clasp: one at the V of her neckline; the other at the swelling of her fount, so that her thighs and bare belly, including her gemmed belly button, were intermittently revealed, and the dress's languid motion seemed constantly to promise greater revelation. Already tall, she seemed to tower, since her heels were a good seven inches in height, and needle-pointed like her peeping toecaps. She smiled, her eyes deep and lazy, at Jane's approach and lifted her cigarette arm in greeting. Jane folded hersef in its embrace. Edwina gestured to a tray, and Peake helped himself to a bright red cocktail. Under the liquid was a fresh cherry with leaf and stalk.

'It's called "Schoolgirl's Bottom",' said Edwina. 'My own recipe, of course. Strawberry juice, vodka, brandy, gin – and if you get to the bottom you reach the cherry.'

'Happy birthday, mistress!' Jane blurted.

'And what have you brought me, Jane? Look at all my tribute! Perfumes and gewgaws and chocolates and super things; a kind offering of wine from your gentleman, who does not know me. Your flowers are passable, but I see nothing gift-wrapped in your hand. Of course I know how beastly poor you are. How dreary it must be!'

'I brought . . . I hope . . . I do want to be super for you, Edwina – mistress – O, perhaps I have done the wrong thing. Well, here is your gift-wrapped offering.'

Jane suddenly let fall her sable coat to the floor, where it was whisked up by a male attendant almost before it had reached the carpet. Edwina laughed in delight.

'Why, the best offering I could imagine, Jane! You have brought me yourself . . . your true self.'

Jane was arrayed in the clothing of a junior schoolgirl. She wore a diaphanous white silk blouse,

41

which clearly displayed her undergarment – a dark blue camisole – together with a pleated blue and white tartan skirt that was so short her blue knickers, suspender belt and the tops of her rather daring fishnet stockings were on show. She wore a striped school tie, carelessly knotted. Edwina clapped her hands and said she was delighted.

'And the house tie,' she cried, 'how splendid. Only –' her hands went to Jane's neck, and tightened the tie into a perfect knot '– there – a small imperfection, which we have put right. Tut tut, Jane! Our dear old school taught us that imperfection is a horrid thing, didn't she?'

'Yes, mistress,' murmured Jane.

'Well! I may decide to overlook the matter, since it is my birthday. On the other hand –' she chucked Jane under the chin '– I may not. I think you may help Gervaise handing round the drinkies, my sweet. Be careful not to trip over your leash.'

With that, she took a long, thin golden chain and swiftly tied it around Jane's waist; the other end of the chain was attached to a ring set in the crimson flock wallpaper beside her. A second chain led to another slick young man, bearing a tray of champagne glasses, who was dressed in short grey trousers and a sleeveless pullover, and wore a roundelled schoolboy's cap. His leash was not attached to his waist, but disappeared beneath the snake clasp of his rubber belt. Jane smiled shyly at Peake and went to fetch a tray of bright cocktails, with which she moved amongst the crowd.

'So,' said Edwina, making no secret of her disdainful and very thorough inspection of Peake's person, 'you are the new beau in Jane's little life?'

Peake flushed.

'Why, not at all,' he blurted.

Edwina's eyes lowered for a long moment to Peake's bulge.

'A little trifling with her affections, then?' she

drawled. 'Not so little, by the looks of things. I wonder what treasures you have . . . *dangled* in front of her. But a maid needs some fun. Picnics, punting, riding . . . all the amusements of Varsity life. Such a pity about the dreary books and exams! I suppose you enjoyed a little more than punting on the River Cherwell.'

Peake was silent, contemplating her deep eyes, when suddenly she cupped a hand on the front of his trousers, right around the bulge of his manhood, and squeezed him tightly and with seeming expertise, as though grading a horse. He gasped, and she smiled broadly.

'Quite a stallion,' she said in a loud voice. 'More than a dangler, Mr Peake: a veritable whip. I wonder if you tickled your whip in my little Jane's lady's place. She had that contented, sleepy look . . .'

Peake assured her that absolutely nothing untoward had taken place between himself and Miss Reculver. Edwina looked at him now with narrowed and suspicious eyes. Her hand did not disengage, but squeezed a trifle harder, until the young man gasped quite loudly. He took a nervous sip of his cocktail, coughed and swallowed hard.

'I know that look on her face,' she hissed. 'There was something . . . something that gave her the sweetest pleasure.'

Music filled the room: a scratchy gramophone record of some American jazz, to which some of the guests began a languid jig, careful not to spill their drinks. The woman's hand rested on Thomas's intimate place and she smiled.

'You went to a good school,' she said. 'At Abingdon, they teach manners – that a gentleman must not reject nor rebuke a lady. So I invite you to confess the truth of what passed between you and my maid Jane Reculver.'

'That would be to betray a lady's confidence, Miss Cheshunt,' said Peake. 'Which is not permitted.'

She squeezed him once more, and rubbed, noting his body's response with a purr of satisfaction, then released her grip. She pulled on Jane's leash, summoning her.

'Jane, you were imperfect, you know, having your tie done incorrectly.'

Jane bowed her head.

'I know, mistress.'

'I have been thinking about the matter.'

'I shall make whatever amends are necessary,' Jane whispered.

'Then I think you should go to my room, miss, and prepare yourself.'

She pressed her lips to Jane's ear and whispered. Jane paled.

'Mistress – I beg – not the full. It would be awfully embarrassing . . . just now.'

Edwina paled slightly and her nostrils flared.

'I said you shall assume full position,' she murmured. 'And in view of your insolence – to keep knickers on, indeed, on my birthday! – I have changed my mind. You shall now assume extreme position. Do it now, please. And –' she detached the leash from its fastening '– you may take this with you, for your boldness demands its use. You have two minutes to make ready.'

Jane left the room, her head hanging, attracting only mild attention from the animated throng. Edwina smiled grimly at Peake and excused herself, making her way in Jane's footsteps. Peake was given another cocktail – a blue one this time – and found himself in conversation with a third-year female who introduced herself as Minty Astor, reading Greats at St Hilda's. She was slim-bellied and of handsome athletic build, with a full taut rump and pert breasts, conical in form, evidently one of Edwina's 'horsey' set, but powerfully perfumed and wearing a scarlet gown of the most extravagant frills and flounces, over which her straw-blonde tresses cascaded. She gyrated vaguely in time to the jazz music, and Peake joined her.

'I only answer to "Minty"', she said through bright red lips. 'My real name's Araminta, but don't call me that. Anybody who calls me Araminta gets what for!'

She mimed the action of a riding crop, miraculously managing not to spill her cocktail.

'Like your friend Jane,' she added. 'What a lark! Her bum will be hot, after cheeking Edwina like that!'

Peake asked her what the argument was about.

'Saucy maid wanted to be spanked with knickers on,' she said. 'Well, that won't do, will it? A Newton Abbot girl, frightened of baring it! Full position – legs apart, and bare bum!'

'What about the extreme position?'

'That is everything off – starkers – and ready for tying. Hence the leash. Bound hand and foot, you know. And more than a spanking, too. The sight of a juicy bare bum, and a helpless maid all tied – well, a spanking scarcely seems to be enough. I shouldn't be surprised if Miss Reculver can't sit down for quite a while. Still, she knew that when she became Edwina's maid. O, I wish *I'd* been at Newton Abbot! Some of their games . . . I was at Faversham. We didn't take it bare, but on knickers pulled tight, and they were wet first, so it came to much the same thing. I suppose you got some frightful lacings at Abingdon.'

'I suppose so,' said Peake, 'but we didn't take it bare. This is . . . rather new to me.'

'Really? I'm surprised. What with owning a sugar plantation in the West Indies. Why, you must know all about the juicy whippings and everything. Don't they still have corporal punishment for naughty boys . . . and girls?'

'I don't think so. I was only there once. I was very young, and don't remember too much. It was very hot.'

The music changed to a slow and plaintive blues song,

and Minty Astor suddenly put her arms around Peake's neck and drew him close to her, saying that they should dance a 'smooch'. Her body pressed to his; quite shamelessly, she rubbed her pelvis against him. Peake put his hands on the small of her back, and as they moved in time to the jangling chords, he allowed them to slip to the tops of her muscular buttocks, which swayed knickerless under the thin cloth.

'How did you know about me – about Abingdon, and the plantation in the West Indies?' he whispered.

'O . . . Edwina must have mentioned it.'

'And how did Edwina know?'

'Don't ask too many questions. Concentrate . . . O, I think you have been concentrating. You're all hard, down there. Not dangling any more. It must be these strong cocktails!'

Peake said nothing, but his breath was heavy as he pressed the woman's body to him.

'Or is it me?' she whispered, licking his earlobe. 'Am I guilty of arousing you – you brute? Must I be punished for being awfully wanton?'

Peake did not answer.

'Please say yes,' she begged. 'I'm guilty as hell. Full position. O, at least full position – I know you are man enough. Brute enough! And afterwards – well, I'll be helpless – I know what brutes want. I shan't be able to resist, shall I? I'll be so guilty . . .'

She drew back, her eyes shining and her lids heavy with desire. Her lips pouted, swollen and flushed, as she mouthed kisses at him, and Peake nodded, stony-faced. She drew breath sharply, as though stabbed with pleasure, and clung fiercely to him. They danced in silence, her head on his shoulder, and her voice crooning softly, 'Mmmm . . .' After a long while, Edwina and Jane re-entered the room. Jane's face was red, and her gait awkward. Her cheeks glistened with tears, and she clung to Edwina's arm, but she was smiling. Minty broke away from Peake's grasp, stroking his cheek and, briefly, his bulging crotch, and joined Edwina for a whispered conclave. She looked at Peake with smiling admiration, then beckoned him. Edwina spoke, frostily.

'Jane has confessed everything, Mr Peake. She had to take her knickers down – of course, her boldness merited the cane: nine with yew, then seven with ash – and I saw your handiwork on her bare. It was yours?'

Peake faced her and nodded, his face still a mask. A faint smile played on Edwina's lips.

'And did she call you master?' she said.

Peake shook his head, refusing to answer.

'A lady's confidence,' he said.

'O, mistress, if I did,' blurted Jane, 'I meant no harm.'

'That is your sweetness, Jane,' said Edwina, stroking her hair. 'The less you mean to err, the greater the pleasure in disciplining your innocent backside. As Mr Peake has found. Well, sir, what's to be done? It would be a shame for us to be rivals, especially when I may have uses for your undoubted talents . . . as a *whipper*.'

Her eyes strayed again to Peake's unabated swelling.

'Minty tells me she has been rather naughty, as I can see,' mused Edwina. 'I think it best if you take her to my bedroom and deal with the matter. Now.'

Her tone brooked no disobedience. Peake opened his mouth, but was stopped by a plea from Jane that he should obey.

'For my sake, master,' she said. '*Please* . . . Edwina must not be angry with her maid. Nor with you, Mr Peake.'

'And were I to refuse?' he said.

'Why, then you may leave, Mr Peake,' said Edwina, 'and return to your wretched books and your solitary punting. Oxford society is more than just the college, sir. It is enrichment of the mind by the philosophical pursuit of pleasure. Look around you – *we* are the true intellectuals.'

Peake followed Minty Astor towards the staircase, attracting admiring glances from the female guests, and Edwina and Jane followed them.

'It is my birthday, and I feel gay,' said Edwina, 'so I shall watch. Pleasure can never be gentle.'

At the foot of the stairs they passed the curiously-accoutred servant Gervaise, with his tray of champagne glasses. Edwina halted and took one, then very slowly poured the champagne over her breasts, wetting her dress.

'Dear me, Gervaise, such clumsiness,' she smiled. 'You must make amends. Precede us to my chamber.'

Without a word, the young man led the way to Edwina's sumptuous bedroom, and as they entered behind him, he was already in position: trousers around his ankles, bottom bare and touching his toes. Edwina held out her hand, looking neither to right nor left. When Jane had placed the ashplant in her palm, she lifted it and brought it down across the young man's bare nates, her muscles rippling fiercely as she applied the stroke. It was followed by twelve more strokes, until Gervaise's buttocks were flushed a deep wine colour. During his beating he made no sound, reacting only by a giddy twitching of his bottom, and a noticeable yet incomplete stiffening of his male organ. Afterwards, he knelt to take the tips of Edwina's shoes full in his mouth and kiss them, then rose silently, bowed and departed, his face reddened by pain but his eyes soft and dreamy.

'That must have brought back happy memories of Abingdon, Peake,' said Edwina. 'See how he took it! And such tight ones.'

She handed him the cane, warm and moist from her grip, and nodded towards the four-poster bed, whose coverlet was still indented with the impression of Jane's body. From each post dangled buckled leather cuffs.

'Now to your business. I'll just watch, without interfering. I want to see how you shape up. O, bother,

I'm still wet from Gervaise's clumsiness. Jane, please attend.'

As Minty Astor stripped herself to her red corselet – she was already knickerless – and hung her dress neatly, Edwina casually unfastened her top clasp and turned slightly away from the others, baring her breasts to Jane's tongue, which began to lick every drop of the spilled champagne from her mistress's skin. Minty spreadeagled herself on the coverlet and placed a cushion under her hips, to thrust her naked buttocks high in the air. Then she hummed contentedly as Peake fastened her wrists and ankles into the buckles. He placed a pillow beneath her head to muffle her cries and told her that she was not to dislodge it, on pain of more severe chastisement; Edwina and Minty both purred in approval. Peake lifted the cane high over the woman's defenceless buttocks.

'This is fun,' said Edwina suddenly, with a wicked stare at Peake. 'When I was caning Gervaise's bum, I imagined I was really caning ... someone else's. I wonder whose bum you will imagine, Peake, as you cane Minty?'

Minty emitted a muffled request to be told how many strokes she was to take. Peake replied that she was to be silent, or be gagged, and Minty moaned softly, either in fear or in satisfaction.

'You shall take as many as you deserve,' he murmured, with sudden anger. 'You slut.'

'Yes!' cried Minty from her pillow. 'Yes . . .!'

The caning began; at each stroke Minty's bare fesses twitched prettily, and a flush of red began to suffuse her bum-cheeks. The twitching became a full squirming of genuine agony, and the red turned to crimson, and then to mottled purple. There was no sound in the room, save for the hard breathing of the four revellers, and the cruel swish of Peake's cane. Edwina's gown was fastened again, her breasts licked dry, and she held Jane to her, her lips moving silently as she counted the cane-strokes.

'O, sir,' Minty groaned, 'you flog so tight! I can't bear it! My bum is on fire.'

Peake told her softly that she was to be quiet.

'But I can't . . . Sir, are you still hard? Does the sight of my squirming bum not make you lewd? Please, cool me with your cream! Spunk all over my bum, sir. Give me all your spunk, please.'

Peake's face flushed in anger.

'You are nothing but filth,' he hissed. 'A whore, a slut.'

'Then spunk on me, spunk on your whore!'

The movement of his arm became a blur as the lashes fell in pitiless succession. The woman's whole body shuddered at each cut, and her buttocks squirmed as though alive with their own fire. Her soft inner thighs, well marked and crimson, were gleaming wet with the juices that flowed from her lady's place. Suddenly Minty cried out very loud, ten or eleven times, in a rhythm that had nothing to do with the caning, and her cries subsided to a soft mewling moan that seemed to make her flogged body glow with pleasure.

'Twenty-seven strokes,' said Edwina. 'Make it an even thirty, sir, and that will suffice.'

Peake seemed aware that a summit had been reached in the ceremony, and delivered three more strokes almost gently; when he lowered the cane, and wiped his brow, Minty began to croon to herself once more.

She was unbound, and raised herself, gasping in pain and delight. Jane handed her the robe and, with her back to the others, she dressed, then slid from the bed and abased herself at Peake's feet. She began to lick his shoes.

'Thank you, master,' she moaned. 'Thank you, my master.'

When she had arisen, there was a single ruby lying at Peake's toes.

'Take it, sir,' said Edwina. 'A maid knows how to reward her master. And now I think we must rejoin the others.'

She led the way, making no attempt to hide the large wet patch at her fount, which was not the spilled champagne. She took Peake's arm.

'You have done well, sir,' she said. 'I take it you will honour us with your presence at my London house? I have parties there, too. You see, there are many women who are rich, and pampered, and ... well, sometimes they feel guilty about it. Jane Reculver – sweet thing! – is one of the richest maids at Oxford. If you wished to become part of my set, I think neither you nor I would be displeased. The services of a presentable and competent young gentleman are much in demand, and amply rewarded. You heard Minty – in her pain, she wanted you to spunk on her. Sometimes rich ladies have the strangest requests. Minty wanted to be punished, then punished more deeply for her very insolence in feeling pain! Posh ladies sometimes do not wish to be pampered, Mr Peake. Or rather, they want to be pampered in unusual ways. Of course, when you are *à deux*, or even three or four, how you treat your maids – your baggage! – is up to you, but I judge from the size of your dangler and plums that you are no stranger to spunking. Minty is a grand girl. She did not attend Newton Abbot, but she is one of us.'

Peake swallowed nervously, but said nothing.

'Well ... things will take their course. Now you must circulate, Mr Peake. Look at these ladies, and their envious glances! And the gentlemen, too. I take it your experiences at Abingdon have made you tolerant? You did not find the sight of poor Gervaise's bum too, too off-putting? I punish the boy – he needs the pampering, the poor spoilt brat – but I admit I can only respect a man, a true brute, who can give it to the bottom of a compliant female, who likes to see her bare bum dance as much as I do: and for who knows what reason? The aesthetic aspect of writhing nudity – we can be Michaelangelos with the teasing of our whips – or simply the purity of revenge, the dominance of one body by another: merciless, primitive and unforgettable. There is hardness beneath your boyish beauty, sir, and I sense that you are such a master.'

Peake was propelled through a glittering swirl of gowns and red lips and eager eyes, names that appeared in social columns and court diaries, faces in the fashionable papers; Gwendoline Hedge, Fleur Dovercourt, Joan Weimaran, Patricia Parcival and Lady Flora de Cante, who kissed him and said he should call her Flossie. There was talk of Biarritz, Berlin, Long Island and Nassau and Paris and Corfu; Peake danced, kissed and was kissed, flirted politely and said little, always examining with gimlet eyes as dainty visiting cards were slipped inside his shirt front, against his skin.

Afterwards, Edwina took him out on to the balcony, which overlooked the river and the spires of the ancient university.

'Oxford,' she said, 'just think! After London, the greatest, most powerful city in the world. Such a collection of wealth and brains . . . and the eager young bottoms of rich women ready for chastisement. It is a cruel world, Mr Peake: whip or be whipped. Kicked out of college! Ha! If I cannot be in it, I shall be *over* it . . .'

Peake consulted his watch, and murmured that it was late, and he must call a taxi.

'You'll have to climb in, I suppose? How childish they all are. But don't snare that lovely bulge on any roses, sir. Here, you will need some cards.'

She handed him a gilt box, which he opened, and found a gleaming pile of gold-embossed calling cards. They read:

'I have already had the foresight to distribute your card to the ladies you have met. It is better to use my address,' she said, 'as I have the telephone, and Gervaise is an adequate messenger. He will run you back to college, and give you a leg-up for your quaint little climbing in. You may receive invitations from time to time, dear Mr Peake, and I trust you will see fit to accept them.'

'I suppose Miss Susan Rattan has something to do with all this,' he said, then asked how Jane was to get back to town.

'Yes,' said Edwina, 'although we must call her Mrs Harold F Parkhurst from now on. And as for Jane, why, she is staying overnight with her mistress. I think she will enjoy eating the chocolates you brought; I shall serve them very slowly, one by one, in our ... special way. We Newton Abbot girls stick together, Mr Peake.'

4

Masquerade

'These scrambled eggs are jolly good,' said Binky
Bevercon. 'I say, Peake, you look a bit cheap. Been on
a bender?'

'Not really. I didn't get to bed. Had to climb in.'

Peake helped himself to more coffee, the steam
wafting up to the nostrils of the ancient scholars whose
solemn likenesses adorned the hall.

'Drop of port is what you want,' said Binky
authoritatively. 'A livener, what? I've got a couple of
bottles of decent stuff in my room, put a sparkle in the
eye. Had a fine day on the nags yesterday, thing came
in at Cheltenham at 11–1. Got a tutorial today, bother!
But my tutor doles out a decent drop of sherry and
Dutch courage is definitely in order.'

'Iberian courage,' said Peake.

After breakfast, they went to Binky's room and drank
port.

'Only an oik doesn't drink in the morning,' said
Binky. 'Far too many oiks in college these days. You're
a gentleman, Peake old chum. Old school. Sugar money.
Tote that bale, carry these bananas. Have some more
port. Fine drop, ain't it? I say, lend me a tenner till
teatime. There is this dead cert at Doncaster, and . . .'

Peake handed over a banknote, which Binky accepted
without any sign of thanks or acknowledgement, in the
manner of a gentleman.

'You are a bit of a dark horse yourself, Peake, these days. I expect you are porking some St Hilda's hockey bint.'

'Not really,' said Peake.

'What do you mean "not really"?' cried Binky. 'Either you are or you aren't. Or is it moonlight strolls, holding hands and spouting poetry, souls mingling, and all that rot?'

'Something like that.'

Binky sighed and belched.

'I suppose I should get a bint,' he said lazily, 'I mean I've had dozens – scores – but honestly they are so much trouble. Always wanting things! And when you get to the business – all that squelching and squealing, and soppiness! Just show me one of these so-called modern gels who is modern enough to put her hand in her purse when the dinner bill lands! At least with nags, you can actually win money off them, and give them a lathering when they need it, and when they whinny, it is not personal. Hmmph! QED, old boy.'

'I'm not sure all women are like that,' said Peake. He fingered the thick ruby in his pocket. 'Some of them are generous, and can take a lathering, too. These girls' schools are surprisingly tough. And they don't always whinny, except with pleasure.'

Binky scrutinised him through his port glass.

'You seem to know a thing or two,' he said, then sighed that a chap knew where he stood with a glass of port, a decent nag, and a page or two of Horace. There was a knock at the door, and Binky called, 'Come!'

It was Brewer, the college servant, who emitted from his gnarled visage the intelligence that there was a Mr Gervaise at the porter's lodge, with an urgent message for Mr Peake.

Gervaise bowed to Peake and handed him a cream envelope sealed in red wax, then departed without a word. His gait bore no evidence of the tanning he had taken the night before. Peake rubbed his eyes, frowning,

55

and pocketed the envelope. He returned to his friend, who opened the second bottle of 'decent'.

'Gosh, that looks important,' said Binky.

Peake slit open the letter, and found inside a note in green ink informing him simply that he was bidden to attend Lady Flora de Cante at her house at Victoria Park, the following Saturday evening. It was signed 'Flossie', and the covering note from Edwina curtly urged him to obey.

'It's . . . it's from my aunt,' said Peake. 'She's coming up to town next Saturday, and I'll have to meet her at the Ritz. What a bore! She'll want me to squire her around, and I don't suppose I'll make the last down train. Do cover for my absence from college, Binky.'

'Of course, old chum, but I thought you said you didn't like your auntie very much. That you hated her for having you beaten all the time, spare the rod and spoil the child and so on. Cripes, we got enough of that at Abingdon, didn't we? But you know, in a funny sort of way I miss it. Bending over for a tight sixer . . . Very bracing in a way, makes a man of you. Didn't get where I am today without it. Still, a bint imposing it seems a bit rum.'

'O,' said Peake hastily, 'she's changed, now I'm grown up. She has become sort of friendly. Likes a drop to drink.'

'Women!' said Binky broodily. 'I dare say I'd be more attractive to them if I didn't drink so much. They seem to mind that, somehow. Jealous of a man's best friend, his bottle! But otherwise, how would I put up with not having a woman? Not,' he added hastily, 'that I haven't had –'

'I know,' said Peake, 'scores and scores.'

'What do they want?' said Binky.

'I am so glad you got here safely. So, Mr Peake, I want to hear all about life in the romantic islands!' cried Lady Flora de Cante.

Peake stood in the vestibule of a large town house, overlooking the sward of Victoria Park, with its rear garden giving on to the Grand Union Canal. The house was decorated in white, with furnishings that were crisp and abstract in the futurist style. His hostess, however, wore a voluminous and low-cut gown of purple velvet that recalled the Edwardian, and Peake's eyes strayed with unconcealed and amused interest toward the generous scallops of her breasts framed against white lace trim. Her waist was pencil-thin, her blonde hair swirling upwards in a beehive. She wore white shoes.

'The cabbie knew the way,' he said, 'but I shouldn't have. A long way from town. Yet so pretty.'

'Yes, the East End is so romantic – although this isn't the East End proper. It's my little secret. Belgravia can be so dull. The folk here are so mysterious and brutal and . . .'

'Romantic?' said Peake.

'Yes, that's it. My other guests haven't arrived, Mr Peake – we are all alone. My butler has the evening off. He's Morrie Lenkowitz – you may have heard of him from the tuppenny papers. Such a resourceful man! He said he had business to attend to. I couldn't refuse! It makes me shiver to think what sort of business it is. He is so . . . brooding.'

Peake followed her into the spacious white salon, where a refreshment buffet awaited on a table of translucent marble rimmed with chrome strips, in the shape of a nude female. The carpet was fluffy white, like a cat's fur. Lady de Cante invited him to make them both cocktails.

Throw in anything, as long as it's colourful,' she said. 'I feel rather gay tonight.'

Peake obeyed, and sat beside her on a white leather sofa.

'Now you must tell me all about yourself, Mr Peake, all about St Botolph and Mayfair, and Susie Rattan – I gather you were well trained under her attentions! – and your maid, dear Jane Reculver. Her bottom is testimony to your masterful prowess. A man who is prepared to make a lady squirm is most fascinating. How I love fascinating men!'

'It seems there isn't much to tell, Lady de Cante –'

'Flossie, sir. It's how I'm known in the Mile End Road.'

'Well, you seem to know all about me, Flossie. And as for being masterful, well, I admit that Jane did deserve chastisement, which I administered.'

'And Minty Astor! The lucky girl!'

'Flossie, you must not exaggerate,' said Peake with a smile. 'You make me some kind of monster.'

She shivered with delight.

'Are you? Mr Peake, you must know that there is no goddess so powerful as the goddess Rumour . . .'

Peake remarked that they were alone.

'Actually, I made sure you were the first, Mr Peake, because I want to ask your advice. Isn't that shameful of me? About my costume, you see. I thought this frock would be frightfully daring and retrograde, but I'm not so sure. Is it too, too old-making? Is my corset too obvious? Too tight? Gosh, it feels like a claw! Everybody else will probably be wearing their little black dresses, with flat bubbies and flat tummies, and I do want to make a splash, but it is so confusing being a girl. Will you help?'

Peake assented, and Lady de Cante said he should sit, and she would change into some 'little numbers', one after the other, and he must not comment until she had finished. Then he would be so kind as to choose. Peake said that her corset was a great adornment, and Lady de Cante smiled shyly.

She left the room, and returned minutes later wearing a white silk dressing-gown, which she opened with a fanfare from her lips, then discarded.

'There!' she said. 'I'm not sure ... Well, look, Mr Peake. Give me instructions about turning around and suchlike, but don't give me a verdict till I'm finished. It shall be like a modelling parade in Paris, and you shall be my couturier.'

She was wearing a short one-piece white dress in gauzy voile, which allowed her white corset, panties and stockings to be seen clearly. She was still wearing her white patent shoes. The corset was a 'waspie', and exceedingly tight, yet looked moulded to her figure, allowing her waist to swell into generous full buttocks covered only by the flimsiest and thinnest of silk knickers. Peake ordered her to turn, and she pirouetted, showing him her buttocks separated only by the thin silk strip clinging to her furrow. The tight panties showed the peach-ripe swelling of her fount.

'Am I too daring?' she said. 'Or perhaps white in a white room isn't ...'

'You look lovely, Milady,' said Peake.

'No! Don't say. You mustn't give a verdict ... Do you really think I look lovely? O, thank you, mast – Mr Peake.'

Lady de Cante sped away, and Peake sipped his drink, without expression on his face. She returned and removed her robe with the same flourish, this time to reveal herself in a corset of shiny red satin, even tighter than the white waspie, and matching underthings and shoes. The garments were trimmed with frilly black lace, and she carried a little stick with bells, which she jingled.

'I am a Pigalle can-can girl!' she exclaimed, swirling and dancing before him.

Peake smiled as she thrust her pelvis suddenly and suggestively before him, and then she was gone, to return naked, swathed in transparent chiffon, her hair cascading artfully so as to cover breasts and belly, and a chiffon figleaf at her fount. Despite her flimsy modesty, the big strawberry nipples atop the thrusting

59

ripe breasts were clearly aroused and swollen; behind the figleaf, the thick slice of her fount was gleaming bare and quite shaven.

'A shorn Lady Godiva!' said Peake. 'I like that.'

Her next appearance was as a schoolgirl in a grey pleated knee-length skirt and demure white blouse, rather like Jane's accoutrement at Edwina's party. She was still obviously corsed, for her breasts thrust tightly against the shirt fabric, and the stays were visible. Her costume was piquant, since the size and fullness of her upthrust breasts, and the amplitude of her croup, belied her girlish appearance. She grinned mischievously and swirled her skirt, so that her stocking tops were visible; then she turned and, with a dramatic twist of her waist, allowed her skirt to flounce up, revealing her naked buttocks framed between stockings and garter belt. She wore no panties.

'A naughty schoolgirl!' she trilled. 'No knickers! Whatever is school coming to? Six of the juiciest on the bare, eh, sir? It's the only language these gels understand!'

Suddenly, she scooped from the corner a black gown and schoolmaster's mortarboard, and a short crook-handled cane, and donned them over her schoolgirl's uniform. She completed this ensemble with a pair of half-moon spectacles, over which she peered sternly.

'Peeping, sir? Well, we know the punishment for that! A dozen of the best, sir, bum spread and naked for my cane. That will teach you a lesson, and I'll cane those beautiful arse-globes for the crime of being juicier than my own!'

'I scarcely think that, Flossie,' drawled Peake, as he lit a cigar. 'Your globes are perfection itself – juicier than any I could imagine, and –'

'And what, sir?' she panted.

'Why, if I didn't know you were playacting, I'd say they were begging to be spanked.'

'My bum spanked, sir? Bare, I suppose? The very thought!'

Her peals of laughter echoed up the staircase, and her face was flushed with excitement when she reappeared, carrying a feather duster. She dropped her robe to reveal herself in frilly black skirt, white apron and blouse open to well below her bosom, and black knickers, shoes and stockings, all revealed fully by the frilly upturned skirt. Below her blouse, a black corset peeped sluttishly, thrusting her breasts impossibly high and tight together. Her long blonde hair was loose, and cascaded over her naked breast-flesh.

'A maid for you, sir? I shall dust and dust, and if I am naughty, master, I suppose you will spank me. But look, I am skilful at my duties. I can be your table as I work.'

She bent double, her hair drooping over her shoes, and placed herself before him, almost as though she were 'in position'. Her buttocks, almost completely revealed by the thin black thong at her furrow, became taut and thrust up to form a table. Peake placed his drink on one bare buttock, and she began to polish his shoes with her feathers.

'An ashtray for your cigar, sir,' she whispered, and one fesse magically trembled. Peake tapped the end of his cigar, and an inch of ash fell neatly into her furrow, which she clenched as though awarded a prize.

She held position and waited until his cigar was smoked, his cocktail drained, and her furrow brimmed with ash.

'I like you as a maid, Flossie,' said Peake.

'Thank you, master,' she replied. 'and do you approve of my portion? My bum? I love the smell of a cigar.'

'You have a most intriguing portion.'

She wiggled the globes of her portion and the ash cascaded to the floor in a swirl of powder which speckled the white pile of the carpet. She began to dust, ineffectually.

'Silly me,' she murmured.

'Silly you,' said Peake.

'I am a bad girl, a naughty clumsy maid.'

'What's worse, you've dirtied my shoes with the ash. Clean them, maid. Properly. With your tongue.'

Lady de Cante knelt, trembling slightly, and began to lick Peake's shoes, all the while allowing him a full view of the shivering jellies of her buttocks. Then, without a word, Peake took her by the hair and pulled her so that she was spread across his knee, with her buttocks up.

'You have time to spank me, master, before the guests arrive,' she whispered.

'Yes,' he said. 'I want you to remove those panties, for you'll take it bare.'

'O, master! You are a brute!' she cried. 'My panties are so small, I am almost bare!'

'The panties, Lady de Cante,' he said.

She obeyed, and wriggled out of her panties, which she handed to him, turning her face away in shame. He pulled her hair to bring her face towards him. Her eyes were heavy, her lips full and slack. He balled the panties and thrust them into her mouth to gag her.

'That way, the neighbours shan't hear you squeal.'

Peake lifted his arm and began to spank her bare buttocks. At first his blows were slow, but quickened and became harder as her bottom flushed, grew pink, and then bright red. He spanked her for a very long time, and at the end of her punishment, the slaps were so strong that at each spank her legs jerked straight out behind her and her bottom squirmed in real distress. When he released her, the tight skin of her bum was deep crimson at the edges, where his fingertips had caught her. Her eyes, like her inner thighs, glistened with moisture. Peake removed her gag and threw the panties to the floor. Her lips trembled.

'My bottom is so sore! Mmm, she smarts. We are all alone, master. Please do not hurt me any more.'

'That is for me to decide, maid,' said Peake. 'Who are Lady Flora's guests?'

'O . . . Joan Weimaran, Gwendoline Hedge, and their chaps, of course.'

'And where are they?'

'I . . . they . . .'

'There are no guests, are there, Flossie?'

'N – no, master.'

'So . . . you are a liar as well as a slut.'

'Mmm! May your slut serve you to eat, master?'

Peake nodded agreement, and Lady de Cante went out, returning with a goblet of wine and a loaf of French bread.

There was neither plate nor cutlery; she approached the sofa and positioned herself between Peake's legs, then slowly leaned backwards with perfect poise until she was supported by her shoulders on the cushions, and her thighs and fount formed a table for the goblet and bread. These she placed on herself, the wine poised on her tensed flat belly, the bread nestling between the glistening folds of her naked fount.

'There is sauce for your bread, master,' she whispered, opening her thighs to reveal the moist pink flesh within, gleaming with her juice.

Peake broke off a piece of bread, dipped it, and thoughtfully chewed the sopping morsel, which he washed down with a draught of wine.

'I have come here to meet gay society,' he said, 'and I find nothing but a lying slut, attempting to show disrespect. What are you, Flossie?'

'A lying slut, master.'

'And what happens to lying sluts, who let down the honour of the school, the good name of Newton Abbot?'

'Why, they are punished most sternly, master.'

'And these guests, who have shown disrespect also – all of them deserve to be punished, I think. You shall be

63

Joan and Gwendoline, Flossie, and they shall each confess the truth about themselves, they shall take the appropriate punishment – and then Lady Flora de Cante shall be chastised last and fiercest. You have a cane there – good. I have no time to catch the last train, so we have all night, as long as our just chastisements do not wake the neighbours.'

'I beg you, master, show mercy!' she cried.

'The cane will do . . . to begin with.'

Peake ate every scrap of moistened bread and drained his goblet of claret. Then he took another cigar and ordered her to light it. When it was smoking, he took the mouth and placed it firmly between the fleshy, swollen lips of her lady's place, ordering her to puff vigorously so that the cigar did not go out. Her hips and belly writhed as plumes of the cigar smoke from her fount wreathed Peake's nostrils, and he sat in silent contemplation, occasionally retrieving his cigar from its holder for a mouthful of smoke. When his cigar was finished, Peake dipped the end in his wine glass, where it fizzled briefly, then disposed of the sodden cold stump by pushing it into her lady's place. Driblets of brown juice mingled with the liquid that glistened on her thigh.

'O, master,' she moaned. 'You humiliate me so cruelly.'

Peake indicated to Lady Flora de Cante that her masquerade should now begin. Trembling with joy and terror, she scampered from the room. After a few minutes, the front door opened and closed, and Lady de Cante's voice was heard in the vestibule.

'Flossie! I do hope I'm not too early.'

'Not at all, Gwen dear. There is Mr Peake already – the most charming, brutal sort of man. I am frightened to be alone in the house with him. He makes you do and tell things that seem awfully blush-making.'

'But I bet you like it, you minx,' said Gwendoline.

Lady de Cante's voice announced, 'Miss Gwendoline

Hedge,' and into the salon tripped a figure adorned with black curled wig and a tight dress that covered her neck and wrists, but stopped well above her white-silked knees. Her corsing arrangements had somewhat flattened her breasts, in the flapper style, but nothing could disguise the ample swell of her proud buttocks.

'You must be Mr Peake,' she lisped. 'Flossie has told me you are a very wicked beast. I'm all shivery! Mix me a cocktail, please.'

Peake did so, and handed it to her, then patted the sofa beside him. She sat down and raised her heavily-painted face. The visage of Flora de Cante had disappeared, and the nymph's countenance of Gwendoline Hedge had taken its place.

'You are far too young to be drinking cocktails,' Peake drawled. 'I should punish you, really, for your boldness. I don't hold with these ways of "modern" young gels.'

'O ...' blinked the supposed house-guest. 'You wouldn't spank my bottom, would you, sir? To see my knickers all trembling and squirming, that would be awful.'

'Certainly not,' said Peake. 'Spanking a girl's bum is scarcely modern. And as for knickers, why spoil nice silk when nudity is so accepted amongst the fashionable set? Bare is much more hurtful, humiliating and satisfying to both parties. I should not spank your knickers, Miss Gwendoline: I should cane you ... on the bare.'

'I promise not to drink any more cocktails, sir!' cried 'Gwendoline', draining her glass, which Peake rose to refill.

'The damage has already been done, miss. Yes, I think you shall be punished. Lady de Cante has shown me a nice whippy cane, and I think that would redden you satisfactorily. But first I must know something of the chastisement to which you have been accustomed at school. You shall please tell me about the *régime disciplinaire* of Newton Abbot.'

Gwendoline sighed, and crossed her legs, exposing a long thigh shining in white silk, and above, the frilly stocking tops and the tiny white triangle that scarcely contained the swelling of her mound. She began to tell of the horrid punishments the sixth-formers devised for the fourths and fifths, and which she later administered with vengeful enthusiasm in her turn, as though punishing her younger self for having accepted them, and even – she blushed – having naughtily enjoyed them. All girls love attention, even when it is humiliating, for chastisement confers importance: a girl unwanted will be unpunished.

There were canings, of course, usually on tight-pulled knickers, sometimes on nighties, again pulled tight, and sometimes on the bare, with knickers dropped or the nightie lifted humiliatingly to the neck. But there were more subtle refinements of humiliation. A girl might be punished by a tribunal of her peers, five or six girls who would join in the sport. She could be tied hand and foot, usually blindfold or hooded too. Sometimes she had her left hand tied to left ankle, and right hand to right ankle, skirt raised and was obliged to hobble past a gauntlet of her peers, each of whom would deliver a cane-stroke to her knickers, or perhaps her naked cheeks.

A variant of this was the 'pin-cushion', where the victim was stripped of her knickers, and had to hold a full pin-cushion clenched painfully between her fesses, to receive a stroke on each cheek separately from the gauntlet. A particularly cruel variant of this was the 'crawl', where the pin-cushioned girl had also to hold a mouthful of marbles, and crawl on hands and knees to receive her strokes, with double penalty as the punishment for opening her mouth to cry, and spilling her cargo of stones. Or there was the 'posy', where the

66

flogged girl was again knickerless, and must hold a posy of violets or bluebells inside her fount, without dropping any as she squirmed under a caning.

One senior girl named Phydia Marchant had equipped a special 'playroom' where there were shackles and chains and flogging-frames, just like in a real dungeon in history. She liked to make a girl 'ride the rail', which meant squatting knickerless, and holding her skirts up, on a very narrow and sharp plank, which bit cruelly into furrow and lady's place, in order to receive a caning on the fleshy top part of the buttocks, where it was exceedingly painful. Or else Phydia would tie a leather thong securely around the girl's waist, and suspend her from a chain anchored in the ceiling, pushing her back and forwards to receive a cut with the cane at each end of her arc. This was called the 'swing'.

There was the 'freezer': a girl who resisted her punishment, or blubbed, or protested her innocence – ('The absurdity, sir! What girl is innocent?') – was stripped entirely naked, and placed in a lidded box which was filled with ice-blocks obtained from the school kitchen. The lid was closed and she was left, gagged to prevent shouting for help, until she had decided to be sensible and accept her punishment. Since she was well chilled and insensitive, the punishment – the normal number of strokes, be it thirteen or twenty-one – was automatically doubled, and since she was nude, a whipping was added to the bare shoulders, comprising seven strokes with a cruel flail of nine knotted leather thongs.

Gwendoline had taken and administered each and all of those things.

'And I hated it!' she cried. 'I would do anything to avoid punishment, especially from a cruel, cruel master like you, sir. Please have mercy on me.'

'Anything is unfortunately not good enough, Miss Gwendoline,' said Peake. 'I have decided to cane you –

as I think you are well aware – but there shall be a refinement. I shall hobble you, and you may walk around the room with your dress up – it is already shockingly short! – and your knickers around your ankles. I shall have fine sport taking you at a run, with the cane on your bare backside. And if you topple and fall, the punishment begins all over again.'

Gwendoline emitted a gurgle of despair and fear, but agreed to take the punishment for her lewd and disgracefully 'modern' behaviour. Facing Peake, she blushed as she raised her skirt up to her breasts, and held it with her chin as she lowered her panties to reveal the shining, naked mound prettily framed by the belt and stockings. When Peake had bound her, he placed a gag between her teeth: a rose upon which she must bite, and which she was forbidden to drop.

She began to hobble, her bared nates gleaming in the soft lamplight, and Peake lifted the crooked cane to bring it down on her skin with a loud swish. It left a red mark. For the second stroke, and every stroke thereafter, he went to the far end of salon and ran at her, so that the marks of the caning were at once vivid. Twice she dropped her rose, and twice she toppled. He helped her to her feet, and the caning began again, so that when Peake announced the termination of the punishment, the woman had taken twenty-seven strokes of the cane on her bare bottom.

'O! O!' she moaned when he released her. 'You are such a brute, Mr Peake! My bum is smarting so cruelly. I shall tell Flossie! I promise!'

She smoothed down her skirt, over white soft thighs that glistened with oils from her fount. The petals of the rose she had held were washed in her tears. And she ran from the room, clutching and rubbing her bottom with exaggerated motions of anguish. Outside, there was an animated conversation between 'Gwendoline' and Lady Flora, and they were joined by a third voice, the subject seeming to be the horrible brutality of their male guest. After a few minutes, Peake was joined by a new figure, a young lady who introduced herself shyly as Joan Weimaran.

She wore a dress of lime-green chiffon, almost transparent, and so flimsy as to scarcely exist. Her stockings and panties were of the same hue, and the skirt was not one piece, but slit into a myriad gauzy ribbons. Over it she wore a bolero jacket, but with very wide lapels, double-breasted, and below, with no attempt at modesty, shone the jet black of a corset trimmed in frilly green lace and leaving most of the breasts sluttishly bare, almost to the nipples. The naked flesh was adorned by the cascade of blonde hair which dangled carelessly on her bosom.

'O, Mr Peake,' she said, 'Flossie and Gwen have told me how cruel you are. They have had to go and put ice on their flogged bottoms. I hope I don't do anything to merit chastisement. I don't think I could *bear* to have my bottom flogged – certainly not on the bare.'

She laughed with a soft contralto, and said that she hoped Mr Peake appreciated her little joke.

'Bear – on the bare. You see?' she smirked.

'I certainly do,' said Peake, 'and I must tell you that while I am quite tolerant in most matters concerning female indiscretion, there is one thing I do not like, and that is attempts at humour. This is carrying being a "modern woman" much too far, Miss Weimaran. One minute, a girl makes a joke – the next, two. Who knows where it will end? It must be nipped in the bud, and so I must warn you that I intend to punish this impropriety most severely. You shall be flogged, miss, and on the bare you seem so fond of. There is little distance to travel between nudity and your frightfully immodest dress, miss. More "modernity", I suppose. Well, I am traditional, and wield a traditional rod on a lady's bottom, to teach her decency.'

'Joan Weimaran' gasped, and put her fingers to her rouged lips. Her eyes moistened with tears.

'You don't think me pretty?' she wailed. 'My best new dress, improper? O, no! I suppose I truly must be punished for my wickedness, sir. Are you sure caning is enough? Gosh, I am always being punished, but no one ever seems to punish me enough. Why is it that everywhere I go, a cruel master finds a new fault with me, and my poor body is whipped?'

Joan sat and began to tell Peake of the parties at Edwina's, at Fleur's or Minty's or Patricia Parceval's, where all the girls somehow seemed to be terribly naughty, and all contrived to have their naughtiness 'tickled' from them by a variety of ingenious punishments and equally ingenious masters; how, somehow the tables were turned, and to show he could take it, a master was willing, or obliged by the force of hockey-toughened female arms, to lower his trousers and bend over, for a smart thirteen on the bare with ashplant or even – she gulped – even the rattan!

Peake said he knew a fellow who had taken the rattan, from Susan Rattan herself, and he believed it hurt like the devil. Joan said that Flossie de Cante was chums with Susan, and that Susan had given her a rattan as a keepsake before she went to America, and she kept it by her bed, and –

There was a pause. Peake looked into Joan Weimaran's trembling eyes. Then he whispered that she must fetch the rattan.

A look of horror engulfed her.

'No!' she moaned, in deep anguish. 'I didn't mean . . .'

'The rattan, miss. Go to Lady de Cante's bedroom and remove your knickers. Fetch the rattan, bring it to me between your teeth, approach me on all fours, with your naked buttocks proud, and kneel to present it. At once.'

His tone was mild, but brooked no refusal. Biting her

lip, Joan Weimaran slunk from the room. After two minutes there was a scratching at the door, and she entered at a crawl. The fierce length of the rattan was held between her pearly teeth; her eyes were piteous. She approached Peake, and raised her face, allowing him to take the cane, which he flexed and then swished harshly in the air an inch from her shoulder.

'O please, sir, be merciful,' she gasped, 'I am a naughty girl, I know, and deserve to be caned, but ... the rattan!'

Peake stroked the tip of the heavy cane across the taut skin of her bare backside, the two globes thrust trembling upwards, like puppies begging.

'Three or four perhaps, I could stand. I am bare for you! But no more, I beg you. Please show kindness.'

Peake continued to stroke her skin, inflamed and crimson from previous beating.

'No,' he said. 'Stand up and touch your toes, miss.'

For all her pleading, Joan Weimaran took her caning well. At each stroke, her legs, buttocks and back shuddered in time, like the leaves of a flower, with the petals of her dress fluttering around her naked limbs. Yet there was not a sound from her, apart from one sharp moan as the first cut lashed her bare buttocks, and a strangled sob when Peake put down the cane after the fifteenth. The buttocks were deep crimson bordered with livid streaks of purple. Joan pulled her knickers up and rushed from the room.

Minutes later, there were agitated voices from the staircase: Joan's, and a deeper, apparently male, voice.

'No, Reggie, no!'

'I'll thrash him within an inch of his life! No sister of mine shall be insulted thus!'

'But he is strong ... brutal! And I deserved it! Deserved to be flogged. He will fight.'

'Then I'll carry him upstairs, and truss him to the whipping post, and flog him like a common sailor!'

'No, Reggie, no!'

With that, the figure of a well-muscled young man burst into the room, clad in a naval uniform, but barefoot, with blond hair coiffed in a rakish shock above the forehead. Peake sprang forward. The fight was brief but fierce, with Peake delivering several crushing blows to the soft breast and belly of the intruder, who eventually grunted and gave up with a moan of despair, although the muscled body still seemed to throb with a strength that had not been put to complete use in the combat.

Peake dragged the moaning body upstairs by the hair, which was longer than naval practice might allow, and took it into Lady de Cante's bedroom. There, before him, stood a whipping-frame of dark oak with thongs to buckle wrists and ankles. Hanging on its side was a whip with nine thongs of braided leather, a cat-o'-nine-tails. The officer began to struggle and howl curses. Peake slammed him against the whipping-frame and had him secured by the tight thongs.

'O!' squealed Reggie. 'How they bite! I've had enough. I give in. Do not flog me, sir!'

Peake made no answer. He ripped the cloth from the sailor's body, until 'Reggie Weimaran' was entirely nude but for a black satin woman's corset. This too was unfastened and torn from the body, leaving it quivering and pale in the moonlight that bathed the room. The narrow waist ripened into buttocks that were full and lush and brilliant with the purple of previous chastisements. Peake found cords, and wound them round and around the scented trim waist, binding it in a fiercer corset to the frame, so that the body of the miscreant was entirely helpless. Then he picked up the cat and laid a hard stroke across his victim's straining shoulders. The naked sailor screamed, the voice a frenzied woman's contralto.

'I beg you, sir, I beg you ... Aaaah!' The entreaties

ceased as a second lash left nine imprints across the naked flesh.

After three strokes to the back, Peake dealt three to the upper thighs, right underneath the buttocks, until they too flushed red. Then he alternated the strokes, pacing them at intervals of one minute: three to back, three to buttocks, taking care to stroke the fleshy tops as well, so that their flesh became a mosaic of crimson and purple.

The flogging continued for two hours, during which the victim did not cease screaming, a high ululation of pain that was beyond pain. Peake's admonishment to silence, lest the neighbours awake, was ignored. Intent on his work, he too ignored the screams. Three times Peake paused to fetch a bucket of icy water, which he threw over his trembling victim. The sky outside grew pale.

When the naked body hung limp and sobbing in its bonds, Peake yawned and threw down his whip, then stretched out on the bed and fell asleep, lulled by the soft croon of pain that came from his naked, hanging victim. He awoke to see bright daylight. The naked body of Lady Flora de Cante, livid with the blossom of her chastisements, hung helplessly trussed to the flogging-frame before him.

'If you release me, master, I shall make you your breakfast,' came a small voice.

He stretched and rose, then unbound Lady de Cante. She turned to face him, her eyes bright with joy and her face flushed.

'O, master!' she cried. 'What a night! What a glorious, glorious night . . .'

Naked, she scampered from the room, to return in only a minute with a breakfast tray. She was dressed once more in her frilly maid's uniform, and bore the tray on her back. He ate his breakfast, impeccably prepared, while she crouched motionless before him, her

73

buttocks raised so that as he ate, her purple flesh, tinged with black and trembling slightly, was constantly in his view. He wiped his mouth with his napkin to signify that his meal was at an end, then noticed a small silver dish at one side of the tray. He opened it: inside was a large gleaming emerald. Peake put it in his pocket.

'You were admirably rapid at preparing breakfast, Flossie,' he said.

'O, that was Lenkowitz,' she replied. 'He always has breakfast ready at just the right time.'

'The butler? You mean . . . he has been here all along? I thought he had business.'

'It is usually the sort of business that is over rather suddenly,' said Lady de Cante. 'I told you he was a resourceful man. And besides, he helps me with my costumes. Now, sir, you said that Lady Flora de Cante would be punished last and fiercest. That obligation has still to be met.'

She lifted her skirt to bare her bottom, then bent over in position. She nodded at the cat-o'-nine-tails, and he picked it up.

'Thank you, master,' said Lady Flora de Cante. 'I do hope you enjoyed the party. By the way, there is no need to worry about waking the neighbours, for there is no one at home in the houses on either side.'

'How do you know, Flossie?' said Peake.

'I keep them that way. I own them,' said Lady de Cante.

Her purpled buttocks quivered in joyful anticipation of the new day's whipping.

5

Realism

'O, madam, please do not spank my bare bottom!' cried the black girl, bent over her mistress's knee. Her white panties were a pretty contrast to velvet skin, and the frilly maid's outfit sat so skimpily on the powerful curves of her buttocks and back that it seemed an outrageously amusing conceit.

'I could not bare the indignity of being naked, and having my panties savagely removed, to make my bottom all hot and smarting! I'll do anything – extra drudgery, I'll wash out the stables, clean my master's underthings till they sparkle – anything but a bare-bottom spanking!'

'It is too late, slut!' cried the European woman over whose stockinged knee the black girl struggled. 'You must pay the penalty for your horrid misdeeds, in the traditional fashion of the Lacedaemonians! And if you are wilful and insolent, I'll spank you, not with my bare hand, but with this leather copy of the works of Aristotle, which will hurt much more!'

'Ooo!' squealed the black girl, her buttocks writhing heartily as the white knicker-silk was pulled down and her full orbs were revealed to the spectators.

'All right,' said the woman in spectacles, carrying a large folio of papers, 'that was admirable. Take a break, girls – Lucinda, remember to squirm the bum as much as possible, we can't have enough squirming. It suggests the earthy symbiosis of your relationship. Now what can I do for you, sir?'

Peake introduced himself, and proffered his card.

'You are Juliet Haize, the director?' he said. 'Edwina Cheshunt bade me attend you.'

He pronounced 'director' with sufficient reverence to thaw her intial irritation. The woman nodded her assent. She was a handsome female, full-figured in a sombre grey shirt and grey woollen skirt which did not quite cover her knees: sensible shoes and dark blue stockings. Her hair was knotted in a white kerchief.

'O,' she said, 'you must be the young man Edwina spoke of – I take it you have acted before?'

'Not exactly,' said Peake.

'Meaning no,' said Juliet Haize. 'Why can men never speak directly? Well, Edwina is a flibbertigibbet, and not quite serious – she knows nothing of the plays of Ibsen or Shaw! – but she is a good judge of character. It seems you know all about the Caribbean, and the barbarous practices of our colonial ancestors – well, your ancestors. And ... you look quite strong, which is mostly what the part requires.'

Peake said that Edwina had explained very little.

'I am directing the lost play of Aristophanes, *The Drudges*, she explained.

Peake said he was unfamiliar with the work.

'That is because it is lost,' she said, clutching her brow. 'I discovered it myself, in the Bodleian Library, by chance – or, as I prefer, by fate. Erato, the muse of poetry, sent me there! Of course the professors, blinkered fools, will have nothing of it, they say it is a bawdy seventeenth-century forgery by John Wilmot, Earl of Rochester. The University dramatic society spurns it, which is typical. Why, they refuse to let me direct Molinari or Astrakhan or Witz or Gudenowsky, preferring sugary romantic confections which, like their beloved Shakespeare, have no ideas in them. So I have taken this hall in unfashionable Jericho – with Aristophanes, I shall rouse the working classes away from their beer and skittles.'

Peake asked what his role should be, and was told that he was to play Phryne, an oppressive slave mistress.

'*The Drudges*, you see, concerns a slave uprising in ancient Lacedaemonia, or as we know it, the militaristic society of Sparta. The Spartan men are away at war, leaving their womenfolk as mistresses of the city. The female slaves, tired of constant punishment for their misdemeanours, revolt, and subject their erstwhile mistresses to the same humiliations as they themselves have endured. But the trick is ... when the men come back, and liberate their women, they find that they do not want to be liberated! They like being freed of responsibility, having the noble toil of the drudge, and it must be said, frequent spankings and, sort of, whippings.'

'You can't really have sort of whippings, Juliet,' said Peake. 'Either they are whippings or they are not.'

'Well yes, whippings then. That is where you come in, as Phryne the slave mistress. You see, you don't have many lines, but in a way you are the lynchpin of the whole thing; you administer punishments impartially. Only mimed, of course, for the stage, but mimed realistically. The modern theatre must be realistic above all things.'

Peake asked what the conclusion of the play was.

'Actually, the fragment is unfinished. A shame – but it is fairly clear what Aristophanes meant to happen. You see, he was a free thinker, a feminist, before his time! He meant for not just the womenfolk of Sparta, but the menfolk too, to accept the just and vigorous dominance of the working classes. Also, they become vegetarians and dress according to the principles of the Rational Dress Society: the whole thing is a symbol of the overthrow of bourgeois culture and the victory of

77

the proletariat and the oppressed females. Thus, all the parts, even the male ones, are played by females – except yours. You are the symbol of oppression, you see, and though you are playing a female, it is ironically obvious that you are a male actor. Witz calls this *Wirklichkeits-befragung* or "questioning". And to make it more realistic, I've transposed it to a near-modern setting – to a slave island in the Caribbean.'

Peake said that he was interested in playing the part, and that, since it was nearly twelve, he might offer Juliet luncheon at the fashionable Cap and Bells in the Woodstock Road. She accepted with surprising enthusiasm, and dismissed her actors, then excused herself to visit the powder room. When she returned, her blue stockings had been replaced by white silk, her kerchief was gone, revealing abundant bobbed auburn hair, and she had removed her heavy spectacles and put on lipstick. Although her frame was narrow, her breasts thrust very full, evidently unsupported, and her bottom was clearly large, the large peaches tight against her skirt. Peake told her she looked very pretty; she seemed unsure whether to frown or smile, and ended up doing both.

'So, Mr Peake,' she said, 'your part demands a strong arm to do a lot of pretend spanking and whipping. I hope you are both strong and subtle for the part. Edwina says you are.'

Peake assured her of his utmost attention. They took a taxi to the Cap and Bells, where Juliet seemed rather suspicious that the flouncy young host greeted Peake with familiarity.

'I am sure dear Edwina made the right choice,' she said as they were seated at a window table. 'You *are* thoroughly bourgeois. One of the oppressor, male carnivorous class.'

Peake said he had not thought much about the matter.

'Men never think!' she exclaimed. 'Apart from Bernard Shaw, and Witz, and Gudenowski, that is.'

She ordered the largest sirloin, very rare, and when the food arrived, she attacked it as though the red meat were a class enemy. Peake asked gravely if she were not a vegetarian. She waved her fork, and said with full mouth, 'Don't you see that by eating as a carnivore I am ironically mocking the male bourgeois carnivore class according to *Wirklichkeitsbefragung*? And anyway, since the carnivorous bourgeois phallocracy is doomed, if you are on the *Titanic* you might as well travel first class.'

Peake said he supposed his own steak was not ironic, though it no doubt tasted as good. He asked about the actress Lucinda, a genuine black female. Juliet's eyes glowed, and she took another hefty gulp of Burgundy.

'I had thought of casting her as Phryne,' she sighed, 'but that would have been too ironic for the public. She is so strong: the thought of her artful hand beating all those bare white bottoms, helpless under her female anger! O . . .'

She wiped her mouth nervously.

'Lucinda Lalage is a jazz musician and a dancer, you know. She has performed with Josephine Baker in Paris: so strong and tender and beautiful! In the play she is to be the leader of the slaves' revolt. A special friend of Edwina's . . . You must be careful when acting with her, Mr Peake. The spanking must all be strictly mimed. She has a harsh temper: I dread to think of her spanking in vengeance, on a bare bottom . . . yours, or even on my own.'

She sighed again, and blushed. She explained that dress rehearsal would be in two weeks – the script was very simple, and Peake's part exceedingly so – and the production for one week after that. But before she accepted Peake, there was an adjudication she had to make, for which it would be necessary to return to the hall. There was no further rehearsal this afternoon, but she had to make sure of his suitability, and to that end Lucinda Lalage would attend them after her own luncheon with Edwina. Edwina had been most insistent that Mr Peake should show his mettle. It was a bright autumn day, and they decided to walk back, their two bottles of claret making them good-humoured. Once or twice on the way, Juliet pretended to slip, and clutched Peake's hand for reassurance. She seemed both expectant and relieved at Peake's easy acceptance of her demands. At the deserted hall, she carefully closed the door; Peake asked for a script, assuming he would have to read some lines.

'The script is not important at this stage. Your lines are mostly simple commands, to strip or bend over for punishment. I must audition you for what happens afterwards.'

'You mean . . . miming a spanking?'

'Not strictly mime. The spanking must be just hard enough to make a convincing and realistic noise. I am to play a token role, as a female slave, therefore you will attend to my bottom, please, Mr Peake. Are you shocked?'

Peake gravely shook his head, and said that realism was essential to art.

'Perhaps you are not as bourgeois as I thought,' said Juliet with approval. 'You had better take me over your knee, I suppose. There are twenty-three females to be spanked in this play, Mr Peake, and you shall have the lion's share of the spanking. I wish to be sure of your stamina.'

The stage set represented Phryne's drawing room, where much of the action took place. There was a sofa and armchair, a table and various fans and tropical accoutrements. Juliet ordered Peake to sit on the sofa.

'Right!' said Juliet. 'I shall bend over your knee – you must hold me down, for I shall pretend to wriggle a lot – and you must give me a spanking. Not hard enough

80

to hurt, of course, but hard enough to make a good cracking noise. Lucinda should be here, to stand at the back and judge – O, where is she? Bother, we shall just start without her, to get me – to get you accustomed to things.'

She lay down rather gingerly across Peake's thigh, then allowed the weight of her body to press fully on him, totally relaxing her muscles in a position of complete helplessness. She lifted her skirts, revealing a pair of very high white panties and a garter belt of lace which was surprisingly frilly. Peake lifted his arm.

'Have't you forgotten something?' she said. 'Spankings are given on the bare, aren't they? I'm rather new to this.'

Her voice dropped to a murmur as she said this, and had the resonance of untruth. Peake pulled her panties down in a swift motion, to reveal two full round fesses, taut and already clenched in expectation of his blows. The panties became wedged at her stocking tops, and she said he should undo her straps and roll the panties down to her ankles, for realism. He did so, and she murmured that he should unroll her stockings too, as it would look more humiliating. He took his time at this task, rolling the sheer silk over long, smooth legs whose tender pale skin was just as silky.

He began to spank her bare bottom, laying quite delicate strokes on the skin, and at each slap she trembled energetically. After a while, she said he was not doing it hard enough. For realism, he must hurt her a little bit, must feel angry at her, and then she would feel angry too, and her squirms and cries would be most realistic.

'Imagine that I've delivered some terrible insult,' she said. 'That I've said – what is it you say to men? – that you've got a tiny dangler. Yes! You've got a little tiny dangler, Mr Peake.'

Peake laughed, and said that this would scarcely be applicable to the female Mistress Phryne.

81

'O, you confuse me. Well, your master has a tiny dangler! So there!'

Peake began to spank her bare fesses with force. Now her wriggles came in earnest, and as a delicate pink suffused her bum-flesh, her cries of 'O!' and 'Ouch!' and 'Steady on!' while not seeming particularly theatrical, did not seem feigned, either. Peake asked mildly if he was hurting her, but as he did so began to spank even harder.

'You know you are! I don't like it one bit. Edwina was right, you are a brute. But it is important to – O! O! O! – to have realism. God, that smarts, sir. You are cruel, do you know? I bet you have spanked many girls before. Ouch! O! My bare bum! You horrid man!'

She was gasping for breath now, her bare bottom a squirming mass of mottled crimson, and Peake had to hold her firmly to keep her on his knee. His hand began to spank her below her buttocks, on the tender skin of her thighs, and her legs thrashed. Now she greeted each spank with a shrill yelp, interspersed with sobs, and her whole body was trembling as his blows rained on her buttocks.

'Don't stop,' she panted. 'Ah! Aaah! God, my bum is on fire! I've never had such pain. I feel this is my finest performance. There will be headlines in the *Daily Herald*. Such realism!'

'My dear,' came a smoky, velvet voice from the door of the hall, 'you'll have to be much more realistic than that. I can hardly hear your whispers.'

It was Lucinda Lalage, who was to play the leader of the slaves' revolt. Juliet made as if to rise, but Lucinda waved her to remain in position. She sauntered towards them, smoking from a long black holder.

'O . . . Lucinda. Have you met Mr Thomas Peake? He is to be our Phryne, and I assure you he has a very strong hand.'

'Then he was certainly holding back, Juliet. I have

seen caterpillars wriggle more than you did. I know you
are the director, but ... you do have a spanking role,
and I think my comments are apposite. Of course,
Phryne's hand will not touch *my* bum – I am a dancer,
and my wriggling shall be feigned but superb. But you
English girls are more reserved, and need a proper
spanking to make you perform.'

'Shall we go again, then, Lucinda?'

'I think you'd better. Harder this time, Mr Peake.'

Juliet emitted a rueful groan as she resumed position
and presented her crimsoned bottom once more to
Peake's attentions. Lucinda asked how many spanks she
had taken, and Juliet, flustered, said that it had been so
painful she had not counted. Peake murmured that he
made it seventy-seven slaps.

'That is not very many,' said Lucinda, approaching,
and stroking her friend's mottled buttocks.

Her suit of thin red silk clung to the powerful curves
of her buttocks, thighs and breasts, as though daring
any spectator to rip the flimsiness from her and be awed
by her nudity. It was plain that beneath her tight skirt
she had no underthings.

'Still ... a nice flush. Perhaps you are not used to it,
Juliet. You should have been schooled in the West
Indies.'

'I certainly am not used to it,' cried Juliet. 'Well, not
really. I've been spanked, of course – everybody has! –
but not on the bare, always with knickers. And never
seventy-seven ...'

Her voice tailed off, as though awed at her own
prowess.

'I think Mr Peake's strong arm can take you to the
century,' said Lucinda, 'and if he tires, then I can take
over, and your spanking can really start! Realism, dear
Juliet, realism. We owe it to the Muse.'

Juliet gulped that she was ready, and promised to do
her best to squirm convincingly, although she thought

she would need little acting. Peake recommenced his spanking, and almost at once Juliet began to squeal as her bum writhed piteously under his strokes. His face was set in stone and betokened no mercy, to Lucinda's evident approval. She purred like a cat as the colour of Juliet's naked flesh deepened under the spanking, until every inch of her bottom was a shade of red, ranging from flushed pink to the deepest purple, and even verging on black in the centre of the bum, by the cleft, where she had been taken most fiercely. He dealt the strokes fast, with Juliet's bare croup writhing on his thigh like a trapped eel, and it was not long before Lucinda said one hundred had been reached.

'Still not squealing quite loud enough, Juliet. You must breathe, intone, project. This training is good for you in your directing of others. Here, I'll show you.'

Juliet was ordered to rest and observe; gingerly, she rose and replaced her stockings and knickers, miming an 'ouch!' as the cloth enveloped her glowing purple bum. Gaily, Lucinda handed her the cigarette holder, and swooped on to Peake's knee, with an easy flick of her arm raising her silk skirt to reveal the lustrous dark flesh of her naked buttocks, which gleamed huge and proud as mountains. The red of her garter belt and frilly stocking tops made a lush conrast to her chocolate flesh.

Knickerless, she spread her thighs very wide, even excessively so, and showed the folds of her lady's place and the tight wrinkled jewel of her anus, as though her pretend spanking was an excuse to show off her naked charm. She reminded Peake that he was to mime vigorously, but on no account touch her bare flesh. Juliet was ordered to clap her hands loud at each stroke, an effect which the stage hand would duplicate for the actual performance. Lucinda looked up slyly at Peake, and asked him if he was shocked by a lady with no knickers. He shook his head, and said it was a lady's privilege to be at her ease.

'Of course, for the play, I shall be wearing a frilly maid's uniform, as you saw,' she said. 'But where I come from, frilly knickers – any knickers – are for the rich folk. I am true to my roots, Mr Peake! And I do like being comfortable. Being spanked, which was often, wasn't comfortable. And after I turned eighteen, it wasn't with bare hand. No, it was with a pawpaw branch, or a switch of sugar canes, or even a whorled conch shell.'

Her voice was smoky rich, and tantalised like lush fruits dangling on the tree just too far out of reach.

'Can you imagine what that makes an eighteen-year-old girl feel, Mr Peake?' she murmured. 'To have her bare bum laced with a conch shell, by a master or a mistress, publicly?'

Peake replied that he could not, and she ordered him to begin his playacting. Dutifully, he raised his arm, and knotted his brow to feign anger. As his hand fell to within an inch of the ripe black fesses on his thigh, Juliet clapped her hands, and at each crack, Lucinda began to wail and babble in most convincing anguish.

'O, Mistress Phryne, you lace me so hard, I can't bear it! I can take no more, my bum is a hot coal. Please desist, mistress, I beg you, from your cruel punishment of my innocent croup!'

Her buttocks and thighs squirmed in voluptuous rhythm, as though she were dancing. She seemed like a mighty dark fish, flailing in exquisite torment. She balanced herself on her pubic bone, as though swimming, and Peake scarcely needed to hold her perfectly poised body in place. Her belly squirmed hard against his thigh as though in attack, or trying to burrow into him. On his trousers, spreading below her crotch, was a shiny dark wet patch. Lucinda, in the thrall of her mimed punishment, was seeping with her lady's juices.

Suddenly she cried that it was enough, that she had

showed Juliet how to perform and it was now time for her real spanking. Juliet paled and trembled as Lucinda said she would take charge, and she would have to take more than mere spanking. Juliet was to have the lash as well as the bare hand, and always on her naked fesses. Lucinda took her place on the sofa, bending Juliet over her red silken thigh.

'Lucinda, darling. I am the director, remember,' stammered Juliet.

'Then direct me, miss,' sneered Lucinda. 'You wanted realism.'

Her hand fell in a blur and smacked Juliet's bare bottom with a crack that echoed through the hall. Juliet howled, both in surprise and anguish.

'Interesting, my dear,' murmured Lucinda. 'That was no harder than the smacks you got from Mr Peake – though your bum's probably a bit more tender now – but because he is a male, you could accept it. Is that it?'

Her hand spanked the trembling bare bottom of her director, again and again, to a dozen times. Her voice silky smooth, Lucinda asked again for direction, although Juliet was moaning so loudly that she might not have heard.

'Do you want me to continue the spanking?' asked Lucinda.

Sobbing, Juliet nodded very slightly.

'I repeat, do you want it? Direct me!' Lucinda insisted.

'Yes ... O, yes! What are you doing to me? Yes, damn you, spank me! Make my bare bum dance for your wicked hand! Spank me till I faint ... please!'

There were no further words; Lucinda spanked with serene determination until the writhing croup before her had taken two hundred slaps and was now the deepest purple, the woman's buttocks in poignant harmony with the velvet skin of her tormentor. She giggled, a deep throaty giggle of pure malicious joy.

'You English girls have to take a lot more than us to go a pretty colour. Our bums don't bother going pink: they turn purple straightaway. We are more ... realistic.'

She paused to stroke her victim's inflamed skin with long fingertips, her manicured nails gently scratching the livid skin like a hawk's talons, then recommenced the spanking. Juliet seemed now no more than a squirming bottom, as though her inflamed bare nates were the whole of her spirit. Gone was the bespectacled bluestocking, the coy luncheon companion; she was only a naked female croup, shuddering in her willing, strange submission. Her gulps and squeals were choked by sobs. Lucinda kept taunting her with cries of 'Enough?' and, at each demand, the broken woman shook her head. At last, Lucinda released her but held her by the hair.

'You want it, don't you, bitch?' she hissed. 'You all do. Stand up. Hurry! Bend over. You –' she pointed at Peake '– fetch a cane, or a stick.'

Peake obeyed, and rummaged amongst the stage props until he found a wicked four-foot planter's cane of mahogany with a silver handle. He gave it to Lucinda, who had Juliet bending over and touching her toes, her knickers and stockings forlornly cast around her ankles. She flexed the heavy cane, then tapped Juliet on the lips of her fount.

'Legs as wide as you can,' she said briskly. 'I shall want to take you well on the inside of the thighs, and the backs too could do with some nice crimson. I think fifteen should be as much as you can bear, Juliet.'

'O! So many! It is frightful! I . . . Aaah!' wailed Juliet, her words cut off by a fearsome stroke of the cane across her bare bottom.

Lucinda took her time, counting each stroke as she laid it with oiled precision on the tender parts of Juliet's body. Her deftness led the cane's tip right into Juliet's furrow and up on the soft inner thighs a hair's breadth from the swelling of her fount-lips. Juliet's shrieks were shrill, and yet in her squirming torment, as her flesh darkened under the lash, a glisten of oily wetness bathed her thighs. Fifteen strokes were counted, and Juliet's shrieks had become a kind of unearthly braying. Lucinda again asked her if she had had enough, and Juliet sobbed that Lucinda was her director.

'Flog my naked bum, you bitch, till you tire, and then I can still take it,' she whispered.

'No, miss, I have dealt my fifteen,' gasped Lucinda, her voice almost as agitated as her victim's, 'and now it is Mr Peake's turn. *He* is the one you are auditioning.'

She threw the cane at Peake, who took his stance and began to cane the bare globes quivering before him. He caned steadily, until he heard moans rising above the wailing of Juliet. He turned; behind him, Lucinda was shuddering herself, her hand frantically twitching underneath her wet silk dress, at her lady's place. When her own sobs had died to a moan, she gasped that the caning should cease. Juliet did not bother to pull up her stockings and panties; instead, choking with sobs, she threw herself to kneel at Peake's feet, and clung to his ankles as she kissed the tip of his dangling cane.

'Yes, yes,' she whispered through her tears. 'You have got the part . . . master!'

Rehearsals proceeded smoothly. Peake spanked hard and often, but was careful not to push the willing girls to beyond their desired limit of chastisement. Bums were reddened and then compared with laughter and much rubbing of sore skin; it was agreed that Peake made an admirable Phryne. One girl in particular took it well, a sturdy hockey type from Somerville named Leslie Scammon, distinguished by her large and pneumatic bottom which gracefuly adorned a figure of boyish slimness, so that her bosom was scarcely more than that of a well-muscled male. Her cheerfulness made up for what many females would have considered a drawback, and her handsome face beamed under its short, mannish haircut, as if to dare anyone to question her essential femininity.

In view of her 'tomboyish' demeanour (an American expression, it seemed) she was elected to double her role: as well as a slave girl, she would play the part of the chief male Lacedaemonian whose resistance to the female cause led to his receiving a proper flogging; that is, to be whipped with a flail, bound standing to a post and naked but for a loincloth. Peake expressed admiration for the tightness of her loincloth as they rehearsed this scene, and the sturdy bulge which was visible in every manly detail beneath. She smiled, and said that realism was the watchword. Peake seemed cautious as he lifted the heavy cat-o'-nine-tails with which he was to whip Leslie's naked back, but she told him not to be a dunderhead, and to lay to with a vengeance.

'We men can take it, can't we?' she chirped: and take it she did, like a man, not uttering a sound of protest as the thongs laced her bare back, although afterwards Juliet said she should moan and wriggle a little, for verisimilitude. Leslie offered to take another twelve, and this was accepted. Peake recommended flogging the already reddened back, and laid his strokes harder, taking care to restrain himself to the shoulders and avoid the sensitive lower portions. But he said 'oops' in false excuse as on several occasions he allowed his whip to slip, and deliver firm strokes right across the juicy full buttocks, protected only by the tightest, thinnest cloth, and on these occasions Juliet pronounced herself gratified by Leslie's startled wail, as though the flesh there was tenderer than her muscled shoulders.

'Or perhaps she enjoys it, darling,' drawled Lucinda.

Everything was satisfactory, although Juliet frequently said the spanking scenes were well enough learned and did not need to be repeated as often as the girls demanded. She did seem to be dithering a little as to the conclusion of the unfinished play, until Peake himself arrived with a few pages of his own handwriting.

'You were right, Juliet,' he said. 'The Muse Erato is directing things. I was in our college library, and I was mugging up on Aristotle's *Poetics* – we possess a priceless copy of Caxton's first printed edition, with marginalia by Erasmus, Sir Thomas More, Dr Bentley, and other hands. Imagine my surprise when I discovered a lengthy gloss, in Greek, which has proved to be the lost fragment of Aristophanes' *The Drudges*, used by the annotator to illustrate some point about the nature of comedy! I copied it down, of course, and here it is. You can't,' he added quickly, 'see for yourself, I'm afraid, as our college library, being priceless, is off limits to all females.'

There was nothing for it: copies were made, and the text learned, despite Juliet's increasingly feeble objections that the whole feminist message of the play was turned upside-down. Phryne became the central character, and ruler of the Lacedaemonians, after it was revealed that she was in fact a male all along. This revelation was celebrated by a mass ceremonial flogging of all Lacedaemonians and Phryne's announcement that henceforth and always, the males should be dressed as females, to cast aside their warlike natures and symbolise the glory of the female principle. This message was greeted with joy by the entire cast, who thought it proper for a real male to be in charge of their punishments, especially dressed in pretty female robes, and any unease at being spanked by a 'female' was thus dispelled. Eventually even Juliet decreed that this message was suitably non-carnivorous and 'vaginocentric', despite the iniquity of having been discovered in a library closed to women.

Everyone who was anyone in the Oxford smart set was to be at the opening performance, including of course Edwina and her friends. There was great excitement at the rumour that Edwina was to bring Josephine Baker, the darling of Paris, who was visiting England and, though busy at the Lyceum, would come up from town to see the presentation. Lucinda Lalage's arrogance was matched only by her nervousness: would the great dancer say a word, notice her, remember her even? She vowed to give the performance of her life, and taunted Peake that the perfect gyrations of her chocolate bottom would make him ache with regret he was not allowed to touch her skin with a proper bare spanking! Peake smiled, and said that he must always respect a lady's wishes.

The play went even better than hoped for: the audience laughed and booed and 'aahed' in the right places, and thrilled to Peake's vigorous spankings, marvelling that such cruel acting could be so lifelike. Peake and his co-players had reached an understanding: the stage manager was not required to make cracking sounds as he spanked one bare bottom after another, and each slave girl coyly and naturally added her own bit of 'business', pirouetting after her chastisement to show her bare nates glowing crimson to the delighted audience. All eyes, after such moments, turned to the mysterious figure, blue-veiled and robed in shimmering orange silk, and glittering with jewels like some glorious creature of the harem, who sat beside Edwina. Her beringed hands led the applause at each scene of chastisement: the fabulous Miss Baker!

The moment came when Peake, as the slave mistress Phryne, was to give Lucinda Lalage, as the rebellious slave leader, her deserved chastisement. Lucinda sneered as she lowered the white silk panties and stockings of her frilly maid's uniform and presented Peake with her naked buttocks, thrust tantalisingly and taunting him with their swelling velvet perfection. Peake wore at his belt a short flail, like a cat-o'-nine-tails, and Lucinda gave this a nervous glance.

'I don't remember that from rehearsal,' she whispered as she positioned her belly across Peake's silk-sheathed thigh.

'O, mistress!' she cried to the audience. 'I beg you, do not beat me! Do not humiliate me thus! Is there no end to your wickednesss and cruelty?'

'Silence, minx!' thundered Peake, as Phryne. 'Your naked bottom shall bear the scars of your insolence, I warrant you! And she shall taste the kiss of my quirt if you persist in your unruly behaviour!'

'You said you wanted to give the performance of your life, Lucinda,' he whispered, 'and don't forget, Miss Baker is in the audience.'

With that, he brought his hand smartly across her naked croup, so that she squirmed and yelled in real dismay.

'O! O! That hurts!'

The audience roared their approval. Peake continued to spank with full hard strokes on the bare bum, whose globes rapidly turned hot purple.

'I'll get you for this!' sobbed the writhing Lucinda as the spanks rained on her flesh, and Peake tightly pinioned her shoulders below his knees.

'O, mistress!' she gasped loudly to the audience. 'My bum smarts so, she burns like the coals of Hephaestus, she shall melt like the wings of Icarus in the sun's heat if you continue with your cruel beating! I pray you, desist, for my squirming bottom tells you my punishment is sufficient. Ouch! O! O! O! God, that was tight! You bitch!'

'You seem to have strayed from the script, Lucinda,' whispered Peake. 'I think that must be properly punished, don't you? We'll give you a round two hundred spanks and then see.'

'O! O! O!' wailed the squirming woman, her bottom a picture of glowing tormented beauty. 'O . . .'

When her nates had taken from his hand two hundred

spanks, Peake reached smoothly for the quirt at his belt, and raised the sharp leather thongs, to further tumultuous cheers. Then he began to belabour the groaning woman's croup with the vicious little flail, making her writhing into a real dance of agony. She took thirty-three strokes until her squeals and sobs almost drowned out the continuous applause. The purple on her bottom was now so dark from the flogging that it seemed beautifully at one with her ebony skin. When Peake finally released her, there was a soaking-wet patch on the thigh of his dress, and Lucinda departed yet again from the script, falling to his feet and kissing them fervently.

'O . . .' she sobbed. 'I've never felt so . . . I've never known anything so . . . *firm*, not even back on St Botolph! Thank you . . . mistress!'

The chastisement of Lucinda received a standing ovation almost as long as the final scene of the mass flogging, where the entire cast, including Juliet, bared their bottoms to Peake's quirt, and he performed his strenuous duties, flitting from croup to croup with balletic and severe grace. All agreed that the play was a triumph, right down to the artful ebony maquillage of the slave girls.

After the performance, Miss Josephine Baker graciously accepted Lucinda's curtsey and permitted her hand to be kissed. She did indeed remember Lucinda, and begged her to call if she found herself in Paris. Then she wafted away in a haze of perfume to Edwina's waiting motor-car. The players enjoyed a drinks party, and afterwards Peake strolled contentedly back to college, just in time for the front door. He went to Binky Bevercon's room, bearing two bottles of vintage port.

'Virtue is rewarded, Binky,' he said, 'and here is your reward for being so adept at imitating the Greek of Aristophanes.'

'Gosh, thanks!' said Binky. 'I wonder what the reward for vice is?'

'I have no idea,' said Peake.

Back in his own room, he penned a short note to Miss Jane Reculver, to the effect that impersonation of an august lady such as Miss Josephine Baker was a grave misdemeanour. To receive her just reward, she must present herself for tea at the Randolph the following Sunday afternoon, prepared for further action to be taken, and must open her purse to him, to show that it contained her knickers.

The play was a resounding success, with packed houses for its week's run. It was 'noticed' by the London papers; the Oxford University Press grudgingly admitted that there might be some substance in the lost text of Aristophanes – the last act being particularly convincing – and that, after suitable research, it might be possible to bring out a scholarly edition, in, say, fifteen or twenty years' time.

At the party on the final night, Juliet took Peake aside, and whispered that she knew all along.

'Knew . . .?'

'About the fragment of the play. You made it up, didn't you?'

'I must be modest, miss. I didn't make it up.'

'And that wasn't Josephine Baker at all, was it?'

'You would have to ask Miss Baker.'

'Ha! Another of your tricks . . . to bamboozle poor Lucinda.'

'She didn't seem to mind.'

'You must make amends, sir. I suggest you take me to luncheon at the Cap and Bells, and then punting from the Cherwell boathouse. I believe you are familiar with a very nice birch grove, past the Moorings pub.'

Peake said it would be his pleasure.

'And when we get to the birch grove, don't think you're going to bamboozle me, and get me to take my knickers off, and use my poor bottom for your cruel sport.'

94

Peake raised an eyebrow.

'You shan't get my knickers off – because I'll have them in my purse . . .'

6

Dothemaids Hall

One pleasant Indian-summer afternoon, after a lot of rather good lunchtime port, Binky agreed to accompany Peake to the bathing place known as Parson's Pleasure, a little enclave of green grass where the River Cherwell formed a pool. He was rather nervous as they approached the sign which read: MEMBERS OF THE UNIVERSITY ONLY.

'No togs, eh?' he said.

'No togs,' said Peake firmly. 'Everybody is nude – that's the rule. It's fun. Why, you'll probably see your tutor there, and the Dean, I shouldn't wonder.'

'You're sure there are no females?' said Binky. 'I mean, I've often punted through, but always looked the other way.'

'Of course not,' said Peake. 'Females have to get out when you haul the punt up the rollers, and rejoin on the other side of the bathing pool. Anyway, if you were to get . . . excited, you could always hide behind that port bottle. Bathing nude is most exhilarating. Our ancient Greek chums knew that.'

'But they were a bit – well, you know . . .'

'It is all most decorous, Binky. Here we are. Now – drop your bags, and be a man about it.'

They found themselves on a lawn covered in the white or pink bodies of naked University men, most reading, drinking, or smoking, as though this were an extension

96

of their leathery common rooms. Only a few of the more epicene dons – lecturers in English, with 'poetic' forelocks – gave them more than a passing look, until Peake removed his own clothing, at which point the organ which hung between his legs attracted general attention which must be, he assured Binky, purely academic.

Even Binky was curious, and was rather embarrassed at being curious. Peake aired his genitalia with mischievous arrogance, and allowed his dangler to wobble in the breeze before settling down on his towel with a beaker of wine. Binky lay on his stomach; both men gazed placidly at the trees, the water and the passing punts, and sighed with contentment. When there were no boats, they could observe the vigorous testicle-scratching habits of the male liberated by nudity.

'You don't have to be polite, when there are no bints,' said Binky. 'Jolly refreshing. Although . . .'

'Although what, Binky?'

'Peake . . . How many bints have you had?'

'You wouldn't believe it if I told you. Not as many as you, certainly.'

Binky sighed.

'Sometimes I wonder what a real woman would be like. I mean, all this romantic stuff. These scores and scores of bints I've had – truly, Peake – well, my dad's in the army. I went to St Theobald's C of E school in Port Said, you know. In Egypt, it's cheap. A belly dance and a grope, and you give a couple of piastres and you spunk, and it's over.'

'Hmmm,' said Peake. 'Spunking is pleasant, and we all do it . . . but it means loss of energy, what they used to call "spending", just as you spend your capital. Women don't mind a man who has other women – look at the harems of old – but they sense when a man has spunked too much, and hasn't enough of the life energy they crave. They want a powerful man, Binky, full of brain power, to show them who is master. Look at the power of priests, who are celibate! I don't recommend celibacy, but I think spunking is valuable only with the right female ... one who is so womanly that she can abase herself entirely to her master. Women want to be slaves and playthings, Binky. They want to be bound in a slave's attire – what are corsets and stays and high heels and girdles, but modern slave's attire? – and made to kneel and serve, because only thus do they feel wanted. Especially rich women, the sort we see here at Oxford. They don't want to be pampered – why, they are quite capable of pampering themselves. The so-called modern woman is an unhappy sham, her modernness a cry for a real man to tame her.'

A cheerful voice interrupted them.

'I say, chaps, may I join you? Spiffing weather.'

A tall figure shadowed the two males, the shape of a truly majestic dangler merrily blocking the sun. The voice was melodious and fluting, as one might imagine a poet's. Peake peered up, and nodded his assent. The nude body plumped down beside them.

'Binky,' said Peake, 'this is Leslie Scammon. A second-year man at ... at St Edmund's Hall. Jolly good chap.'

Leslie Scammon shook hands with both of them, although neither pretended that the enormous shaft of her, or his, dangler was not intriguing. A sly brown floppy thing, it curled over Leslie's thigh, the helmet dipping on the grass. It was huge! Lesle grinned cautiously at Peake, and he grinned back. Atop the dangler was a forest of curly hairs, concealing whatever sealed this cunning rubber prosthesis to the woman's fount.

'Teddy Hall,' said Binky. 'Rugger bugger, eh? Have some port, Leslie.'

'Rugger?' said Leslie, accepting a beaker. 'Er, yes ...'

'Leslie's a jolly useful prop forward,' said Peake.

The disguised woman awarded him a grateful look.

98

She lay down on her back, beside Binky, who remained resolutely on his stomach. Despite her male appurtenance, Leslie's female perfume must certainly assail him.

'Nice to get away from bloody females, ain't it?' said Leslie. 'Starkers – naked as nature intended. 'Course, at a sporting college like Teddy Hall we spend a lot of time at horseplay in the showers. Not that there's any hanky-panky. We're all chaps together, eh? Of course we've all been to boarding school, done our share of you know what . . . With a juicy bum like that, Binky, I bet you were quite a catch. And don't let's pretend we didn't enjoy it at the time.'

'I say, really . . .!' Binky exclaimed.

She gave him a resounding smack on his bare bottom, to his great surprise, then sat up.

'I'm going to do boxing next term,' she said. 'I think my pectorals are tough enough. Here, feel!'

She took Binky's arm and awkwardly placed it on her bare breast, making him squeeze and tug as she flexed the taut muscle beneath. Her breasts were indeed like a heavily-muscled male's except for the strawberry areolae of the nipples, which at Binky's touch noticeably stiffened. Brightly, Leslie said they should all take a swim, but Binky refused, blushing, and seeming to burrow into the grass with his loins, as though terrified of discovery. Peake joined Leslie, and they scampered to the water's edge and plunged in, disturbing a colony of frogs.

'Well, Leslie,' said Peake with a thin smile, 'you are a mistress of disguise. Or should I say master.'

'She does everything a real dangler can do,' said Leslie merrily. 'I call her she because she is so lovely and soft and cuddly. But when she gets hard, and spurts . . .'

Peake looked down and saw the rubber organ standing stiff and high almost to Leslie's dimpled navel. He gasped.

'Little air pouches hidden in my lady's place,' she

99

whispered. 'When I squeeze – so yummy! – my friend stands up. And when I fill my pouches with cream, I spurt just like you! It's a lark! I say, I'm having a get-together tonight, at my digs in the Iffley Road. Lots of beer ... hearty talk. Just chaps. Why not come along?'

Peake excused himself. He was bidden to attend a gathering at Nuneham Courtenay, at the house of Miss Katharine Mann. Leslie said mysteriously that she knew of Katie Mann and her 'jammy' ladies' academy.

'Edwina Cheshunt and her chums certainly have you marked, Mr Peake ... Well, if you won't come, I'll have to drag your friend Binky. He really has got a lovely bum.'

'I'm sure he'll attend,' said Peake. 'Just chaps, eh?'

'Chaps ... like me,' said Leslie, lowering her eyes and giggling. 'Edwina would cane me bare if she knew.'

She pouted and smiled shyly.

'I think I'll make sure she knows ...'

The great house at Nuneham Courtenay was very like Edwina's, with the addition of a meticulously painted sign in gold leaf which read: DOTHEMAIDS HALL, K MANN, PROP. The driveway was well furnished with Daimlers, Chryslers and Bentleys, and Peake's taxi looked quite out of place. He ordered the driver to wait, as he would be leaving at about eleven o'clock. There was a warm, flowery scent of early evening in the air; all around stretched the lush green fields of England, and in the distance the purple hillocks of the Chilterns. All was peace.

The front door was opened promptly by a maid, a young lady of his own age dressed in a frilly costume which was pretty but impractical: it consisted of a very short skirt of dark green, with a white apron, lime-green panties and stockings whose lacy tops plainly showed; white shoes, very high and pointed, and a tight green

100

blouse open to reveal generous breast-flesh, the pert teats themselves held in a bra whose two conical cups projected somewhat cheekily.

'You didn't bring your things, sir?' she said, curtseying in a most submissive manner.

Peake wore his evening dress; he explained that his taxi would wait for him to finish his evening.

'O, but the mistress expects you to stay – the guest room is prepared – and there are the school sports tomorrow!'

Without consulting Peake further, she stepped over and ordered the taxi to go. As she bent over, her buttocks were fully revealed, encased in tight green knicker-silk which clung to the orbs like the skins of grapes. There was a fine net pattern to her stockings, and up the back of her legs snaked a dark green seam, like a vine. Then she smiled again and returned to Peake in submissive mien.

'You mustn't worry about being out of college, sir,' said the maid as she led him through the vestibule and took his coat, gloves and hat. 'The mistress is very friendly with your warden . . . and his lady wife.'

A smile played across her face as she curtseyed again, and showed Peake into the salon. A number of guests were already there, animated with champagne flutes. A tall woman detached herself and swanned towards Peake, hand outstretched and long ballgown flowing white behind her: she seemed the only woman to wear a dress that covered her knees. Her face was tan, and her hair was auburn flecked with gold; pearls sparkled above her deep bare cleavage, the skin of her breasts notably golden, as though the summer sun had washed her whole. She announced herself as Katharine Mann, 'but of course you must call me Katie.'

Peake was served with a glass of champagne by a maid dressed in the familiar frilly uniform, but pink; other maids were in pale blue or yellow.

'Such a treat for them,' said Katie Mann. 'The colours are a mark of status; the doormaid was so thrilled to be awarded green!'

Peake asked what the colours signified, and Miss Mann replied that they meant different levels of scholastic achievement, and correctness of discipline.

'We are a proper academy, you know,' she said earnestly, 'with everything that entails, including lavish fees – even if it is only, as it were, part-time. But the maids must wear proper uniforms of grey skirts and white blouses, and these frillies are really a pretty treat for them. Some of my maids are of a certain age – but being back at school makes them feel so young and girly! And of course, Mr Peake, a stern mistress, or better, a stern master, is part and parcel of every maid's favourite schoolday. Edwina speaks most highly of you. And I saw *The Drudges* – three times. You were wonderful! I knew I had to have you at Dothemaids. You won't mind judging the sports tomorrow afternoon? In the morning, you shall see our classrooms if you like.'

Peake made small talk, and it was evident from the ladies' sparkling eyes and coy lips that he had something of a reputation. He remarked on the charming name for the academy and said that referring to the 'Dotheboys Hall' of Dickens, it was amusingly tongue-in-cheek. His words 'tongue in cheek' were repeated with merriment quite beyond reasonable expectation, and all agreed that Mr Peake was very droll. They sat to dinner, served on silver by a bevy of the frilly maids, who curtseyed, bowed, spooned and ladled with the sweetest deference and the most seemly prancing of silked croup and bosom.

The service was according to their colours, the soup-wench, as Miss Mann called her, being inferior to the fish-wench, and so on, until the grandest of all was the pudding-wench, who served the most sumptuous cake with meringues and caramel and cherries and cream, in the perfect shape of a schoolgirl! The figure lay face-down with meringue knickers around her ankles, skirts up and her bare cream bottom well laced with raspberry jam, the product of a whip whose thongs were of spun sugar. The proud pudding-wench was the girl who had admitted Peake to the house.

Peake, in place of honour beside his hostess, was served a portion of the left buttock, with a piece of meringue ankle and a gooseberry nipple, and pronounced it an excellent confection. A gobbet of cream fell on the front of his trousers, and Miss Mann remarked on this, saying that he had better wipe it off before anyone else thought of it. She said that his suit would be cleaned tomorrow; since he appeared to have come without a change of kit, such would be provided for him. There was wine and port in abundance, and Peake remarked on the excellence of her cellar.

'You are acquainted with dear Susie Rattan, I believe,' Miss Mann said over the hubbub. 'I fear she will not enjoy her wine over in America. It is forbidden, you know. Barbaric! Yet that is how Mr Parkhurst makes his money. I do hope Susie is all right. Some of Mr Parkhurst's business associates carry dreadful things called Thompson guns.'

She shuddered, then put her hand quickly on Peake's for reassurance. She looked at him earnestly, her own grey eyes deep mischievous pools.

'A personal question, Mr Peake,' she said. 'How well do you know Susie?'

'I should very much like to know her better,' he replied. 'Our acquaintance was short.'

'And sharp?' she said, eyes twinkling. 'I mean, did she cane you?'

'Why . . . yes, if you must know.'

'On the bare?'

Peake nodded, his face stony.

'It is her speciality. And did you like it?'

'It hurt abominably!'

'That is not what I asked. You see, I watched you as Phryne, and you were not just acting. There was real fury, real vengeance, in your chastisement of those bare bums. There is such a fine and lovely thread separating mastery from submission!'

Peake said Miss Mann seemed to know him very well.

'These two maids know you too, Mr Peake,' she said, drawing to her a girl in yellow and a girl in pink by clasping their pert bottoms.

'Yes, we've met,' said Peake. 'At Edwina's . . .?'

'And again!' said Miss Mann. 'You met them at dear Flossie de Cante's cottage . . . You must remember Joan Weimaran and Gwendoline Hedge!'

All three women burst into melodious and half-mocking giggles, which Peake acknowledged with a wry smile of submission. After that, liqueurs were brought, and conversation flowed into the small hours, until shufflings and exclamations of surprise at the time indicated that the party was at a close. Miss Mann bade him goodnight with surprising formality.

'Till we meet again, dear sir,' she intoned.

Joan and Gwendoline showed Peake upstairs to his guest room, which was equipped with the softest of beds, a scented bathroom and every convenience, including a trouser press. There was a wardrobe in which he would find adequate kit for the morrow. He slipped into the green silk pyjamas folded on his bed, and then between the silken sheets.

After a time, the door slid open and admitted a shaft of light together with two female bodies. Peake moved his head, and saw Miss Mann and the pudding-wench in her green costume. Miss Mann was holding the maid by the ear, like a naughty schoolgirl.

'Ah, Mr Peake,' she said, 'still awake, I see, and I trust not too tired to undertake a trifling task. You are

104

to supervise the sports tomorrow, sir, and I must be absolutely sure of your prowess – of your willingness, I mean. Do you find the colour green attractive? It goes so nicely with a reddened bottom, I always think. My head prefect here expressed doubts about your prowess – the minx! – as though the word of several ladies were not good enough for her. And as it was she who spilled cream on your mess kit, you will agree she must pay a good price for that. The cane, sir, the cane. Let her taste your work.'

She let go of the girl's ear and opened the wardrobe, whence she extracted a gleaming heavy ashplant, which she swished approvingly in the still night air. Peake got out of bed, rubbed his eyes and took a sip of water from his carafe. He said that he was most ready.

The green girl bent over in position. She did not need to lift her skirt, for the frilly, skimpy thing flounced charmingly up by itself to reveal her bottom. Then she lowered her knickers to her ankles, revealing the white orbs of her buttocks shining pale in the moonlight, which bathed lime-green mesh stockings with their livid snake seam, the white bare bottom, the frilly dress and Peake's green pyjamas, and the white shimmering robe of Miss Mann.

'I hope you like your pyjamas, sir,' said Miss Mann. 'My husband in the Lancers brought them from India. I do hope he will bring some more some day. Miss Mann being my maiden name, of course . . .'

Peake took the cane from Miss Mann and flexed it.

'O, sir, I beg your pardon for spilling cream on you,' said the girl. 'I know I must be beaten on the bare, but I beg you to go easy on my poor bottom. Please say you will.'

Peake was silent.

'Well then! I think I'll take twenty-seven,' said the girl, sounding suddenly very businesslike. 'We'll see if you can make me squeal before that. You should be able to, a strong man like you. Otherwise I might think you soppy.'

Peake ordered the girl to take her knickers right off, and spread her thighs as wide as she could. Both women nodded approvingly as this command was obeyed, and the girl handed Peake her knickers. He balled them – already well moist – and put them in her mouth. Then he lifted the cane, and brought it down very hard across the girl's naked buttocks. They clenched, but she did not make a sound. He caned her quite rapidly, varying his target so that all the flesh was kissed by the rod, yet still she did not cry out. At each stroke, her buttocks and back shuddered, and the dangling mink-hairs between her thighs began to glisten with her moisture.

He applied the cane to the insides of her thighs, close to the furrow, and at that she seemed to need all her strength to repress a squeal. When he reached the penultimate stroke, her buttocks were glowing dark crimson, but she still had not cried. Then he twisted and dealt a stern stroke lengthways, slapping across her furrow with the tip of the cane snaking inside, to land squarely on her exposed brown anal bud. Through her gag, she emitted a bellow of agony.

She got painfully to her feet and began to rub her sore bottom. There was moisture on her cheeks, and on her thighs too, and her voice was choked. She removed her gag.

'That was pretty tight! Those cuts to the thighs – how a girl hates that! I think you'll do, master,' she said, holding out her hand. 'Now that I've got to know you, I can be introduced.'

Miss Mann spoke.

'Thomas Peake – Miss Phydia Marchant,' she drawled. 'A splendid prefect at Newton Abbot, and now at Dothemaids.'

Peake said that Miss Marchant's reputation had preceded her, and that Lady Flora de Cante had spoken highly of her. He added that green and crimson made a pleasing combination.

'She spoke highly of you too, sir,' said Phydia Marchant, 'and I don't think she was mistaken.'

She took the ashplant from his hand and tapped the straining silk of his pyjamas.

'Your dangler,' she breathed. 'Such a beautiful flagpole.'

'Quite appropriate for sports day,' said Miss Mann.

Peake went down to breakfast wearing brown plus-fours in a dashing Prince of Wales check, which, of the male attire in his wardrobe, seemed to him the most suitable for 'the country', as Miss Mann referred to Nuneham Courtenay. He also equipped himself with a stout walking cane of silver-topped teak, from a generous selection of instruments of which most were clearly disciplinary. Breakfast was served by the same maids as had attended the party, but was a much brisker and more solemn affair. The maids wore sober school uniforms of grey pleated skirt, white socks and blouses and black buckled shoes, with black knee-socks and striped neckties. The other diners were faces Peake recognised from the night before: they too wore businesslike school-mistress dress, and Miss Mann herself was arrayed all in black, with a gown and school mistress's mortarboard beside her on the table. The white blouse was open to reveal a generous cleavage of tanned breast, topped by a golden neckchain. She too had a cane at her belt, a thin, whippy implement with a crooked handle that was not for walking.

'You are examining my suntan, Mr Peake,' said Miss Mann. 'I expect you wonder where I got it. Don't deny.'

Peake did not.

'Well,' she continued, 'I understand you are a regular at Parson's Pleasure, so it will not shock you to learn that I am a devotee of the all-over suntan, or, as the popular press calls it, "nudism". I believe in a healthy mind in a healthy body. I frequent a little island off the southern coast of France. My husband's family owns it, actually. Something to do with the Second Crusade. And of course I put my principles into practice here at my little academy. My girls learn the bliss of practising their compulsory sports quite naked, like the ancient Olympiasts. You shall see.'

Peake said that he looked forward to it with pleasure, and Miss Mann signified that it was time for classes to begin. The other diners got up and left, after bowing to their Head: it was clear they were the class mistresses. Miss Mann took him through some quaintly winding corridors and explained that there were four classes at the moment, of nine girls each, and that they learnt proper lessons – receiving, she added slyly, proper punishments for error.

'Nudism teaches a healthy mind in a healthy body,' she said, 'and I add the doctrine of Newton Abbot – a healthy mind in a well-disciplined body.'

They came to a classroom, where nine attentive ladies appeared to be studying geography. They had uncomfortable wooden desks, with maps, exercise books, quill pens, blotting paper and inkpots. Peake recognised some of the maids from the night before; all were now neat in their school uniforms, their hair tidily braided or pinned, and all rose on his entrance. The mistress was a tall female not much older than Peake himself, and dressed in the same uniform as her charges, but her spectacles, gown and mortarboard gave her a stern appearance. She stood at a high lectern, upon which lay, most conspicuously, a cane. Miss Mann nodded and the class resumed their seats after she explained that Mr Peake was a visiting master who would observe their deportment and studiousness, and would be giving out the prizes at the sports that afternoon.

'And what is the capital of Hungary?' asked the mistress. 'You, Letitia.'

'Er . . . Bucharest, miss,' stammered a blonde girl with

108

pigtails, whose full figure seemed to burst from her tight and skimpy school things, as though her uniform had been taken from a drawer where it had been lovingly mothballed in remembrance of innocent youth.

'Wrong!' rapped the mistress.

There was a disapproving murmur from her classmates.

'I mean Vienna, miss?' said Letitia miserably, aware she was clutching at straws. The mistress tut-tutted.

'You have not done your homework, Letitia,' she said, peering over her spectacles.

'I promise I did, miss!' wailed the blonde girl, her pigtails shaking in agitation.

'Falsehood compounds your error, Letitia,' said the mistress. 'You will approach my desk, if you please.'

Trembling, the hapless Letitia did so. She was ordered to stand with her bottom facing the class and bend over to touch her toes. When she had assumed position, the mistress picked up her cane by the tip – which was wickedly splayed into two tongues – and inserted the crooked handle into the waistband of the girl's white panties. With a tug, she pulled the panties down to the girl's knees so that her bare bottom and thighs were exposed, gleaming above her woolly socks. The mistress lifted her cane by the handle and swished it so that it cracked on her desk top. Letitia shuddered, and there was a gasp of awed anticipation from the class.

'You will repeat a penance for me,' said the mistress. ' "I promise not to be a lazy slut in future." '

'I promise not to be a lazy slut in future,' moaned Letitia, and then jumped as the cane landed hard across her bare fesses.

'Again!' snapped the mistress.

'I promise not to be a lazy slut in future – Ooo!' cried Letitia, squirming violently as the cane lashed her again, harder, in exactly the same spot.

'Again, Letitia,' said the mistress.

Letitia repeated her penance a further five times before she was allowed to rise, pull up her knickers, and return sobbing to her desk.

'I think that should be a lesson to us all,' said the mistress, 'and I want no further error, especially as we have a distinguished master observing us.'

She smiled shyly at Peake.

'The capital of Hungary is of course Budapest,' she said. 'Now, Gladys, the capital of the United States, if you please. Let us try to impress our guest and Miss Mann.'

'That's easy, miss,' smirked the girl Gladys. 'New York!'

The mistress sighed, with some agitation in her face as she observed Miss Mann's own frown.

'The answer is Washington. So, Gladys, it seems I must make an example of your cockiness,' she said.

Gladys too had to put down her pen and approach the desk.

She assumed the position, and her bottom was bared like Letitia's. Her penance was to repeat: 'It ill becomes a lady to be a know-all'. She was obliged to repeat this lesson nine times – seven strokes, with an added two for her cockiness – before the mistress permitted her to go back to class, crying softly and rubbing the generous crimson that adorned her flogged portion.

The next two questions were answered correctly, until a girl named Constance said that the Alps were in Asia Minor. This earnt her seven strokes on the bare, and the homily: 'A lady must not hesitate to climb the mountain of knowledge'. However, despite these fierce penalties, the tide of ignorance flowed unstemmed, and some of the girls bent over to take their bare-bum canings with unashamedly proud looks at Peake. The mistress was growing increasingly flustered, as though the ignorance of her girls – wilful or not – was a measure of her own error.

Miss Mann's frown grew dark. With a tight smile, she

said that perhaps the visiting master would care to put a question, as all good girls would wish to please a master. Peake obliged by hurriedly asking the class to name an island in the West Indies.

'You – Eulalia Preen,' said the mistress to a svelte, dark-complexioned girl whose lustrous raven hair and olive face was in delicious contrast to the crisp white blouse of a demure English schoolgirl. Her brown eyes looked straight at Peake.

'Please, sir – St Botolph,' she said softly.

Peake expressed his satisfaction and surprise.

'Well, sir, it is the only one I know,' she said, smiling with her moist pink tongue rubbing her teeth.

The lesson resumed but, despite Eulalia Preen's success, the record of accuracy remained dismal, and more canings were applied to bare bottoms before Miss Mann whispered to Peake, 'Isn't it interesting how they take it, Mr Peake? Some, like Phydia last night, take it with only the mildest flinching; others squirm and shiver like demons, or shudder as though their bums were on fire. Variety, I always say, is the satisfaction – the spice! – of discipline. And there is little so pleasing as the sight of two bare fesses, well reddened and dancing under a stern cane. However, discipline must have a certain democracy, just as an officer must be prepared to undergo the same hardships as his men.'

They observed two further canings of nine strokes, for cockiness, and Miss Mann said that every girl except Eulalia Preen had now taken punishment. The class-room was a rustle of dresses and knickers as bottoms were shifted in seats to ease their smarting.

'We can't have Eulalia top of this morning's class by default,' she said. 'So another test for you, Eulalia – Mr Peake, please do the honours.'

With a smile, Peake asked her the capital of France.

'Madrid,' she answered promptly, with a cheeky and quite malicious grin at her questioner.

111

'O! This is an outrage!' cried the mistress.

'I agree,' said Miss Mann smoothly. 'An insult to our distinguished visitor, and a shame on my academy. Accordingly, I think it fitting that Mr Peake, as master, should award chastisement.'

Eulalia drew a deep breath that was almost a sigh of satisfaction, and gaily took her position before the class, pulling down her white knickers over the velvet skin of her naked bottom, which shone with mysterious innocence as Peake raised the cane. He asked how many strokes she should take.

'Seven,' said the mistress.

'And another two for outrage,' added Miss Mann.

'Beg pardon, miss,' murmured Eulalia from her stooping position. 'Are you sure nine is enough? I have been awfully cheeky, you know.'

'Well!' cried Miss Mann. 'You certainly have now! I don't know what you expect to gain by this – this impudent showing off, but you shall certainly pay the price. Give her thirteen, if you please, Mr Peake, and tight ones. And not a squeal out of you, not a murmur or a sob, Miss Preen, or each and every cut will be given over again.'

Peake delivered thirteen strokes of the cane to the dark girl's naked bottom, and not once did she show any sign of distress, save for the lightest of shivering as his cane stroked her bare skin. She clenched her buttocks tightly at the first lash, and maintained them in clenched position throughout the beating. At its end, her bum was coloured the deepest purple. She rose, and stiffly pulled up her knickers with a very small grimace and a gasp, which were rapidly replaced by a glowing smile at her chastiser.

'Thank you, sir,' she whispered, the deep brown pools of her eyes fastened moist and adoring on his.

Miss Mann halted Peake as he was about to return the cane to the mistress's desk, and said there was further use for it. She looked reprovingly at her mistress, who lowered her eyes.

'An officer is accountable for his men, and a mistress for her charges. I believe you know what is in store for you, miss.'

The mistress bit her lip, and removed her spectacles, placing them on the desk where the cane had lain.

'Yes, Miss Mann. I must make amends for their – for my error.'

'Nine, I think, one for each of these girls and her disgraceful error. And since only a master may chastise a mistress, I ask Mr Peake to oblige us once more.'

'A master must use his own cane,' whispered the mistress.

Peake replaced her school cane on the desk beside her spectacles, then lifted his own heavy teak instrument.

Trembling, the mistress removed her gown and mortarboard, and touched toes in position. Slowly she raised her skirt, to reveal knickers of the brightest crimson silk, framed by a garter belt of black lace, and silk stockings of fine mesh, with the sensuous snake-vine at their seam. Peake used the cane's silver top to pull down the tight panties until they dangled at her shivering knees. Miss Mann murmured that she expected the girl's bottom to match her panties. In silence, Peake dealt nine strokes of the cane to her bare backside, very hard and very slowly.

The atmosphere in the classroom was electric; all rustling and shifting stopped as the girls observed their mistress as bare as they had been, and taking the same merited correction. She could not help but moan softly, then with deeper and deeper anguish at each stroke as the cane kissed her fesses. The mistress's bottom was pale as alabaster, and reddened most vividly and most rapidly under flogging; after the ninth, touches of dark purple and even black edged the crimson mass of her naked flesh.

Sobbing, she thanked Peake for his attention, and the trembling of her lip was not to suppress her anguish, but to suppress her smile of gratified submission.

'Well, sir, I must thank you! You were most ... impressive,' said Miss Mann as they proceeded to the next classroom. Her face was flushed, and her eyelids heavy. Peake remarked that there was something familiar about the mistress he had caned. Seen close, she seemed to be wigged.

'Of course she wears a wig, *here*,' giggled Miss Mann. 'I told you I was acquainted with the good lady of your warden! She certainly got her money's worth! School fees are double for mistresses, you see ... I do hope the next classes will not require as much correction as that one.'

Peake discovered that they did.

7

Girl Sports

After a light luncheon, Peake accompanied Miss Mann to the playing fields, where Phydia Marchant was in charge of teams and competitions.

'Modest, but strenuous,' said Miss Mann, clasping Peake's arm. 'Not all of the competitions are in the nude, of course: some things lend themselves to the most delightful frilly costumes. I am fortunate in possessing a rather large demesne, so we have plenty of room, and streams and pools for girls to splash in. There is something so innocent about a girl's bum all white and frothy in the water, isn't there? A boy's bum too, I dare say. Especially a well thrashed one . . . Mann, whenever he is back from the tropics, is keen on all sorts of water games, though not as keen as I am. Visiting masters always enjoy themselves at our sports days. Funny, the girls always seem to react well to a master who is of colour . . . Edwina is well known in what they call the jazz set, and has a most helpful range of acquaintance. You'll do, sir – from the West Indies, indeed! Quite exotic enough . . . I say, I wonder how your chum Binky got on at Leslie Scammon's little do?'

Peake was taken aback at this, and with a sly smile she assured him that in her set, not much went unnoticed.

'You don't think Leslie bearded you at Parson's Pleasure by accident?' was all she would say.

A small marquee stood amid various grass pitches with arcane markings, and a swimming pool, beyond which a pleasant stream gurgled. The girls were all lined up in white frilly gym kit, with ankle socks and pleated bum-hugging skirts, under the supervision of mistresses in similar attire, but with proper stockings and slightly longer skirts, and all curtseyed to Miss Mann and Peake. Phydia Marchant seemed the mistress of ceremonies, and rather proudly wore her green maid's costume. She showed them into the marquee, where a sumptuous tea was laid for later, and suggested that they might like to refresh themselves with glass of port while she organised the first event. They assented, Miss Mann noting with approval that there were plenty of custard creams for their tea. There were, however, no seats in the tent, and she explained a singularity of Dothemaids Hall: the prizes for winning at sports were trifling, but the penalties for losing were quite severe.

'It is just like real life,' she said brightly, helping herself to a custard cream, and hoping that Peake would not notice. 'Most of us lose more often than we win; so the girls won't have any desire to sit down on their bottoms . . .'

The first event was to be a running race, one lap around the field, which was four hundred yards. Half a dozen maids stripped down to bra and shoes alone, with no skirt, blouse or panties – Miss Mann explained that they were permitted this one essential support – and lined up to await the start. Phydia blew the whistle, and at the same time cracked a rather fierce horsewhip, which was even louder. The girls set off and struggled around the track, which dutifully managed to muddy their bare limbs even on this sunny day.

The winner received a kiss from Miss Mann, the losers had to bend over, their faces pressed firmly and humiliatingly in the mud, while Phydia dealt them each four vigorous whip-strokes on the bare buttocks. Then winner and losers went to the river and were ordered to plunge into the water to cleanse themselves. They did so, giggling and rubbing their flushed whipped bottoms, to loud cheers from the assembly. Miss Mann said naked young bottoms were so charming when bathing, yet so wicked when bared for the merited cane, as though all girls were two beings in one.

Next there was a swimming race, for which the contestants were entirely nude. It was organised as a tournament, and the overall victress received a kiss, while the others had their penalty meted in the same way as before. Peake's role in the proceedings was to announce the name of the winner in a thunderous and therefore masterly voice, as though the authority of a male bestowed favour. At his proclamation, Phydia brought him a glass of port, with which he toasted the victress, with every sign of enjoying himself. While the whippings were dealt, to the great enthusiasm and acclaim of the crowd, Miss Mann absented herself into the marquee, and returned wiping crumbs from her lips. She glanced at Peake with a guilty smile or, rather, a smile that was supposed to indicate guilt.

The sports at Dothemaids were chosen for their 'piquancy', as Miss Mann explained. In the wheelbarrow race, both wheeler and wheeled were naked females, scampering along the muddy track with the 'barrow' propelling herself on her hands, her legs rigid behind her, while her comrade steered her by holding her ankles. The race was run twice, with the roles reversed in the second course, and points were deducted if a girl permitted her legs to buckle, with inevitable whippings for the bare-bottomed losers.

There was a form of football called, curiously, 'hogball', because its naked players snuffled like pigs as they pursued a large striped beach ball of rubber, which they were obliged to propel on all fours, using their bare breasts as mallets. Some of the girls seemed eminently practised, and were able to 'pass' and 'dribble' with great skill, using their swinging teats to whack the ball. These were usually the girls with the most pendulous breasts. After hogball, the losing team was honoured by taking their whippings from the visiting master himself: Peake obliged conscientiously, delivering the lash to the eager bare bums without expression and with solemn fierceness, which seemed to excite the recipients considerably, and their exaggerated squeals of anguish, feigned or real, rang through the scented air. After he had whipped the losers, Miss Mann, wiping crumbs from her mouth, smiled pointedly at Peake's manhood.

Two forms of polo were played, both water polo and the terrestrial variety. Water polo was played in the swimming pool, with two teams of giggling naked women, the players hoisted on piggy-back and battling over the rubber beach ball, the aim of the game being to score points not by propelling it into a goal, but by striking the opponents with it on the points of their nipples. Points were awarded for the number, accuracy and force of these impacts, and the losing side, after their customary whippings, had bottoms just as reddened as their bruised bare breasts. Even though the losers' beatings were largely ceremonial, and the posture of submission more important than the pain inflicted, nevertheless Peake was able to ensure that a few strokes raised vivid crimson on the girls' bums.

Field polo was played with the riders carried in little dog-carts, like Roman chariots, drawn by naked maids who were harnessed, reined and blinkered as 'ponies'. From their carts, the riders swung mallets at a hard croquet ball, and spurred on their steeds with cracks of their riding crop to bare backs and buttocks. No verbal instructions were permitted, so that all communication between rider and pony girl had to be by whip-stroke. Peake learned that the role of the pony girl was the most prized in this particular sport. He said to Miss Mann that the ponies looked very pretty, like real horses, and even as the losers lined up to receive their beatings, they still whinnied and pawed the ground and snorted as though they enjoyed their equine status.

Every girl got to participate in some sport, and as the afternoon wore on, there was not one whose bottom was without the glow of 'penalty crimson'. The final event was to be all-in wrestling, an elimination contest, in which every girl would take part. Before that, there was an egg and spoon race – with, as Miss Mann coyly indicated, a slight difference. The runners were nude, and on all fours, as in hogball. There were eggs, but no spoons; instead, the girls were obliged to spread their bare fesses, and take the ovoid firmly pressed inside their anus. Like this, they raced around the field, their progress interrupted by frequent loss of their cargo, at which the luckless runner had to squat and without using her hands, manoeuvre her buttocks to pick up the egg again before proceeding.

Some girls were disqualified, with suitable chastisement delivered on the spot by Phydia Marchant, for squeezing too hard and breaking their eggshell. Sobbing, they would endure the shame of bending over and taking their beating on bare thighs and buttocks streaked with sticky egg yolk. Only one girl never dropped her egg at all, and she won easily. As Phydia removed the eggs from the contestants, she had to pull quite strongly at the winner's, as it seemed to be stuck. Miss Mann demanded to see it, felt it, and glared at the girl, who bowed her head in shame.

'A cheat!' cried Miss Mann. 'You glued your bumhole, miss! That means a proper chastisement. Phydia, bring the blackboard and the chalk. Miss, you shall write twenty lines, "I must not be a slut"!'

At this, the girl began to sob.

'Not the blackboard, miss! I beg you! Let me take the

master's cane, if you please. I'll take twenty . . . thirty . . . as many as you like. But not the blackboard!'

But the blackboard was duly positioned, together with a tub of chalk powder. The naked girl stood trembling before the board, and Miss Mann said she should have her wish partly granted, as it was a nice sunny day: she would take nine from the master, and her penalty was reduced to fifteen lines. The girl seemed absurdly grateful, and touched her toes to take nine efficient cuts from Peake's teak cane.

She never moved or complained during her beating, but there were tears in her eyes as she rose to begin her punishment with trembling fesses glowing crimson against the blackboard. She dipped her fingers in the chalk dust, and began to write her lines on the blackboard, the squeaking scratch of her fingernails making the audience clasp their ears in horror. Even Peake grimaced. But Miss Mann was immovable, and waited until the girl had scratched her penance on the blackboard with her bare fingernails, the ordained fifteen times. Miss Mann looked at Peake in triumph, as though to show him that she was not afraid to inflict *real* chastisement.

After that, the wrestling match was greeted as light relief. The rules were simple – there were no rules. Peake beheld a mass of naked females transformed from the most sweetly decorous of assemblies into a collective fury of kicking, scratching and pummelling wolverines. Girls left the fray when they had been savagely beaten, either by one, or a gang of the others, to the point where they wailed submission. The winner was crowned by the master with a wreath of laurels, after she had engaged in single combat with a girl twice her size, darting and twisting in a blur of glistening naked flesh to deliver kicks, scratches and even vicious gouges to the tenderest parts of her opponent's body in a veritable frenzy of aggression. Smiling, she thanked the master for her award: it was Eulalia Preen.

120

Since every girl except Eulalia had, technically speaking, lost in the wrestling match, Peake was invited to deliver a penalty chastisement to the bottoms of all. The naked girls presented a tousled and muddy spectacle of livid bruises and scratches, all rubbing their pummelled bodies even before receiving their beatings. This did not dissuade Peake from an energetic correction of tender bare skin, to moans and squeals and sobs. Miss Mann pronounced herself much pleased with the master's performance, and enthralled by the variations in response of the flogged girls.

'Like the colours on an artist's palette,' she said dreamily, 'some muted, some bright . . . How you tease a lovely painting from them, sir, like the artist you are.'

The girls splashed in the swimming pool, dressed again, and eagerly trooped in for tea. As *victress ludorum*, Eulalia was allowed the lion's share of the custard creams, although it was glaringly obvious that a large portion of them had already disappeared.

'You must have tea with me in London, master,' she whispered, and drew a printed card from inside her knickers.

Peake took it; it was sodden with warm moisture. Her face was very close to his, and she twirled with a little laugh, so that the pleat of her skirt brushed against the swelling of his manhood. The card gave an address in Greencoat Place.

'Convenient for the Colonial Office,' she said. 'Of course, in London, you'll have to call me Lady Preen. Bit silly . . . Preen's the under-secretary, you know . . . Still, gets me a good box at the opera. But the sight of you caning all those girls has made me feel most frightfully juicy, you know. I feel I've been left out. Didn't you see the horrid way I fought that poor girl so cruelly? Lucinda Lalage – now *she* can put up a fight. When we've had our tea at my house, I think you should chastise me properly for my wickedness, master.

121

I have canes – you may take your pick, and then I'll bend over bare for you. I don't expect seven, I don't expect thirteen or even twenty-one, I expect you to give me a lovely slow beating . . . with no holds barred. Will you? You know you will be properly rewarded.'

Peake nodded his agreement.

'Wonderful! I am so wet just thinking about it. My Daimler is waiting, I must go before I do something very silly and lovely and embarrassing! By the way, you won't mind if my maid watches my chastisement? She likes that. In fact it would be awfully nice if you chastised her too, a lovely naked caning, her frillies up round her neck and her knickers down, while I watch. She is a wonderful maid – a great help and provider – and that's why I married him . . .'

Eventually, the girls had sated themselves on tea, glad farewells were cooed, and the driveway echoed to the purr of departing motors. Some of the girls insisted on curtseying and taking the hand of the master 'who has made me smart so beautifully'. And small glinting objects were pressed into Peake's hand, along with shiny visiting cards. Peake was left alone with Miss Mann and Phydia Marchant. He said that he too, would be going.

'Why, Mr Peake,' exclaimed Miss Mann, 'you have not yet had your reward for your sterling service today. And before you have that – why, your service is not complete. Didn't you notice what a naughty girl I was? Helping myself quite shamelessly to more than my share of custard creams?'

Peake smiled thinly and said that he had considered it impolite to mention.

'Well, we know what must happen to naughty girls,' said Miss Mann with sudden coyness. 'And as for a naughty mistress – one who is supposed to set an example . . .!'

Gravely, Peake accepted her hand, and her invitation to return indoors for the matter of her correction. And the Mistress of Dothemaids Hall did indeed require more subtle and arduous chastisement than an errant schoolgirl.

'I have said that a woman is two beings, Mr Peake,' she said. 'The bright side of an innocent young girl, and the dark side of a mistress. In life, we must balance these two sides. In a mistress, the dark must dominate, but sometimes she needs a master, to ... illuminate her darkness.'

'Do males have a dark and light side?' Peake asked.

She looked at him and touched his lips with her fingers.

'Let us see,' she said. 'Master.'

They ascended to a dark room which Miss Mann said was her study. Phydia lit scented candles, and Peake said it looked more like a dungeon than a study: there were no books, just instruments of correction and sinister frames of constraint. Miss Mann said that it was for the study of real things, the arts of submission and discipline.

'You shall make me your slave, master, if you please,' she said humbly. 'Soon you shall be gone. All my students have departed, and I shall be alone in my school, and want the memory of your attention. Sensation, Mr Peake – my body must glow in her submission to you. You are the dark fire, the bright scent and colour of the hot lands, come to breathe pain and life into my cold northern flesh. Phydia shall be first; you shall whip her, please, to make me shudder at the thought of what is in store for me, knowing that you will punish me ten times more harshly.'

'If you wish,' said Peake.

'No, master!' cried Miss Mann. 'It is precisely what I do not wish. I must submit to your will.'

'You are aware I shall hurt you most severely,' said Peake.

She smiled with fierce joy, her face flushed, and panted with real, evidently satisfying fear.

123

'O, *please* don't, master! I beg you!'

Peake ignored her entreaties. Phydia stripped, and stood naked as Miss Mann opened a seaman's chest which was full of shiny black rubber fabrics. She extracted a long thin ribbon of latex and began to wind it efficiently around Phydia's body, starting at her collar and binding the breasts securely, but leaving the big cherry nipples exposed. The binding continued across the belly, which was pressed into the tightest of corsets until the waist seemed no more than two hands' girth; the fount was left bare, as were the buttocks, but soon every remaining inch of Phydia's body, including her dainty feet, was a thin shell of gleaming rubber, like a second skin or the carapace of a scarab. Her feet were fastened into thick boots anchored to the floorboards, about four feet apart, and Miss Mann tightened their screw fastenings until Phydia moaned and begged her to stop. She did stop, but only after tightening the boots a few more notches until Phydia's spread bare buttocks trembled violently, and she wailed. She placed a black rubber hood over Phydia's head, encasing her with only an aperture at the nose for her to breathe.

Then Phydia held out her arms and her wrists were cuffed together in metal bracelets attached to a chain pulley through a ring in the ceiling. This was tightened until her whole body was stretched and her arms high and straining above her head. The other end of the chain split into two strands, one shorter than the other. To this was attached a large steel buckle with tiny spikes, and these were threaded through piercings in each of Phydia's nostrils, giving her the aspect of a tethered cow. The other chain was similarly adorned, and the wires of the second buckle passed through the pierced lips of her naked fount.

Three more chains were fastened to her body, one from a fixture on the the far wall, through her furrow to the fount-buckle; the others from the opposite wall, which clamped her bare nipples and pulled her breasts grotesquely out from her body. The chains were fully tightened, so that Phydia's rubber-encased body was a trembling arrow whose slightest brusque movement would cause her some discomfort. Peake asked if the maid was ready to be whipped on the bare.

'Not yet, Mr Peake. She must first beg to be whipped. That is the sweetest part of her enslavement.'

Miss Mann took a long goose-feather and inserted it delicately under Phydia's buttocks, until its tip was stroking the swollen pink quim-lips. Then she began to tickle her fount and inner thighs, withdrawing from time to time to tickle her bare bum and the tender skin of the furrow at her anal bud, through the chain-links which kissed the girl's perineum and tender region. Phydia started to tremble, and gurgling came from her throat. She clenched her buttocks as though she were already receiving a flogging, and as her body shook, the chains slapped tight against her rubbered flesh, causing her little moans of discomort as her bare nipples and labia were pulled.

'O! Aha! O! Stop, stop, stop! Please . . . it's cruel!'

'Why, Phydia, if you can stand my tickling for only five more minutes, then you shall be spared Mr Peake's cane,' said her tormentor mildly.

Phydia continued to wail and moan, until she squealed that she would rather have the cane – please – anything but the horrid feather! Miss Mann selected two implements from her cupboard, and handed them to Peake. One was a thin, whippy yew, about four and a half feet long, and this was to be used on the buttocks. The other was a short tawse of black thick leather with three wicked tongues. This, Miss Mann indicated, was suitable for use on the breasts, the teats and areolae being well stretched to present a target. Peake began with the breasts, taking care to make the tawse-thongs flick hard on the nipples, which soon became dark red under his strokes, while the soft breasts themselves trembled beneath their rubber binding like jellies. Phydia's moans at her tickling were nothing compared to her wailing as her nipples were flogged from both sides of her trussed body.

All the time, Miss Mann stood humbly, watching the torment of her maid with bright eyes, and her arms folded meekly in front of her. Intent on his work, Peake looked at her rarely: at each glance, her fingers seemed busier at her crotch, and the wet on her thin dress had spread. When Phydia had taken forty strokes of the tawse to her bare nipples, Peake laid down the implement and took up his cane. He stood touching Phydia's arse-chain, pulled on it roughly to still her, and took aim.

At his first stroke her wailing became quite pitiful, and at each subsequent stroke her voice blubbed and choked and sobbed, without avail. His caning was hard and regular, and by the time he had delivered the fortieth, her bare nates were a mass of purple and crimson and her twitching and squirming were a frenzy that took no heed of the jangling chains that chafed her tender parts. She hung, sobbing and broken in her bonds. The inner thighs of her black rubber carapace gleamed moist; on the floor beneath her naked fount glistened a little pool of oil. In a small, choked voice, she begged to be released, and her mistress complied. As soon as she was free, Phydia knelt on the floor, groped sightless for the master's feet, and began to kiss them with her lips and tongue straining against the thin rubber of her face hood. One hand clutched Peake's ankles; the other rubbed feverishly and without shame between her thighs.

'Thank you, master,' she moaned, 'thank you. O! Ooo . . .!'

As Phydia's body convulsed in her joy, Miss Mann swiftly stripped herself and stood naked before her master. Her body was golden with an unblemished sun-bronze, including the lush swelling of her fount, which was shaven clean of hair so that the lips glistened pink and wet and swollen under the smooth golden hillock of her mons. Her breasts stood firm and proud, the nipples already erect like dimpled tangerines, and her thighs glistened with the oils she had seeped on watching Phydia's torment. She smiled shyly, and held out her scholar's mortarboard.

'I must be bound, too, master,' she whispered, 'but otherwise I must, as mistress, wear my mortarboard.'

She twisted the cap, and it seemed to snap in two, then uncoil so that the headpiece was revealed as two large cylinders of stiff black cloth, bound by the silk band. Peake expressed admiration for this device, and she told him he must make her wear it. She knelt and spread her buttocks and fount-lips, and Peake gingerly inserted the two solid prongs into both her anal orifice and her fount. She ordered him to push deeply; he obeyed, and was rewarded with a groaning and twisting of her nates, as she grunted in satisfied pain.

'O, that hurts,' she gasped. 'Right up my bum! God, it's good! She's elastic, isn't she, master? Can you feel how she gives – you push and push, and then you slide in like a greased thunderclap . . . That's the glory of a bum-fill, it always feels like the first time.'

Phydia removed her hood. Miss Mann could not give instructions to her master, she said, so she whispered suggestions to Phydia who then conveyed them to Peake. In this way the mistress of Dothemaids organised her own trussing. The prongs were fastened in her bumhole and slit by the simple knotting of the silk band around her waist and furrow, whose pressure was reinforced by a heavy chain panty, like a mediaeval chastity belt. When Peake remarked on this, pulling the garment tight around her fount, she murmured that in fact it was just that.

Her hands were roped behind her back and she was forced to adopt a kneeling, submissive posture, with the soles of her bare feet peeping up from under her buttocks. Peake knotted the wrist-ropes securely and with much show of expertise, and took care that Phydia should not see they were simple slip-knots, from which escape might eventually be effected by a disobedient slave. Then her upper body was draped with heavy chains, each of which was fastened to a buckle on the floor, giving her the aspect of a tent or flagpole held precariously upright. Her breasts were clamped with pincers and fastened to a pulley from the ceiling; her scalp was hooded, and held uncomfortably back by a chain that fastened to her shackled ankles.

A leather sheath, like a corset, pinioned her thighs together, and her naked breasts were forced upwards by a steel corset over her chains, which seemed even tighter than the rubber which had bound Phydia's belly, and pressed the already biting chains still further against her body. Finally, she was gagged, with a harsh, studded leather thong whose studs faced inwards, and her mouth was filled by a steel ball which depressed her tongue and made her cheeks swell as though she were hiding an apple. Her eyes gleamed bright and fearful at Peake as he took up the tawse; she insisted on being able to see as he beat her breasts.

Phydia had taken forty on her breasts; her mistress took twice that, and without squealing. Her only noise was a sigh of satisfaction as she squinted down from her head's twisted position to see her breasts reddening to crimson under Peake's lashes, and the nipples jumping in stiff pain as the tips of the quirt flicked them harshly. Then her bare shoulders had to receive the cat, a vicious flail which Phydia kissed before handing it to the master. The slave maid was quite blatant about rubbing her own fount as Peake whipped her mistress; when Miss Mann had taken four dozen on the shoulders with the cat, leaving her back a criss-cross of savage crimson, it was time for her bare-bum caning. She was trembling now, and her eyes and cheeks were wet with tears. Her buttocks shivered as though in song.

The chains which bound her left a clear space for the cane's attention. Peake had to sweep low with the long springy wood, and lifted his arm to full height, so that each impact travelled far and made a resounding crack as it stroked her bare flesh. At each stroke she shuddered, and after a dozen, Peake shifted, without warning, to flog the exposed soles of her tender feet. This caused Miss Mann to howl, and dance within the strenuous bonds of her chains, which rattled cruelly at each stroke. Again and again he flogged her helpless bare feet, while Phydia moaned in pleasure, hand busy at her voluptuous frottage. At intervals, Phydia moaned loud and long, and her black body shuddered in a spasm, like an insect dancing on a pin.

When the mistress's shaking feet were prettily criss-crossed with red, Peake completed the caning of her glowing bare nates. The crimson was darkening to purple with blackened stripes at the centre, where the heavy cane's tip caught her, squirming, again and again with pitiless force. She took six dozen strokes of the cane before Peake pronounced her chastisement at an end – with one for luck. At the last stroke she groaned aloud, and the floor beneath her wet thighs was a pool of her seeped oil.

'The chastisement is over,' he said, 'but not the punishment.'

Suddenly, he grasped Phydia, and before her pleasure-sated body could attempt to struggle, he had her clamped by the waist in a steel body-cinch attached to a sort of mediaeval stocks. She squirmed and squealed, and he said he should be forced to gag her like her mistress. Then he bound her wrists and ankles, using the same ferocious-looking but easy knots which bound her mistress. When this was done, he surveyed the two trussed and helpless females, facing each other in staring, impotent fear.

'I'm going to leave now,' he said pleasantly, 'and I have no intention of coming back to release you. Just think, ladies, you are all alone in the house, unable to move or speak ... Bound in helpless submission, forever and ever.'

Miss Mann's reaction to this dire information was extreme. She began to strain against her bounds, and her fesses and fount writhed against the prongs that filled her bumhole and slit, as though she were trying to impale herself. She squealed louder and louder through her gag, and seemed to be trying to speak. The oils could be seen flowing quite copiously from her swollen fount-lips.

'Mmm! Mmm! Mmm ...' she moaned. The words escaped in distorted form. 'Again ... Say it again!'

'Unable to move or speak,' Peake intoned, 'bound in helpless submission, forever and ever.'

Miss Mann screamed. Her body seemed about to burst in torment as her screams rose in a helpless crescendo of pure ecstacy, dying down very gradually to a mewling sob of contentment. She looked after Peake with glistening, grateful eyes as he closed the door behind him.

Downstairs, he telephoned for a taxi. As he got into the cab, he felt something hard in each pocket. In one was a gold-wrapped custard cream. In the other was a diamond, as hard and precious as the diamond that reared from his balls.

8

Miss Leslie's Bash

'Have a good win at the geegees, Binky?' drawled Peake, refilling his glass of port and holding it quizzically up to the light, in the fashion of a gentleman, to suggest that every mouthful was a matter of great deliberation.

'I did, actually,' exclaimed the red-faced Binky. 'No outsiders, plunged on the favourite – money in the bank. It came in at six to five. Don't mind telling you, Peake – you're my best pal, Peake old boy – won a packet! Pass the port, old boy. Did I ever tell you you're my very best pal?'

'You must have had quite a stake,' said Peake. 'Six to five is short odds. Whence the boodle?'

'O . . .' said Binky with a furious blush. 'You'll never believe me. That Leslie Scammon . . . what a girl! You know I went to her bash in the Iffley Road the other night. I bet you are dying to hear what happened!'

'Not at all, Binky,' said Peake. 'What passes between a gentleman and a lady is their business alone.'

'Peake, you're my best pal! Heavens, my glass is empty. Thank you, that's better. You must be itching with curiosity. Not a bad drop, eh? And there's plenty more.'

'Binky, I should no more demand your confidences than expect you to demand mine. Silence is golden, old boy.'

'You don't mean that!'

'I do.'

'Honestly?'

'Honestly.'

Binky subsided for a moment, and applied himself to his port glass. He smiled, the smile turning to a giggle. He stared at the ceiling, then the wall, then at Peake. He broke the silence.

'Not a bad drop, eh?'

'Very sound, Binky.'

'Well, since you ask,' said Binky, as if it had just occurred to him, 'when I got to the house in Iffley Road . . .'

Binky's narrative was in turns coy, delighted, amazed, enthusiastic, rambling, shocked and exuberant. Peake listened impassively as the port was consumed.

Binky had brought a bottle of white wine, but Leslie Scammon opened the door and cheerfully informed him that they preferred champagne.

'And we take it in a rather special way,' Leslie said mysteriously.

Binky entered to be agreeably surprised that Leslie's table groaned with every kind of beverage, including some very decent brandy and port, which Leslie insisted on mixing for him in a special cocktail. Soon the animation of the group seemed great fun, and Binky got over his initial surprise that he seemed to be the only male there, apart from Leslie and a rather daredevil black fellow who was apparently the latest 'hot diggety' in the Chicago jazz scene. There were plenty of people dressed as males, 'sort of like that fellow Charlie Chaplin', but they were all female! Leslie brushed aside his query by saying that one was never sure what sort of chaps would turn up.

Some of the other females were dressed in awfully sweet girly outfits, all frills and taffeta and pink and yellow and white, with lots of knickers and garter belts

132

rather daringly on show beneath little pleated skirts. He recognised some of the actresses from *The Drudges*: all seemed to have extraordinarily narrow waists. Other females wore quite bizarre costumes in black or purple, made of leather and even rubber, and some had masks and were festooned with chains, with little canes or whips dangling at their belts. Leslie, coat off, was wearing just such a costume, to Binky's surprise, and so was Lucinda Lalage, whom he recognised from the play.

After a couple of cocktails, Binky thought it tremendously jolly. There was jazz music on the gramophone, and some tinkly coloured music called blues, and he found himself much in demand as a dance partner. There was no charleston or black bottom or any of these energetic modern things, much to his relief; instead there were slow, intimate dances which the girls called 'smooching' and where they pressed their bodies against his, very tightly, grinding quite lasciviously with their hips, so that his reaction was what any normal young fellow's would be, and they didn't seem to mind, in fact they seemed pleased. He was pleasantly reminded of the *bonhomie* in the stews of Port Said, only here it seemed genuine rather than mercenary.

It seemed quite natural that the girls should dance with each other, and that some of the girly ones should allow their dark partners to feel their breasts or even hold their hands inside their short frillies while they danced. Binky was rather taken aback when Leslie invited him to dance, but agreed to, thinking it a bit of a lark. Leslie smelled funny, but nice, like a girl, and Binky drew back in shock when Leslie began to rub most naughtily against his crotch and murmured that it was all right, for she *was* a girl.

Binky had to have another cocktail to steady his nerves but soon began to see the funny side. And, in truth, the pressing of Leslie's body had made him excited, but now he did not have to feel guilty about it,

133

so returned to the smooching with great enthusiasm. Leslie explained about the rubber prosthesis, or *obispos*, with which he should be familiar from the poems of Hesiod: 'the forbidden poems,' she giggled. If he did not believe her, he only had to feel for himself. She raised her short black leather skirt to show her net stockings and a ribbon of white flesh between stocking tops and black skimpy panties of shiny rubber!

She took his hand and plunged it right inside her panties, on to her mons, which was now smooth as silk and quite shaven of hair; then made him put his fingers inside her lady's place, which was all soft and wet, just like the real thing! Well, it was the real thing, she insisted as she tongued his ear. Binky was quite excited by now and kissed Leslie, reminding himself that she was a proper girl – well, maybe not proper, but certainly real. Leslie broke away and said it was time for some fun, despite Binky's protests that he was having fun already. Consoled with another cocktail, he watched as the girly girls stripped themselves of their tops and revealed themselves to be all wearing corsets of pastel-coloured shiny silks and satins, trimmed with frothy lace. That explained their narrow waists.

The girlies lined up, giggling and simpering, and Lucinda Lalage passed along the line putting her hands around their waists; those whose girth she could not encompass were singled out and ordered to be spanked. Those chosen bent over quite merrily and, with lots of squealed protest allowed their frilly panties to be pulled down, then were spanked on their bare bottoms quite severely by Lucinda, by Leslie, and by one or two of the females in leather, who did not stop at hand-spanking, but used their whips on the shivering bare bums too. The girlies took it in good sport, and then Leslie said they should have fireworks as their reward.

All the girlies clamoured to have fireworks. Binky was mystified, until he saw crates of champagne. The bare bums of the girlies were spread, giving a clear and very immodest view of their pink quim-lips, and then bottles of champagne were shaken vigorously, uncorked, and as the wine frothed from the bottle, the nozzles were pressed against their open slits, causing them to shriek with merriment. The wine cascaded down their thighs and was eagerly licked up by the kneeling leather-clad women, whose tongues did not stop when the champagne was finished, but lingered to lick the girlies in their bum-cracks and even on their quims themselves, with much oohing and aahing from the shivering maids, their bums bobbing red from the spanking as the liquid cascaded. Binky admired their genuine pleasure, for in the stews of Port Said he had only been familiar with feigned pleasure.

The leather women now selected various girlies and started treating them as their servants, slaves or pets, commanding them to stand and beg, kneel, sit or apply their tongues to the exposed quim-lips of their mistress, who would roll down her rubber or leather panties and reveal her bare fount for this act of obeisance. If they did not lick hard enough, they were awarded a crack from the cane or whip across their bare shoulders, on the corset or even down on the fesses themselves, already crimson from spanking. Leslie intitiated the next stage of the proceedings; she removed completely her own skirt and panties and stood only in a black leather corset studded with sharp silver knobs, with her whip in hand.

Deftly, she fitted on her massive *obispos*, the rubber phallus which was so lifelike at Parson's Pleasure. Then she selected her girly, spread her buttocks and rammed the rubber organ deep into her slit, moving in and out as though she were a male pleasuring his female. The groans and cries of pleasure were most realistic, especially Leslie's, for the dusky jazz musician was helpfully tickling the front of her labia, where, Binky had heard, ladies had a 'pleasure button'.

Soon Leslie panted and moaned and cried out in a spasm of joy that sounded perfectly ecstatic. Binky was enjoying the spectacle hugely, especially as he was propping up the comfortably lavish bar. The other mistresses followed their hostess's example, donning rubber appliances and inserting them between the compliant buttocks of their subservient 'slaves', and not just in their lady's place, but in their bumhole as well! While they were penetrating the girly's fount, they would rub the front of her quim-lips with their fingers; if they had chosen their girly's bumhole, they would rub themselves, unless the jazz singer was there to oblige.

The dark man had a notable bulge in the front of his trousers as he performed this servile task, and soon there was wild, ragged applause as he divested himself of his trousers and revealed an organ that stood gleaming like an enormous ebony tree. Now when a mistress was inserting her *obispos* into the willing holes of a slave girl, the jazz man had his organ plunged into the bumhole of the mistress herself, to make a pretty tryptych of amorous sport. He seemed quite superhuman, not allowing himself to spurt, but passing from one bumhole to the next with a gentleman's politeness, and making sure that every lady had her pleasure from him.

He would accompany his thrusting by vigorous slaps to the bare buttocks of his ladies, which increased their own ardour and their cries of 'O! Ragamuffin! You gorgeous brute!' The whole thing seemed to the imbibing Binky like a choreographed, if rather blurred, ballet. At last, the jazz man had brought one particularly fierce mistress to evident pleasure, in her quim, and withdrew his organ, which was still massively stiff and glistening with her juices.

Leslie promptly grasped his waist and knelt, to take his organ between her lips. She began to suck vigorously, as on a lollipop. Not only that, but she swallowed the whole shaft of his manhood right down to the balls, straightening her neck to allow the giant ramrod to penetrate her throat in a technique that suggested much practice. At last the jazz man clutched her hair and began to sway and cry out and moan, as though he were spurting, and Leslie's throat swallowed convulsively. His organ seemed to wilt a trifle and she released him, wiping shiny cream from her smiling lips. Binky clapped loudly, and all eyes were suddenly on him.

He felt himsef pinioned, his nostrils assailed by heady perfumes of female juices and lust, and was powerless to resist as his clothing was stripped from him. In truth, he did not really want to resist. Naked, he was stood beside the black man, who put his arm in friendly fashion around his shoulder and pointed at Binky's organ, which in his embarrassment had quite wilted from its former eminence. The black man's organ, too, was flaccid; someone produced a tape measure, and Binky was the butt of derision, as he had evidently lost in a comparison of size. Now Leslie kneeled down and began to lick his balls, while Lucinda Lalage did the same to her fellow countryman.

The two organs, pink and ebony, rose majestically to their full height, and this time Binky was proclaimed equal, to his great pride and satisfaction. The black man whispered congratulations and said that he had 'held back a bit', in sympathy. He took hold of his organ and whirled it around like a toy windmill; then he grasped Lucinda Lalage, who laughed and pretended to resist, and made her bend over to touch her toes, bare bum raised. He whipped her with his organ, which made a fearful slapping, though Binky did not suppose it hurt very much.

It undoubtedly hurt Lucinda, though, when she scuttled on all fours to return with a cane in her teeth, which she presented to the black man, making his organ stiffen again to the full. She begged him to attend to her bottom; he gave Lucinda thirteen very juicy ones on the bare, and she took every stroke without a sound, with only the slightest trembling of her clenched dark fesses, which Binky thought so pretty as they purpled that his own organ grew stiff again.

At this, Leslie pointed, and proclaimed him a naughty boy worthy of punishment. Despite Binky's protests, which he admitted were only half-hearted, he was pinioned by a group of eager sweating girlies and obliged, in fun, to don a girly's outfit: panties, stockings, corset, the lot! The corset in particular was awfully tight; Leslie produced a curly blonde wig and he had to wear that too. Oddly, he accepted the fun, as it reminded him no little of some of the high jinks in dorm after lights out at school, so it didn't seem any harm.

It did seem a trifle odd, though, when Leslie ripped down his new frilly knickers and began to spank his bare bum with her hand, making him bend over and kiss Lucinda Lalage's shoes as she did so. He took it without too much protest, but when the hand was replaced by a cane he shrieked in anguished surprise, and had his voice muffled by Lucinda's leathery palm pressed tightly on his lips. Struggle and squirm as he might, he was obliged to take four tight ones from Leslie, and as the tears welled in his eyes, he heard the girls taunt him, saying 'Look at her bum shiver', 'Isn't she pretty for the cane', 'What a juicy little madam', and suchlike.

After the four stingers he thought it was over – but no! The cane was passed to another mistress, her face unseen, and he took another four, even tighter than Leslie's. Pain and tears blurred his eyes, but his comforting cargo of drink made it seem not too bad, and strangely distant, as though the pain belonged to someone else. He had to admit to Peake – he wouldn't breathe a word, would he? – that after a while he was actually enjoying it, looking forward to the next searing cane-stroke, and exaggerating the squirming of his bare backside to enjoy the coos and thrills of his audience. It made it all the more pleasant when he was allowed to pause between latherings and have another cocktail, and wonder if his wig was on straight and his stockings and skirt not too rumpled, and all that lovely girly fussing.

Binky admitted ruefully that he must have been very convincing as a girly, for when his bum was smarting like the devil, and his squirms under the cane were in no way feigned – he reckoned proudly that he must have taken at least three dozen tight cuts – Leslie decided that to appreciate true chastisement, he needed to know what girlies really had to put up with. To Binky's horror, the cheeks of his smarting bum were stretched wide and he smelled Leslie's magical, excited scent as she straddled him and pushed her greased rubber organ right into his anus! He groaned and squirmed and shuddered, but he could not resist, and after she had pushed really hard, suddenly it seemed to give way. She simply shot inside him, filling his bum completely, and he moaned and sobbed, to great girly mirth, because he did not want to resist. And they knew it!

Leslie's was not the only *obispos* which shafted his defenceless bumhole; the girlies and mistresses took it in turn to poke him, taunting him that it must remind him of boarding school, and he could not honestly deny that it did, nor that being poked by a girl was infinitely better than ... well, you know. As he was attended to, lips licked his balls and he felt feathery fingers and soft moist lips caressing his organ to a maddening stiffness.

The girls frigged their pleasure buttons against his raw whipped bum, and each of them had some devilish squeezy contraption in their stiff rubber organs, so that when they had pleasured themselves to their own satisfaction, they would cry out, just like a chap at *that* moment, and spurt hot cream right into Binky's convulsed anus! He was quite delirious with unimaginable pain and unimaginable pleasure, and at last, to his horror – it must have been his sixth or seventh bumming – he knew he was about to spurt. He did so, crying out in a spasm of joy, all over Leslie's face.

He dimly remembered being seated and dressed in his frillies again, upon which he received showers of happy kisses as the girlies told him what a wonderful sport he was, and so on. Happily, the cocktails were constantly replenished, and Binky did not remember too much after that, except that in the morning he woke up dressed in his own clothes, heading back to college in a taxi. At home, he stripped to take a bath, and to his astonishment he was still wearing his frilly girl's knickers as a memento of the party. But the garment was not the only memento – the panties were stuffed full of five-pound notes!

'So now you know how I had the stake money for that nag, Peake old boy,' he concluded. 'What an experience! I never knew bumming could be such fun! I mean, in Port Said, I always had to give the bints money . . . And here were bints giving me money! As though I were some kind of whore. I say, Peake, does that make me a whore?'

Peake smiled for the first time.

'Yes, Binky, it does,' he said. 'Enjoy it.'

As Peake refilled their glasses and produced Havana cigars, there was a knock at the door. It was Brewer, with a message for Mr Peake. The Dean requested his presence.

Peake's interview with the Dean was preceded neither with an invitation to sit, nor the customary glass of sherry. It was brief and grimly to the point. Peake stood unblinking as his dossier of sins was read to him: fined on numerous occasions for climbing in after hours; the bulldogs had been detailed to watch his movements;

140

mingling with a set quite unbecoming to a member of college, such as Miss Edwina Cheshunt, Lady Flora de Cante *et al*; time frittered away in scandalous theatrical productions; trips to London, weekends spent away from college, all in flagrant breach of the rules. Mr Bevercon's well-meaning excuses were now useless: the warden, possibly under the influence of his lady wife, had showed an unaccountable leniency concerning Mr Peake's activities, but was now leaving for Cambridge.

'I believe there is a university at Cambridge,' said the Dean, peering malevolently over his pince-nez spectacles, and pronouncing the word 'Cambridge' as though it were some unpleasant bodily function. 'No doubt at Cambridge they will be delighted to attribute this contemptible playlet of yours to Aristophanes, when any worthwhile scholar can see that it is nothing but some trumpery from the charlatan Apollonius of Euboea. That disgrace to scholarship alone would quite justify your being sent down from college. Your days with us are over, Mr Peake, and you shall make arrangements to depart by the week's end.'

The Dean added as Peake left that in view of the warden's imminent departure, there could be no appeal within college, and he should not waste time going to Convocation or the University authorities, as the Dean had troubled to consult them first, and they were in complete agreement.

'Goodbye, Mr Peake. Do not forget to settle your battels before going down; I believe your account at the wine cellar is quite substantial.'

'Gosh,' said Binky, on Peake's return, 'I suppose this calls for rather a lot to drink.'

Peake agreed; they had rather a lot to drink.

'I say,' slurred Binky some time later, putting his arm around Peake and waving a port bottle as though to give authority to his words, 'did I ever tell you, Peake, you're my best pal? What are you going to do? Go back

141

to Kent? Gosh, the country must seem so boring after Oxford, and being in town so much.'

Peake said that Binky was right about the country, and added that the only person who might make it interesting had long departed for America. He would stay in town for a while, and then he supposed he would go to the West Indies, to claim his inheritance in St Botolph.

'It is not technically my inheritance yet, since my uncle isn't dead, but he is getting on a bit, and I dare say he will be glad to have me help out.'

'Are you all right for money, Peake?' said Binky. 'You see, I'm not short any more, and I don't think I shall be, because ... Well, you remember what I said about Leslie Scammon's bash? I didn't mention –' he grinned shyly '– that she's asked me back. Not just her, but Lucinda Lalage, and a whole lot more. Seems I am quite popular, so I reckon I'll be quids in from now on. While it lasts, of course.'

Peake told him that to enjoy being a whore, it was simply necessary to enjoy being a whore. It was a question of getting one's mind right. He said that he was not short of money, and allowed himself a few careful revelations about his own activities amongst the smart set. Binky said 'gosh' several times, adding that he was scarcely any nearer to knowing what women really wanted. Peake smiled.

'A good thrashing is the simplest answer,' he said. 'Whether to take one, or to administer one. But it all boils down to money. Money is power, and women respect that. You have learned from Leslie that people like to pay for pleasure; it puts things right. They are suspicious of getting something for nothing because they suspect it to be valueless. That is why your knickers were stuffed full of banknotes, my friend. And long may they be so! As long as you don't mind baring your bum for a lady's pleasure. As for myself ... Well, there are some women who want to thrash, and others who want to be thrashed. Who knows why? Perhaps it is a form of sensual revenge, or a form of equally sensual penance. I take it you are familiar with the poet Mallarmé.'

Binky said he was quite familiar with Mallarmé, but not his works.

'Mallarmé said that every human conversation may be reduced to a silent exchange of money,' Peake said. 'But I would add that every conversation between male and female can be reduced to the wordless crack of whips.'

They got rather merry, and went to the post office, where Peake made a telephone call to London, and then sent a telegram to 'Mayfair Plantation, St Botolph, West Indies'. Peake explained that the plantation was called Mayfair because its inhabitants, whether workers or overseers, had a reputation for fancy metropolitan airs. Business accomplished, Binky and Peake had a riotous supper at the Turf Tavern, and then proceeded to the twilit streets of Jericho, where they went into a public house. Peake said that it was refreshing to mingle with the working classes, who were the salt of the earth and the backbone of England.

'They understand life in the raw, Binky. There is no statement of account here, only hard cash.'

Binky said nervously that there were a lot of painted women, and that they seemed to be gay girls.

'Then we are amongst colleagues,' said Peake. 'Why, hard cash is the gayest thing imaginable.'

He engaged one of the gay girls in conversation. Her name was Flora, and she accepted a large port and lemon.

'Flora is a most aristocratic name,' said Peake. 'So tell me, Flora, do you like to play aristocratic games?'

'That depends on who's paying,' said Flora.

She was a handsome, tousled blonde woman with

awkward lipstick, and was dressed gaudily, to please if not to impress. Her scent was cloying and its message unmistakable. She accepted another port and lemon with alacrity, and stared at the fistful of five-pound notes which Peake brandished.

'The Bank of England is paying, Flora,' he said. 'You can take one of thse bits of paper to Threadneedle Street and exchange it for five pounds' worth of gold. That is called the credit theory of economy.'

'You University gents know these things,' said Flora doubtfully. 'But I know a fiver when I see one.'

'To me, it is but a scrap of paper, Flora, and I am quite happy to exchange it for services bravely rendered,' Peake murmured. 'Not just one, either.'

He counted ten five-pound notes and made them into a roll, which he pretended to tuck between Flora's breasts. She smiled.

'There's not a girl in Jericho braver than me,' she said.

More drinks were drunk, and the little party grew merry. Flora acted protectively over her new benefactors, and even curtailed her visits to the ladies', for fear that her gents should escape. She regaled them with stories of her life's hardships, how her husband beat her most severely (though she knew she deserved it, and it was the way of things), how Mr Morris was planning a motor-car factory at Cowley, and her man proposed to get work there and she would have to leave her lifelong home. She spoke as if a move to the other end of Oxford was a move to another planet. She would leave her man if she could, but she couldn't, and that was the way of things too.

Much later the trio proceeded arm in arm to the University Parks for 'a nice walk'. They entered the pasture and Peake halted them at convenient shrubbery. He said he was sure Flora had not forgotten the five-pound notes, and her bravery. She giggled and began to play with the opening of his trousers, while at the same time undoing her dress. Peake removed her hand from his crotch.

'But you have such a big bulge, sir,' she whispered. 'Mayn't I taste?'

'First, you must taste this, Flora,' said Peake evenly, withdrawing a yellow crooked cane from beneath his velour cape. 'From what you say, your bum is no stranger to a thrashing.'

Her eyes widened.

'But that was for being naughty and bold,' she said.

'You are naughty and bold to come to the park with two strangers,' said Peake. 'And wishing to leave your lawful husband – why, madam, I think you deserve a good thrashing for your wickedness.'

'Yes, I suppose I do,' said Flora glumly.

'On the bare,' said Peake.

'You mean – knickers down?'

'Yes. Doesn't your man thrash you on the bare?'

'No! He is my husband, and respects me, though he uses his belt, a great heavy studded thing. Ugh! I hate it.'

'Well, gentlemen use the cane, Flora, and always on the bare – it's more tasteful. The pain is more intense, but you can always run away if you are scared. Look, the street lamp is not twenty yards away.'

'A gent's punishment – I suppose that's all right. I'll take your beating, sir . . . Oo! And bare, like you say.'

Peake ordered her to lift her dress to her neck and bend over, touching her toes, with her knickers at her ankles. She obeyed, shivering, and then Peake held up a shiny red ruby.

'I propose to give you twenty strokes, Flora, for £50, but if you'll take this instead, it'll only be a dozen.'

Her face creased in disgust.

'Go away! Cheap paste! Give me twenty whacks, and honest fivers, sir, like a gent, and don't mock. I can take it!'

She did take it: twenty harsh strokes to the bare buttocks, which left her trembling and red, but she did not cry out, save for a long stifled groan of distress at the eleventh. She rose, and wiped tears from her eyes, holding her hand out for the money. Peake gave it to her, and she put it down her bodice, like a cat cunningly hiding a morsel of fish. Then she knelt and licked her lips, and began to open Peake's trousers, for honest completion of the transaction. She rubbed his stiffness with a coo of genuine admiring pleasure. Peake stayed her, saying that his friend had yet had no pleasure, and that there was another £50 for her.

'Another thrashing?' she wailed. 'O, sir, my bum smarts so! Well, if you are paying.'

Binky took the cane, pondered, then suddenly handed it to Flora. Then he stooped, and bared his buttocks.

'Twenty for me, please, madam,' he whispered, with a shy grin at Peake. 'You don't mind, old pal? It's just that after Leslie's bash, I think I have rather a taste for it.'

Binky's manhood was stiff as he took his twenty cuts on the bare, with much dramatic clenching of his bum, and begging his cruel mistress to stop. Peake smoked placidly as he watched his friend's bare backside reddening. As Binky cried, Flora looked questioningly at Peake, who nodded that the beating should continue, and Flora's eyes burned with a vengeful pleasure that was not entirely commercial. When Binky was squirming and hopping in pain, she said she was an honest woman and gave value for money, then knelt and took his erect shaft between her lips. With swift bobbing movements of her head, she milked him until he spurted in her mouth. She took the rest of the money and tucked it safely away, her face glowing with pleasure.

'Thank you, sir!' she exclaimed, through lips glistening with Binky's spend. 'A hundred pounds! Soon

I can afford to leave him, and move to . . . to Abingdon! I'm sure I'll get a job in a teashop. I can leave him now, for I've already been thrashed for it, haven't I? And do you know, sir, my bum is all warm and glowing, it's the first time I've ever been caned, or even beaten on the bare, and I think I really enjoyed the thrashings, both of them. Bare is the gentleman's way – and there's much to be said for it, and I'm glad, sir.'

'You see, Binky?' said Peake, as they strolled home. 'She thrashed, and was thrashed, with pleasure, because she was paid. She could have had a ruby worth five times as much, and for less pain, but she only believed in banknotes. Pain, pleasure, riches – all in the mind, old pal . . .'

9

Eulalia

Peake dawdled for two weeks at Eulalia Preen's house in Greencoat Place, assuring her more than once that her hospitality was worth more than any University. He arrived one morning, and the door was opened by a handsome maid, as tall as Peake himself, who blushed shyly as she called the porter to attend to his cases. Then the maid showed him to Miss Preen's salon, where Eulalia awaited him with black peignoire and cigarette holder, nursing a flute of champagne. She was naked under her flimsy robe, and barefoot; the maid kneeled to kiss her painted toes before withdrawing.

'Isn't she a darling?' drawled Eulalia, extending a hand for Peake to kiss. 'I can't get used to calling her "him" – my lovely husband Freddie, of the Coo-loonial Office!'

She burst into a musical peal of laughter.

'You are not, of course, shocked,' she said, 'knowing you as I do, Mr Peake. Nor will you be shocked that Freddie is most understanding – grateful, even – for me to have my special needs attended to by a vigorous man such as yourself. It excites him, you see, as though my donation of my body to others somehow confirms him in pride of ownership. Aren't men strange! Well, you are one, so I suppose you should know. Have some champagne, and amuse me.'

They drank champagne and Eulalia laughed at his

story of Binky's evening in the Iffley Road, his expulsion from Oxford, and their farewell celebration in Jericho. Then she yawned and stretched, allowing her peignoire to fall open across her sheeny dark legs, revealing a bare mink gleaming and shaven. She saw Peake's eyes and grinned mischievously.

'How wanton of me,' she murmured. 'Are you shaven, sir?'

Peake said he was not, and she made a face.

'I suppose you have a horrid forest of curly hairs,' she said. 'I must shave you, Mr Peake. Bare is beautiful – bare is clean. I felt cleansed when you beat me at Dothemaids Hall. Now I feel like a spanking; I often take a spanking in the mornings, it cleanses me. I need the clean smack of bare hand on my bare skin, and a lovely warm glow to see me through the day, then in the afternoon a sound whipping or caning, to make me lively for the evening. A lady's life is so busy! You will please attend to me.'

Without more ado, she unfastened her peignoire and dropped it on the white pile carpet, then draped herself nude on Peake's thigh. He spanked her bare bottom a good forty times, while she shivered and sighed with satisfaction as her dark skin purpled. Then she wriggled from his thigh and began to rub his manhood to stiff swelling. Peake did not resist as she unfastened him and released the naked organ, at which she gasped with unfeigned astonishment.

'Heavens! What have we here? Why, Mr Peake, you must stay in my house as long as you please – no, as long as *I* please! See what you've done to me ...'

She rubbed her finger between her naked fount-lips, and withdrew it, to press her oily secretion against Peake's tongue. Then she ordered him to make himself completely naked. He did so, frowning, as she opened her thighs and began to frot herself most blatantly on the dark stiff bud between her labia.

'Miss,' he began, 'you may be sure I wish to give you

149

pleasure with my bare hand, or my cane or whip. And my bare body is yours to examine, or to use. But I've never . . . with a lady.'

'No?' she cried. 'How odd! Well, I must be the first, then. How awfully exciting. Surely you do it . . . you know, yourself, or with gay girls.'

'Not with gay girls,' said Peake. 'It would be improper, miss. I am a master, and if I weakened myself by giving spurt inside a lady, then she might not respect me as master. I should be in her power, rather than her in mine, and what lady would reward a mere slave?'

Eulalia Preen smiled in wonder, especially at the word 'reward', and said he was a brave and true master. But there was a problem: an organ such as his – a 'cock', she called it – could not possibly stay in her house unused and untasted. There were ways to compromise.

She began to stroke massive purple bulb of his organ, and he did not resist, although his breathing became sharper as her nimble fingers caressed his peehole. Then she grasped his balls and squeezed them quite hard, making him start, to her grinning pleasure; she transferred her hand to his shaft and began to attend his cock with both hands, one at the helmet, alternately stroking with fingertips and palm, and the other vigorously rubbing the shaft up and down. It was not long before a white droplet appeared at the peehole and she sighed with delight, making her rubbing of the shaft harder and the stroking of his helmet more delicate.

'Excruciating?' she murmured.

'Excruciating,' he sighed, then gasped as a mighty jet of spurt burst from his peehole, over Eulalia's bare breasts.

She continued her massage until the last shudder had subsided from his cock, and then, rubbing the creamy fluid into her skin, she kissed his peehole with puckered lips. She gave him champagne, but did not release him.

Peake drank thirstily, until she began her tickling of his softened cock and balls all over again and he rose to his former stiffness. She rubbed and rubbed, like a tiger at its prey, and then squeezed his cock between her breasts, rubbing him with her velvet skin and telling him that he must spurt like a fountain and wash her petals with his cream. Peake did not resist as the soft pressure of her teats brought him to spurt once more.

The operation was repeated a third time, and Peake was flushed with exertion, pleasure and champagne when he finally groaned that she had him well drained. She did not stop rubbing his cock, and made sure it was standing hard again, then said he was now in the correct priapic state, and it was time for her pleasure. Peake was made to lie on the carpet, on his back.

'Do not worry, sir,' she said, pulling on a bellrope. 'You have been milked, and there cannot be a drop left in you. But you will stand as long as my pleasure dictates, won't you? I have sent for my maid. She may watch my pleasure, and take her morning punishment at the same time. And then I shall be in the mood for shopping.'

Eulalia opened her thighs and squatted over Peake's massive organ, then parted the lips of her fount to reveal her oily wet pink lady's place. She snapped her lips over his helmet and suddenly sank on to him, taking the cock into her right to its hilt. Only his balls were visible; she gave them a playful squeeze and began to rub her stiff nympha as the squeezed his cock and slowly writhed on top of him.

'My, you are big,' she gasped. 'What did you do to become so huge? It must be the tropic heat, Mr Peake. I think you are dark inside . . . you are one of us!'

She slapped her bare breasts quite hard, making the soft flesh tremble, and pinched her stiff nipples, grinning impishly and beginning to suck him harder between her powerful dark haunches.

'I wish Freddie would hurry up!' she cried. 'She'll get extra slaps for her tardiness.'

There was a scratching on the door, and Eulalia bade her maid-husband enter. Freddie looked on the two naked bodies with a raised eyebrow and a purr of satisfaction. Eulalia allowed him to stand watching as her gyrations grew more profound and the movements of her fingers more intense as she gaily frotted herself until Peake's belly was shining with a pool of her moisture. She swivelled, so that her back and buttocks faced Peake's head, and called for her cane. Freddie knelt and shuffled to fetch a short ashplant, which he picked up with his teeth and gave to his mistress, then assumed a posture of submission, kneeling on all fours with frilly skirts raised, so that he straddled Peake's legs. Eulalia brusquely pulled down her maid's knickers.

'Peeking at your mistress while she is at sport!' she cried gleefully. 'You know what that deserves, maid. A sound thrashing on the bare. Doesn't it?'

'Yes, mistress,' quavered the delighted Freddie. 'O, make my bum all hot and red with your cane, mistress. Hurt me frightfully, it is all your naughty maid deserves.'

As she frotted, Eulalia lifted the cane and dealt a fierce slash across her husband's bare fesses, followed with another, and a third in swift succession. She flogged him rapidly and efficiently, seeming to match her cane-strokes with the rhythm of her squeezes to Peake's organ, and the hefty flick of finger on nubbin, until she squealed joyfully in a very loud spasm of pleasure.

'O! O! O!' she gasped. 'Had enough, maid?'

'No, mistress,' panted Freddie. 'How it smarts! I shan't be able to sit down. But my wickedness has not half been punished.'

The maid took thirty stokes of the cane on the bare, until her buttocks were well-mottled and flushed a deep crimson. Then Freddie begged his mistress's permission to dress, as there was an important meeting at the Colonial Office on the Bechuanaland question. She assented, but said that Freddie was to keep on his garter belt, suspenders and stockings, and wear tight trousers, so that the straps should be visible. As she spoke, Eulalia did not stop her frigging, nor her writhing on Peake's cock.

'How mortifying!' cried Freddie with delight as he rose, rubbing his bare bottom. 'Everyone will see, mistress! Everyone will know I am your slave, and envy me!'

He left the room, and Eulalia turned to face Peake again, her face well flushed like her spanked bottom; her thighs pumped as her fingers flicked, and she had come to her spend twice more before Freddie reappeared for inspection. Now he was attired in sober pinstripes, grey waistcoat and black jacket, a bowler hat and umbrella under his arm. The straps of his maid's suspenders were clearly outlined under his pinstripes. Eulalia extended her fingers, glistening with her love-oil, and her slave gravely applied his lips.

'Now leave me, you wretched worm,' said Eulalia and Freddie set off, smiling radiantly, to his day's work.

Eulalia exerted herself once more, cooing that Peake was magnificent and hard and a perfect tool of pleasure. She brought herself to another spend, her noisiest yet; in the middle of her spasm, she bent forward to kiss Peake's lips, but he turned his face away, though he permitted himself to embrace her as she shuddered. When her spasm had subsided, she put her head on his breast.

'You were right to refuse my kiss, master,' she murmured, 'Whores do not kiss . . .'

'Blueberry jam,' said Eulalia Preen to the top-hatted attendant, 'and gooseberry and quince. Some butterscotch cream and honey, too – the Malayan bluebell and the one from Amazonian poppies. And, let's see –' she consulted her shopping list '– we want caviare, and smoked salmon and eels and oysters and things – all the usual stuff, Mr Perkins. I'll leave it in your capable hands. Deliver it to Greencoat Place as usual. Well, Mr Peake, that is the hard part over! Now I feel the urge to shop for clothes.'

She handed Perkins the list, and he saluted. Peake found himself in a taxi on its way from Knightsbridge to the Caledonian Road.

'Marvellous little shop,' said Eulalia as they passed King's Cross and its retinue of gaudy street ladies. 'Found it quite by accident. I was on a bit of a racket, and Flora de Cante bet me I wouldn't doll myself like one of these hussies. I must have been awfully drunk, so I did – and I went out on York Way, and had nine men in one day! Sailors mostly. I whipped three of them, and was whipped by two, and once I had three all together. It was such fun. I made thirteen pounds eight and sixpence, and I won a seven-shilling bottle of champagne from Flossie.'

They entered a shabby doorway and descended a flight of creaking stairs, which smelled quite verminous. Then Eulalia knocked in a curious and rapid sequence on a plain wooden door painted prison-green, which seemed the entrance to the meanest dosser's dwelling. The door swung open and Peake and Eulalia were admitted to the apartment by a sumptuous woman in gold and silver silks, with lacquered hair, prominent conical breasts, and an evidently corsed waist, or waistlet. This creature greeted Eulalia with kisses. They were in a large and airy apartment brightly lit and painted all in white.

'Welcome to my little emporium,' breathed the perfumed creature.

All around stood racks of whores' garments and accessories. There were whips and corsets, crops, canes

154

and restraints of leather or rubber, tight low-cut dresses, an ocean of flouncy underthings, or else panties, stockings and corselets in stern black, and cut with holes at navel, buttock or crotch. There were hoods, handcuffs, boots and shoes with impossibly high stiletto heels and brightly painted devices of constraint in the shapes of cucumbers or bananas, designed for insertion into the tenderest male or female orifices. There were garments that were waistbands from which rubber prostheses dangled, like the artificial male organs Binky had described; some of the bands had two male organs at once, one for each orifice it might be expected to service. Eulalia threw her hands up in delight.

'New stock, Jasmine! How marvellous!'

She began to browse, enthusiastically holding the most bizarre garments against her as though they were no more surprising to her than a pair of winter mittens. Jasmine tossed her long blonde hair and eyed Peake coquettishly.

'If sir would care to try something?' she murmured. 'We have many fine accoutrements in leather for the discriminating master.'

Peake nodded in polite demurral, and said that Miss Eulalia seemed quite in charge of matters. Jasmine whispered she was sure Miss Eulalia would not be displeased if the master cared to accoutre himself somewhat individually, and held up a flowing dress in bright-pink gauzy chiffon, together with a pair of silk stockings and a G-string made of two interwoven silver chains. Eulalia smiled approval and laughed at Peake's astonishment.

'Haven't you ever been robed, Mr Peake?' she asked mischievously. 'Robed, and enjoyed it? So many people are unhappy because they have trapped themselves in singularity, they see themselves as only this, or only that, without understanding that in our nature are all things. You *are* a friend of Susie Rattan, are you not?'

'Yes,' Peake replied slowly, 'but I have never been robed as a lady.'

He met Eulalia's smile with a mischievous one of his own, as though daring her to guess, or admit she knew, the truth – that Miss Rattan had robed him as a serving-maid.

Eulalia told Jasmine to put aside the chiffon dress, she would take it whether Mr Peake thought it suited him or not.

Suddenly, she cried with delight at a large cat-o'-nine-tails, with shiny sharp studs all the way down its thongs and a pearl handle. Jasmine purred with satisfaction.

'A wonderful piece,' she said. 'All the way from Stamboul, where I believe it was in posession of the chief eunuch of the sultan's harem, for the chastisement of imperfect odalisques. If madame would care to try . . .?'

With a flourish, Jasmine bent over and raised her shimmering golden dress, with many frilly petticoats, high over her back, revealing white silk stockings and a pair of high gold-spangled panties. Eulalia pulled down the panties and began to belabour the naked bottom with crisp strokes of the cat. She flogged it nine times, gently at first but her strokes growing quite severe, until Jasmine squealed that madame must have made her mind up, and her poor bottom smarted so that she thought her shopkeeper's duties well fulfilled. Laughing, Eulalia said she would take the whip, as it handled superbly. Jasmine, however remained in position, her bottom glowing.

'Perhaps sir would like to test an implement?' she whispered shyly.

Eulalia handed Peake a cane with a sparkling diamond at its tip, and a green leather handle that fitted snugly over the back of the hand, like a 'brass knuckle'.

'That one will be nice,' she said. 'A diamond – it will cut very hard! Give the boy six of the best, Mr Peake, in your best Abingdon manner. I shall watch with interest.'

'Boy?' said Peake, frowning as he took the cane and flexed it.

'Why, yes, sir, don't you recognise me? Recognise my bum, at any rate,' said Jasmine gaily. 'Jasmine is really Jason – Jason Keach. You said I was the naughtiest fourth-former whose bottom you had ever tanned.'

'Well, well,' said Peake, amused. 'Hello again, Jason. You were a naughty boy – and now what?'

'A naughty girl, sir, called Jasmine,' she said shyly. 'Please tan my bum, sir, just like the old times, when you caught me smoking. Schoolday memories are so sweet!'

'I suppose you still smoke, Jasmine,' said Peake.

'O, yes!' cried Jasmine. 'Oodles and oodles. I am a very naughty girl.'

'Six tight ones it is, then,' said Peake. 'Touch your toes, Jasmine, and no girly squealing as I lace you. You'll find my cane much harsher than madame's whip.'

Peake delivered three lines very sharply at the centre of Jasmine's bare buttocks, which flinched tight at each stroke.

'Tell me, Jason – I mean, Jasmine,' he said, 'do you dress like this all the time?'

'Oo! That *smarts*, sir! You are just as cruel as when you flogged me at Abingdon. And ... I liked it then, and I like it now. There! I've confessed! But no, I dress like this for my shop here, and for ... special gatherings. Three days a week I am in pinstripes and bowler, collar and tie at Foulkes and Co in Burlington Gardens. I am deputy to the senior loan officer, western hemisphere! But, in my boutique, and by night, I am beauteous, fragrant Jasmine. Even at school, I always loved dressing in nice things, silk socks and shirts, and the best cashmere. At the bank, I love to have the crispest starched shirts, the whitest spats – a little old-fashioned, perhaps, but so elegant – the sharpest trousers and the shiniest shoes. Women like me, and I have no shortage of intimate ladies. How I love to see them undress, smell the perfume of their bodies and their underthings so wickedly moist ... To feel their bodies, so smooth and silky, to feel my stiff organ inside the hot wet silk of their slits, with their own silk sliding up and down on my back and my bum ... It is heaven. Then one day I thought, why shouldn't I dress in truly pretty things, all the time, as the females I adore so!'

'And why do you like being caned, Jasmine?'

'O! How it hurts, sir! I don't like it at all, not the thing itself. But I like the knowledge of punishment for my impudence of being a girl – the idea of my bare girl's bum helpless under the cane's lash – and having paid for my impudence, I'm free to be a girl. Ooo!'

When her caning was over, Peake told Jasmine that she made quite a handsome girl, except that her dangler was showing. Moreover, the organ was erect!

'That always happens, sir,' said Jasmine. 'When my mistress whips me, or watches me whipped. She is very cruel; she teases me by buying things from my shop, but I know her real purpose is to taunt and humiliate me, and whip my bare bum, and as her joyful slave I am powerless to resist! I must do anything she commands.'

For the next few days, Peake fell into a kind of rhythm at Eulalia's household. His duties as guest remained what they were upon his introduction: the administering of stern discipline both to his hostess and her maid, and the occasional 'virgin roger' as she rather quaintly put it. Eulalia commended his seemingly inexhaustible supply of male essence, and said he was truly 'one of the people' but complained impishly that there was not quite enough for her to take a bath in, so her usual warm goat's milk would have to do. Peake became acquainted with her long hours in the tub, soothing the lines his cane had laid on her bare bum, as well as a succession of 'darling little shops' in places such as Bermondsey, Willesden and Homerton, whose wares were as exotic as their locations. Soon, the day of the party arrived.

'So,' said Eulalia, as she gazed at her startling costume in the glass, 'you remain technically a virgin, Mr Peake: even though you have entered my sacred place, and have honoured my breasts and fingers with your spend, nevertheless you have not spent in my cavern. It is a pretty point of philosophy: I have made you spurt, and I have made you enter me, but not both at once. So you remain master, without my thrall. How exciting! It will be pleasant to see if that mighty dangler can resist the temptation to spurt tonight. A party in your honour; a theme party – and the theme is secret pleasures.'

Ragamuffin was there with his jazz ensemble, five of his sleek compatriots who wore immaculate cream linen suits, red shoes, much jewellery and sunglasses even indoors. Freddie bustled about in his French maid's uniform, flushed with the excitement at supervising things, and with the affairs of Bechuanaland evidently settled for the day. Peake wore his normal evening dress, and Eulalia said he looked divinely exotic – he told her she looked like a wolverine, or a vixen, both of which she took as compliments. She wore a tight black leather corset, rubber panties and rubber stockings, and dangerously teetering high heels on boots that just covered her knees. A wicked whip hung at her belt.

'I don't feel girly tonight,' she said. 'There will be plenty of girlies for you, Mr Peake, and you'll know some.'

She was correct; as the house filled with gay, scented society, Peake saw some familiar faces: Flossie de Cante and her set, Fleur Dovercourt, Minty Astor, Joan

Weimaran, and to his satisfaction, there was Edwina Cheshunt, who entered in the grand manner and threw her sable coat aside – where Freddie caught it with perfect subservience, before it had touched the floor – to reveal herself entirely naked. Her body was adorned with the intricate paintings of stars and flowers, and hung with chains and studs attached to arcane piercings of the most intimate places, including her nipples, her fount-lips and a series of rings on her furrow, nipping her buttocks together like fount-lips. At her waist dangled both a massive twin-pronged rubber phallus, a red cane, and a black six-thonged whip.

Edwina led Jane Reculver by a tightly fastened waist-chain, the younger woman being dressed all in white with a frilly tutu, gold spangles and white silk stockings – with no knickers, and her fount bare! Its shaven mons was bedecked with glittering sequins like the wrapping of a fruit cake. Her cheeks bore large circles of kohl, and her eyes were heavily ringed likewise, with her hair in coy braids, so that she looked like a doll or a sugarplum fairy.

'Master!' cried Jane Reculver, then looked guiltily at Edwina, who smiled and nodded that the address was permitted, then gave Peake her two-inch black-painted fingernails to brush with his lips.

'I heard of your departure from Oxford. But you never summoned me, and I am mistress Edwina's now.'

Peake bowed, and said both ladies had made a perfect choice. As the music slid into its slow and sensual rhythm, Edwina flicked the chain and ordered Jane to dance for them. The girl performed a graceful little ballet, hopping from toe to toe and bending to do the splits, revealing furrow and labia in all their delicate folds. Other couples began to dance. They presented a curious picture, since some were formally and some bizarrely attired, yet all mingled in complete normality. There were searching glances from nearly naked women with piercings and studs like Eulalia's, women in rubber or leather catsuits, even with hoods that showed nothing but lips and eyes; all looked admiringly at Peake as though *he* was the exotic. The glances seemed to fasten on the bulge of his manhood, and Edwina observed that the reputation of Peake's dangler had spread.

'I hear business is good, Mr Peake,' said Edwina, accepting a peeled grape from her maid. 'My friends are pleased with you as master, and I trust they give good value as slaves.'

Peake said it was so, and that he derived satisfaction from pleasuring the errant female by the humiliating chastisement of their bare skin, although he was still unsure of their own reasoning in the matter. Edwina laughed.

'Reason doesn't come into it, my lovely,' she said, pretending to brush his bulge accidentally. 'All women long to be slaves of a stern master, of a big strong *dangler*.'

She trilled in laughter and her bare breasts trembled, causing the rings which clustered from her pierced nipples to ring like chimes.

'Whip and male organ, aren't they one and the same?' she murmured. 'Each whips us into sensation, Mr Peake – small matter if the sensation be pain or pleasure, for at the end of the day, when our bodies glow, who can tell the difference? And there is more: all girls know that at heart they are wicked, and must be punished for their wickedness. We are weak – we weep and tremble, and we must show ourselves strong by taking the lash on our naked flesh. Or,' she added, stroking her maid's hair, 'by disciplining others . . . female or male.'

The orchestra raised the volume of their music, and the cream-suited musicians whirled and swayed in perfect harmony as they played. In the smoky half-light of censers and candles their shiny instruments looked strange, as though in imitation of the outrageous costumes

161

of the listeners. Ragamuffin himself played a sort of saxophone, but elongated like an alpine cowhorn so that the trumpet end touched the floor, its upturned bulb rising into a curve like a mushroom. From its hole came a velvety insistent fluting, like a dance of flower petals.

'Ragamuffin's band is called The Food of Love', said Edwina. 'Isn't that quaint? The black man understands so well the dark rhythms of life which flow in a woman's body. He understands the whip, too. You, Mr Peake –' she squeezed his balls and prick '– are, I think, an honorary black man . . . a Maroon, perhaps. You know that all women long to be slaves, and that is why we devote ourelves to pleasure, for nothing enslaves like pleasure. Only a true master knows that the greatest pleasure is freedom from it.'

Peake drank and made small talk, and here he found that his powers of invention were drawn as the females longed to know about life in the West Indies. Of course, they had all seen tasteful planters' mansions, or peered from cruise ships, but what about the life – the smoky, sweating perfume of raw sensuality? He was much in demand as dance partner for the smooch, and the movements of the women left him in no doubt of their interest. Nor did the reaction of his body to the pressure of urgent loins fail to tantalise the women. He had many quim-scented calling cards given to him, with invitations to intimate conversation, or sometimes a blunt pleading for 'my bare bum to be caned, master'. To all he responded courteously. When not dancing, he was surrounded by a gaggle of females: those who had tasted his lash had plainly adoring eyes, while those who longed to gazed at him with voluptuous curiosity.

The party grew more animated, and more abandoned. Smooching gradually evolved to something else, and gay revellers were shown by the obliging maid, Freddie, to more secluded quarters. Eventually the excitement of lust and drink made seclusion unneeded, and Peake watched open copulations on couch, sofa or even carpet, while the other guests clapped and laughed. Such events caused a sort of chain reaction; at the sight of a near-naked couple in frenzy, women began to stroke their partner, or someone else's partner, most intimately, until they too had joined in coupling. Cracks began to ring out in the smoky perfume; bared bottoms received spankings from hand or whip. Usually it was the females in girly dress who bent over to take a spanking, but often it was the males. Jasmine was there, in a radiant frothy creation of lemon yellow, and she bent happily to receive a dozen on the bare from the cane of a fierce hooded woman in black rubber.

The spankings and canings were often preceded by acts of obeisance or worship by which the victims seemed to earn their chastisement. Several females discarded their upper clothing, or even disrobed altogether from their party dresses, to reveal their undergarments: tight pastel corsets in satin or silk, rubber or even leather; panties and stockings of the same; pointed high shoes which vied with each other in cruelty and outrageousness. Men and women alike prostrated themselves to be handcuffed and whipped on the bare as they took pointed toecaps into their mouths and gurgled with babylike joy as they adored their mistresses; some lay facing up, with heel or toe ground ruthlessly into their gaping mouths.

Edwina took her flail to the bare bum of her slave Jane Reculver, and then, after a few dozen swishing strokes that had the maid squirming and crimson, she thought to enliven her sport by enlisting a kneeling male, naked but for chains, cuffs and harness. He was obliged to lick Jane's tight corset and knickers while Edwina flogged him, and the more fervently his tongue moistened the girl's underthings, the more severe the whip on his bare shoulders and nates.

This scene of worship was repeated elsewhere.

163

Eulalia's feet were sucked by a kneeling female in girly attire, with her frilly skirt raised and her knickers down; Eulalia beat one buttock with a cane, while Flossie de Cante spanked the other with her bare palm. The slaves were copiously served with champagne by the admirable Freddie, who held his silver tray of filled flute glasses under his mistress's spread legs for a minute or so, until the flutes brimmed, and their contents were gratefully gulped by the flogged girls and men.

Some of the girly females divested themselves of their knickers, after much pleading from dinner-jacketed males, who took the moist garments into their mouths, sniffing the stained silk and sighing with contentment. Other men who had stripped themselves were accorded the privilege of wearing a lady's shoe, with which they paraded proudly, making conversation as if having a lady's shoe dangling from one's erect organ were the most natural and pleasant thing in the world. Some yelped in excitement as a lady actually fastened her shoe with a pin.

Some were accorded silk stockings, which they smelled and kissed most voluptuously before wrapping them around their danglers and balls, as though by wearing such a trophy they had enslaved themselves to their chosen mistress. And some hardy males dared to press their lips and noses right into the rubber founts of their mistresses while these delivered fierce floggings to their naked fesses. There seemed to be no item of clothing of the female body that could not be worshipped as an icon.

'Isn't it wonderful?' said Eulalia, cupping Peake's balls, in token of friendly conversation. 'The garment bears the aura of the body against which it rubs: knickers; stockings; shoes ... The part symbolises the whole, and a lady's bare feet are her soul. To worship a lady's bum, whether with lips or cane, is to worship life itself.'

'So many ways of reaching the soul through the

orifices of the body,' murmured Peake. 'So many milk-white bottoms flogged to life by the gentle whip.'

'My bottom is not milk-white, sir,' whispered Eulalia with a sharp squeeze to Peake's balls, 'and she needs flogging nonetheless. My bottom with the whip, my breasts with creamy sperm. All women need it. The leader of the Maroons taught that the human brain feeds on male sperm. Males of course produce their own which, with proper thinking, can travel up the spine to nourish the brain with noble thoughts. Women, having no sperm, are obliged to get it from the male, which is why our brains are in our quims, to be close to the source of supply!'

She laughed gaily and melted away, and Peake's puzzled enquiry as to the Maroons went unanswered.

The males who chose not to kneel or worship were called upon to administer chastisement to the bared nates of myriad females, not only the 'girly' maids. Some mistresses, with wry little smiles, divested themselves of their razor-honed chains and by undoing cunning flaps or fastenings in their leather armour, bared their buttocks to receive the sternest whippings with the chains which had jangled on their own bellies. Many of the women bared their breasts entirely, and like Edwina wore large rings through pierced nipples. It became a party game for a mistress to pinion her slave girl, who squealed with mock-terror and delight, while bulky objects were hung from her nipple rings, stretching her breasts most painfully. One girl had two heavy brass fire-dogs suspended from her breasts, which Jasmine proceeded to bang together in time with the jazz music.

The sumptuous buffet was indeed relished, but its purpose was not only alimentary. There were dishes of curiously unsliced cucumbers, bananas and even turnips, all of which were used for pleasuring the parted slits and bumholes of the girly maids, being vigorously

165

pumped in and out of the glistening orifices while their bare bums were heartily thrashed with rods. Many mistresses now strapped on their rubber prostheses, and when a cucumber or banana had been worn to shreds by a maid's frictive bumhole, it was replaced by the rubber adornment with which the mistress thrust vigorously into the girl's slit or anus, while trampling on another maid's naked belly with her spiky heels as the maid writhed in voluptuous distress. Where a submissive male was trodden upon, the spiked heel rested firmly on his balls.

Flossie de Cante smeared her naked body with mayonnaise and a specially thick helping of mustard sauce in her slit, and writhed in pleasure as several tongues licked her clean; Joan Weimaran did the same, only with butterscotch cream, and made her erect nipples into two little chocolate mountains, with the instructions that they were walnuts, and her admirers must bite on her nipples very hard indeed. Some mistresses put chocolate bonbons into their quim or even bumhole, with the instruction that their maid or slave should extract them with the tongue, like a pig snuffling for truffles. Edwina seemed most fond of rogering other females, and her twin rubber organs were by far the largest prosthetic toy in the throng. Peake watched her flog and roger one maid after the other, taking her in both holes at once to the full depth of her phallus shafts; his face was a mask, but his eyes smouldered.

Still the hypnotic music played; the drummer had replaced his tomtoms with a triple set of naked girls' bottoms, on which he beat a sumptuous rhythm, cupping his palm most artfully to make the different cracking noises. Meanwhile the lilting notes of Ragamuffin's saxophone had turned to a strenuous droning roar, like a foghorn, and the curious design of the instrument became apparent. One after the other, maids lifted their skirts to cool their smarting bottoms by squatting on the shiny metal orifice, which they took right inside their slits, muffling the noise until their bodies shook with the vibrations as Ragamuffin played. Their fingers flicked on exposed bare damsels as the vibrations of the music brought them to their spasms of pleasure. Edwina noticed Peake's attention, and paused in her work with her flail on a young man's bottom.

'Don't you wish you had a slit, Mr Peake, so you could enjoy Ragamuffin's horn?' she said. 'You haven't been doing much. Biding your time, I suppose?'

Peake examined her sweating naked body, the painted flowers seeming to breathe and live as her breasts and buttocks heaved in her exertion, and now he smiled, a thin smile. He murmured to Edwina that she was quite right. Suddenly he grasped her nipple rings and pulled her roughly towards her, stretching her breasts so that she squealed in astonishment and dropped her cruel flail. He made her kneel, her bare bottom high, and pointed to the flail. Shivering, she picked it up in her teeth and gave it to him. There was real fear in her eyes, and she whispered, 'No ... no ... no, master.' Peake shrugged and made as though to release her, but she cried out in a deep sob and dropped her head, at the same time parting her thighs to reveal her furrow, anus and quim-lips fully.

'I have it coming to me. Be gentle, master,' she whispered.

Peake's chastisement of Edwina was watched by the whole company. Kneeling and shaking with humiliation and fear, she bore the weight of fifty whip-strokes with the cruel thongs of her own cat. The whip jangled as it struck the rings which fastened her arse-cheeks, and at each jolt of her body, the skin strained and bucked as though trying to escape from its constraint. When it was over, her bottom was dark purple, and her thighs awash wih glistening oils from her fount. Tears ran down her cheeks and she sobbed brokenly, but had let out no squeal of pain even at the harshest whip-strokes. Released, she knelt at his feet and covered them with tears and kisses. Peake's face was once more a mask. Jane Reculver helped her to her feet and embraced her mistress. At that point Freddie the maid interrupted Peake with an envelope.

'This came earlier, sir,' he babbled. 'I am so sorry, I forgot ... I was so busy. My, Edwina is lucky. So beautiful!'

It was a telegram, which Peake tore open, to read the sender's address as 'Mayfair Plantation, St Botolph'. His face darkened, but he folded the paper quite calmly. Eulalia asked him what was the matter.

'A misunderstanding,' he said. 'It seems that my uncle is not the model of probity I thought. He has run the estate into the ground, bankrupted Mayfair, and taken to his heels. My poor aunt! I shall have to leave for the West Indies at once to sort matters out, for it seems that Foulkes's Bank is intent on foreclosing on our substantial loans, debts of which I was unaware.'

Eulalia bellowed in fury and summoned Jasmine, whom she took by his earring and forced to kneel at Peake's feet to hear what had happened. Jasmine protested that despite his position at Foulkes & Co., he had nothing do do with it.

'Well, make it your business to have something to do with it, Jasmine,' said Peake mildly. 'A stay of execution, until I sort out the finances: six months should suffice.'

Jasmine wailed that her job was in jeopardy, and Peake said that he had seen Edwina under her cat-o'-nine-tails.

'You'll take three – no, four times as much, Jasmine, if you don't comply! Strung up by your thumbs, bound, hooded and gagged, and no respite during the punishment. Think of those wicked thongs, Jasmine, stroking you as hard as I can flog, not fifty, but two hundred fierce ones on your bare skin.'

'I can't!' wailed Jasmine.

'Nonsense!' Eulalia hissed.

Jasmine sobbed wretchedly, but his eyes gleamed.

'I'd fail if I tried, sir,' he stammered, 'so you'd better give me my punishment right away – here and now!'

Peake grasped Jasmine's hair and looked her firmly in the eyes for a moment, then pulled the hair tight. He grinned.

'You shall do what I say, Jasmine, ' he whispered, 'for I shan't punish you now. I shall only punish you when you have fulfilled your task to my satisfaction. Agreed?'

Jasmine smiled and nodded happily.

'You promise, sir?' he said.

Peake departed for Southampton the day after next, and just before his cab took him to the station, he attended most firmly to his naked and trussed hostess Eulalia, and also to the maid Freddie, who said his bum needed to smart well so that he could concentrate properly on the affairs of the Turks and Caicos Islands. As a farewell gift to his hostess, he permitted her to shave his cock and balls completely bare, and robe him in the pink chiffon dress from Jasmine's, before effecting her punishment. He said it made him feel quite serene.

He rogered Eulalia in anus and quim, while Freddie watched from cuffs and harness. Then, as he was whipping Eulalia's bottom, Peake asked her about the Maroons. He learned that they were a tribe of escaped slaves on St Botolph, a nation within a nation, who had fled from tyranny and organised a society which over the years had become a vicious parody of the one they had fled.

'They have lords and ladies, landowners and merchants,' said Eulalia, writhing under her whip, 'courtesans and poets and lovers and, above all, slaves.

Ouch! That really stung, master! They fled from the world of the lash, and since the lash is all they know, their new-created world is ten times as stern. The Maroons, sir – Ooo, how you hurt my bum! Don't stop, I beg you – are a living proof of our dark side, a mockery of our graces, a reminder that all power and wealth and beauty are based on pain and submission. I should know. My friend Lucinda Lalage is one. O! I've never smarted so much! You are the cruellest master in the world, sir. Never stop whipping me, whip me till I scream, till I melt in your sweet cruelty. And – O! Oooo! I'm spending! Yes! Whip me! You see … I am a Maroon, too.'

10

The Taste of Tongue

Rum, fish, sweat and flowers: the smoky scent of the West Indies assailed Peake's nostrils as the ship's dinghy docked at Peake Town, the port of St Botolph. There was an excited crowd to meet the new master; the placid village which bore his name had been founded some three centuries before, and not much seemed to have happened since. Mr Carew, the colonial office representative, was there to greet him, perspiring in his stained white suit and with the only collar and tie in Peake Town. He took Peake to his residence, a dilapidated bungalow surrounded by giggling hordes of children, goats and market women squatting to sell bales of cloth. They took rum punch on the verandah and the official said he hoped Peake would have some success.

'We are rather a backwater here,' he said, mopping his brow. 'Mayfair, your family plantation, is just about all that keeps us afloat, in a manner of speaking. Since we heard of Mr Peake's flight, his dreadful mismanagement and the bank foreclosing, we didn't know what to think. Some say he was in league with the Maroons, though why I cannot guess. There was no hint of any penchant for debauchery. Without Mayfair, we should have nothing. Sadly, we are too far from the coast of Florida to make our money in rum-running, like the Bahamas,' he added a trifle wistfully. 'At any rate, I

171

hope and trust you will get Mayfair back on an even footing, sir, because, frankly, it *is* St Botolph.'

A goat padded up and nuzzled Carew's ankle.

'Well, I suppose I'd better get busy,' he said, looking around rather wildly as though hoping some excuse for business would fall from the humid air. 'You may, of course, count on my every assistance, sir.'

Peake thanked Mr Carew, and said he would like to visit the bank, to which Mr Carew willingly escorted him. The Bank of the Leeward and Windward Islands stood between a rum shop on one side and a rum shop on the other, and only the limp flag outside, showing a galleon and a gold bar, suggested it too was not a rum shop. Peake arranged for a personal account and safety deposit box, into which he placed a small chest. When this was done, he took his leave.

'It may be necessary to make some profitable changes at Mayfair,' he said. 'I trust there will be no difficulties with planning permission, licenses and suchlike?'

Mr Carew looked at him in bemusement.

'Permissions? Licenses? My dear sir, here on St Botolph, the Peake family gives licenses. Except to the Maroons. Watch out for the Maroons, sir.'

St Botolph seemed larger than the map had suggested. Above, the sky was vast and shimmered cloudless. Around the narrow basin of Peake Town, where only small boats could dock, stood a frame of low jagged hillocks, their slopes thick with lush green, dotted with shacks. There were tobacco plants, bougainvillaea and hibiscus and jacaranda trees, and everywhere the fragrance of spices. The dirt road wound around the hills until they levelled into flat savannah, where the flowers and crops grew in small plantations. Men, women and children gaped or shrieked at Peake's passage in the island's largest – it seemed, only – taxi-cab, an enormous Chrysler of pre-war vintage, painted immaculately and shining, its interior and outside bobbing with African charms and amulets while the dashboard boasted a portrait of the heavyweight Jack Johnson.

Ahead of them to the north stretched a jungle, extending halfway up the slopes of the dormant volcano, Mount Sulphur. Beyond that, right up to the the north shore made fertile by centuries of lava and volcanic ash, lay the vast Mayfair estate. Distance and time seemed meaningless here; the heavy moist air was perfumed with indolence. After an hour or two of bumpy progress, the road approached the edge of the jungle and the chugging pace of the Chrysler quickened.

They passed alongside the dense foliage, the drumming of the motor drowned by the cries of parrots and beasts, and the sun powerless to lighten the jungle's gloom. The driver seemed less relaxed, and he assured Peake that they would be past 'Old Suffer' in no time, to his fine plantation, 'where all folks is well bred'. When Peake asked about the Maroons, the driver said nervously that they kept themselves to themselves, and that they were well looked after – 'Mr Christopher had an accord'. Mr Christopher was Peake's departed uncle; Peake asked no further, but smiled as he inspected the perfumed mysteries of his new homeland. The blue glory of the sea was again just visible, as the driver suddenly halted, and leapt from his cab.

'Sorry, sir,' he mumbled, clutching his hat, 'I got five pickneys to feed, and business is business. You'll be OK, sir, you is a businessman, like the mistresses.'

Peake had no time to query or react before he was surprised by a dozen shining ebony bodies which surrounded his vehicle. He had no choice but to obey and get down, and did so without comment. He stood in a pool of sunlight surrounded by a posse of young men wearing only loincloths and carrying machetes, but no guns. Their leader, who had issued the command, was a woman, and she too wore only a loincloth. Peake blinked in surprise at her bare breasts, stiff and conical, with big walnut nipples, which were pierced; from them hung wide silver rings. Her breasts and whole torso were beaded with sweat under a heavy necklace of silver strands studded with jewels; this and her splay-tipped whip seemed her badges of authority.

She was young and smooth of skin, scarcely more than Peake's age, and bore a resemblance to Lucinda Lalage. Her hair was cropped to tight curls, and this manly appearance by paradox emphasised her over-powering femaleness. Her loincloth was tight, her fount swelling proudly beneath.

'I take it you are the Maroons,' said Peake pleasantly. 'Do tell me how I may help you. I say, miss, you remind me most charmingly of a friend in London.'

The young men gaped in awe that their captive addressed their leader with such familiarity. The young woman spat on the ground, and cracked her heavy whip dangerously close to Peake's face. She laughed cruelly.

'Mr Christopher – a bad man!' she hissed. 'He done a bunk, we haven't been paid for months! No rum for my boys, no jewels and pretty things for me!'

One of the males spoke up.

'Have you got rum, master?' he said, grinning hugely.

He was rewarded with a severe lash from her whip across his bare back, which bore the marks of many previous lashings. After a sullen whine, he fell silent.

'He is no master,' sneered the woman. 'He shall be a slave like you boys, and taste my whip like you, unless he comes up with *rhino* and *boodle* and *moolah*!'

She grinned savagely, flicking these words around her tongue like incantations.

'Why, we understand each other, miss,' said Peake.

'You call me mistress!' she cried, cracking her whip.

'Mistress, I have no rum,' said Peake, 'and there might be a delay in getting some moolah, as I should have to send to London. But you know about Mayfair.

If you allow me to proceed, I shall see what there is to give you.'

The mistress gurgled with laughter.

'Ha! You think I was born the day before yesterday? You think I am a coconut? If I let you go, you won't come back. You smartbum white boy, you won't laugh at your mistress when your white arse gets singed by my whip!'

Some of the males were sifting through the contents of his cases, and making faces at finding neither rum nor moolah. The mistress frowned.

'I suppose you want to hold me to ransom,' Peake said, with a sigh. 'Well, let us go to your encampment.'

'No one but a Maroon may enter the city of the Maroons,' said the mistress scornfully. 'How long will it take to get the moolah?'

'Two or three weeks perhaps. It would depend on Eulalia.'

'Eulalia Preen,' she muttered gloomily. 'This is a pickle.'

'You could make me an honorary Maroon for the duration,' suggested Peake. 'I would try not to be a nuisance.'

She pondered this.

'It is possible,' she said slowly. 'It is not unknown. But, smartbum white boy, you shall have to learn our civilised ways. And if the money doesn't come, you shall remain one of us. I am Floella Tarnishe – Tarnishe with an e – and I shall be your mistress to obey.'

Peake said that was understood, and they set off through the jungle.

'Mistress,' he said, 'we are agreed that as soon as the money comes, I am free to go?'

'Yes,' she said. 'And we shall be in accord once more.'

She turned and flashed a white predator's smile. Her nipple-jewels glinted in the sunlight as her breasts moved.

'But until then, Mr Smartbum, you shall be a slave of the Maroons.'

The city of the Maroons was dark when the party arrived after an hour's trek through dense jungle. So tortuous was their path through fronds and creepers that distance was impossible to gauge, and it seemed likely that Floella Tarnishe had chosen a deliberately confusing route. The stars and moon shone from a velvet sky on a slumbering collection of tarpaper shacks, hovels of scavenged brick or mudstone, and even tents made with rubber tyres and palm leaves. There was the customary evidence of pigs, goats and chickens. The humid air was still hot, but without the searing sunlight; nevertheless Peake's linen suit was drenched in sweat. They were formally challenged by a female guard, half-naked like Floella, in a strange singsong language, and Floella answered in the same.

They passed into the city's main and only street; the aspect was of a Peake Town that had fallen on hard times. The central square was dominated by a gallows; Peake shivered but then sighed, seeing that the frightening structure seemed to be merely a flogging-post. When they came to a large barn, Floella halted them and shoved Peake inside, with two of her slaves, who had to surrender their machetes. The rest were to accompany her, carrying the booty of Peake's cases.

'This is your new home, Mr Peake,' she said. 'It is called the dungeon, and it is where the slaves live. I won't say it is cosy, but it befits your new station. Tomorrow you will be taken before the House of Lords.'

With that, Peake was pushed through the rush matting door into a cavernous, foetid chamber, where dozens of bright white eyes stared at him from the darkness. There were small windows open to the sky, and these permitted entry to a wan starlight, but the dungeon was even hotter and more humid than outside.

The floor was rock and dirt. Peake stood rubbing his eyes until he had got used to the shadows. By the door, two women armed with machetes and whips slumbered gently on stools, evidently their guards. There were empty rum bottles, and chicken carcasses, strewn on the ground. One of the slaves, the seeker for rum, pointed to a heap of straw, and said it was his billet.

'It's swelter hot, Smartbum,' he said. 'You'll want to strip to your modesties.'

He gestured to his bulging loincloth. It was indeed sweltering, and Peake stripped off his shirt and jacket. He became aware that of the denizens, at least half were women, naked like the males and jumbled together in sweating immodesty or indifference. All stared at him, and in particular at the bulge of his dangler. They were curious! Peake smiled in the darkness, and said he should prefer to remain clothed, as he did not wear modesties. His companion guffawed loudly, and there was a ripple of amusement. Peake sat on his straw and felt in the pocket of his jacket to retrieve a bottle, then gestured to the young man.

'I have found some rum,' he whispered. 'Care for a snifter?'

The young man, who introduced himself as Spuzzy, did indeed care for a snifter, furtively turning the full rum bottle to the wall to indicate privacy. Upturned faces, male and female, soon clustered, however, and Peake said there was plenty for all, as he had another bottle in his other pocket. There were amused wails and yelps of high appreciation, as Spuzzy proprietorially granted swigs.

'Show us your modesties, white boy,' said a mocking female voice from the rum-scented darkness.

There was the sound of a slap, and Spuzzy said sternly that his name was Mr Smartbum, and he was a white man, and white men did not wear modesties.

'Maybe 'cause they got nothing to be modest about,' said the female, causing delighted titters.

'He's got rum, Vimella, what more do you want?' said Spuzzy crossly.

'You know what we want, Spuzzy,' said Vimella, 'what all of us girls want.'

This caused more merriment and the party grew quite friendly. Peake asked Spuzzy to explain things: what was the House of Lords?

'Why, they are the rulers,' said Spuzzy. 'Apart from the Maroon Queen, who is over them. They are chosen by the guard, which is all women, and they run things around here. Yup, women rule the roost, as they have done from time remembrable. But,' he added proudly, after another swallow of rum, 'we is a democracy. Anybody can get to be in the House o' Lards, if you work hard and take your tongues.' Peake asked what powers the 'lards' had.

Spuzzy scratched his head.

'I don't rightly know,' he replied. 'The powers to do what the women tell 'em, I guess.'

After further questioning, and a sudden show of coyness from Spuzzy, it transpired that being chosen as a 'lard' had something to do with 'the dangler test'.

'So the "lards" are those males with the biggest danglers?' said Peake.

'Never thought of it much before, but I reckon you are right, mister. Well, well . . .!'

And Spuzzy let out a whoop of glee, as if an ancient mystery had been solved. He then informed Peake that girls, who of course had no danglers, could become duchesses, who were part of the Maroon Queen's court. There too, the choosing process was a mystery, but the guards reported on promising females, ones that were 'well-formed with proper bums', and brave under the lash, called 'the tongue'.

'Show me a duchess and under her fineries there are the marks of the tongue,' said Spuzzy. 'Her bum and her shoulders are real paintings! Shows she's proud and

178

wilful. Why, this great city is run by the women and
their tongues, it's the only language we folk understand.
The mighty wise founder of the Maroons, King
Abraham, said so, and then he *abdakeeted* in favour of
a queen, for he said that women were crueller, and
better with the tongue.'

There were other methods of a slave's advancement:
after becoming a free boy or free maid.

'I want to be a hunter,' said Spuzzy. 'You get to wear
a jewel, and you get a big yellow bag to put all the
creatures in for the stewpot – iguanas and geckos and
such.'

Peake asked if it wouldn't be more efficient to hunt
the larger animals to make a bigger stew. Spuzzy said
that if they caught a jaguar, it would feed everybody for
days, then what would the hunters have to do? And the
guards would have no excuses to whip them, so what
would they do?

'That,' he said, 'is democracy.'

Peake asked about intimate friendships. Here they
were, dozens of naked people in a closed space. Didn't
they . . .?

'You mean jig-jig?' said Spuzzy in a tremulous voice.
'Noo . . . Only with the entertainers – or if a mistress or
lard summons you. The guards will tongue us for any
hint of . . .'

'But the guards seem to be asleep,' said Peake mildly.

Sure enough, the rum was having its effect. All
around, black sweating bodies were locked in embraces
that were now playful, now fervent, now quite
unashamed and passionate as the vestiges of modesty
were unfastened and male organs of quite astonishing
length and girth sprang into joyful appreciation of the
naked females who caressed them. Spuzzy grinned shyly
and looked down at his own modesties, which swelled
unashamedly, then at Peake's more reserved linen
garment, which nonetheless showed his own stimulation.

'Well, what's another tonguing?' he said gaily. 'You joining in, Mr Smartbum? I know Vimella there, the cheeky one, she's just longing to see your dangler.'

Before Peake could think of a retort, Spuzzy absented himself and a scented dark body squeezed up beside Peake on his damp straw. Its hand delved inside his trousers and its voice gasped as silken fingers began to squeeze his cock.

'Vimella?' murmured Peake.

'Vimella, big boy,' came the answer.

The smoky darkness was perfumed with magic as Peake allowed himself to be caressed by the lithe young female. She rubbed against him, her bare breasts squashing like fruits on his naked chest. She managed to unfasten his trousers and roll them over his thighs, releasing his cock which sprang to full erection. She stroked his pubis, and giggled shyly that he had no hairs there; evidently this was part of 'Mr Smartbum's' foreign magic. Her hand cupped his tight balls and began to squeeze, while she took his own hand and guided it between her thighs and into her slit, which was hot and oily. With his other hand, he stroked her bare buttocks, and she playfully squeezed his fingers in her elastic furrow, kneading them and directing them towards her anal bud. When his index touched her flower, she opened her buttocks wide and actually took his thumb into her anus, to a depth of half an inch, before she squeezed it and with little moans pressed very tightly. Peake obliged her by thrusting, and soon his thumb, index and middle finger were deep inside her anus and quim, whie she vigorously rubbed his erect cock, with artful little tickles to his peehole that made his helmet clench and shudder. Peake sighed.

'I hope you are not going to spurt before you mount me, boy,' she whispered, biting his earlobe.

Her hand stroked his bared nates.

'My, what a fine strong bum! And what a dangler! I

have never seen such a cock! You would be King of the Maroons, if we didn't have a queen. What a treat it shall be to watch you take your first tonguing! For it will come soon, if I know Floella. You'll be bare, of course, and all squirming and lovely as the tongue bites your bum. Your dangler will rise, too – it always seems to. How I wish I were a mistress, and could tongue you myself. Or that you were a sergeant, and could tongue my bare backside. Just think of it, sir – my bum all dark and blue and squirming for you, and me sobbing and howling as you hurt me. Aahh . . .'

Her cry was of mingled wonder and disappointment, for her fingertip felt the first droplet of seed at Peake's peehole. He grunted, thrust faster and faster with his fingers into her anus and slit, and then could not stop the flood of seed which spurted over her writhing belly. Her hand left his buttocks and crept to her stiff nubbin, which she began to frot most energetically, and as his spurt eased, she groaned in her own shuddering spasm. She cried out very loudly in her pleasure, so much that the whole hut looked at them, and one of the guards stirred. The guard groped for her rum bottle; Spuzzy, busy on top of his own female, had the presence of mind to pass his own bottle to her lips, where she drank copiously, belched and fell back into slumber with her chin cradled in massive bare breasts.

'That was lovely, sir,' panted Vimella, 'but you haven't mounted me yet. I hope you have some creamy spunk left in those big balls of yours.'

Without a word, Peake directed her to recommence the operation, and then whispered that she should have her mounting when it was time. She brought him to another spurt, and then he lay back and said that she must mount him, since he had achieved priapism. She intoned this word with awe, all the time stroking the gleaming stiffness of his cock, and told him he had the biggest priapism she had ever tickled. He covered them

181

in the straw, and abruptly she sank on to the shaft of his cock, moaning that he pierced her like a sword, and that he was to come all the way inside her and poke her till she split.

She began to bounce up and down, her buttocks slapping his thighs, and making a great rustling of the straw. Her yelps of pleasure grew more intense, as did her frenzied frotting of her glistening stiff damsel, which peeped from her quim-lips like a little horn. She rode him for an age, and Peake whispered she could do it as long as she liked; their coupling became slower and more rhythmic, as the other slaves, sated with lust and rum, fell into contented slumbers. Only Peake and Vimella still swived; she cried out louder and louder as her quim juices flowed over Peake's trembling thighs, and suddenly she came to her spend, writhing and howling in a flurry of straw, and her spasming voice rising to a scream.

The guards awoke, blinking in fury at this misconduct, and raging with guilt at their own somnolence. But they had no time to make plans, for the door suddenly burst open, admitting the first faint rays of dawn, and Floella Tarnishe, with her soldiers, stood glowering before them. Vimella fell back in terror, clutching the remnants of straw to her body, which glistened with love oil that was plain for the mistress to see. Peake pulled his trousers up, and covered himself with straw.

'Well,' sneered Floella Tarnishe, 'you haven't wasted much time, Smartbum. Whatever can have made this bitch scream so loud? Maybe you were spanking her, or tonguing her – no matter. You must be hungry for a tonguing. This slut too –' she spat at Vimella '– and as for you two bitches! Call yourselves guards? Give me your whips – you can find straw here, for you're slaves again.'

With fear in their eyes, the two big-breasted guards

handed over their whips and squatted as though to make themselves invisible, covering their breasts in modesty.

'I dare say your fellow slaves will see to you,' Floella told them cruelly. 'I'll make the new slave dance. And Peake at the tonguing-post! The queen will be pleased. I'll tongue your slut, sir, and what she gets, you'll get fourfold.'

'You'll never lash him!' cried Vimella suddenly, embracing her paramour. 'He is . . . special!'

Floella lifted her whip and lashed furiously across Vimella's naked breasts.

'Silence, bitch! For that, you'll get *special* tonguing.'

The pair were grabbed by the young men, and hustled outside, to be bound by the wrists to the top of the flogging-post, with feet on tiptoe in the dust. Floella said that at dawn all the Maroons would assemble to watch.

'Naked, sir,' she said with relish. 'Those trousers off you, and no modesties. Just my whip on your back and bum till you are the same colour as me.'

She cracked her whip once, with furious force, across his shoulders, so that his whole body shook with the impact and livid red appeared on his white skin. Floella licked her lips, and said he would look pretty after a couple of hundred, and would then be broken and fit to serve.

'Don't worry, boy,' said one of the soldiers who had bound him. 'The first tonguing is always the worst.'

'And the second,' said his fellow philosophically, 'and the third. In fact, all of them.'

Peake was left with this thought in the cold dawn light, and listened to Vimella's muted sobbing, the song of parrots and the faint noise of whip-cracks and whoops from the dungeon, where his fellow slaves were whipping summary vengeance to the bodies of their former guards.

With not long until his and Vimella's punishment, the sun swooped high in the sky and his shivering rapidly turned to perspiration. One of the guards brought them a crust of stale bread to eat, and a swallow of rum, which both prisoners accepted gratefully. Then, in the distance, a drumbeat was heard, ominous and growing steadily louder. The young soldiers opened the door of the dungeon, and the slaves – including the two former guards, now walking with discomfort – emerged bleary-eyed and blinking in the sun. They saw the hanging bodies of Peake and Vimella, and their sullen docility turned to excitement at the prospect of a double punishment. A large female, brightly-robed, wheeled round a cart laden with plantains and bananas, and jugs of water, which seemed to be the slaves' breakfast, and soon the square was a happy morass of chewing and spitting. A procession came into view, with Floella proudly at its head.

Ten men dressed in the most outlandish vestments were borne on rough-hewn teak sedan chairs. They wore a mixture of top hats, satin breeches, powdered wigs, gold watch chains without watches, buckled shoes or riding boots and enormous fur or snakeskin codpieces, in the fashion of King Henry VIII. One of them had a highly-polished wooden leg. All were surprisingly young and muscular, like the naked soldiers who sweated to carry them, and all carried whips, chunks of beef jerky and flasks of rum, and were wreathed in the smoke of huge cigars. They cracked their whips on the shoulders of their bearers, to their great amusement and that of their companions, for each lord was accompanied by a vivacious lady in maquillage, jewels and bright silk or chiffon robe, with fashionable London shoes and silk stockings. Vimella whispered that these were the House of Lords, accompanied by the mistress entertainers.

The sedan chairs were set down in front of the flogging-post, and the lords waited contentedly for the spectacle. The drums quickened, as there was another cortege, this time a box-like carriage draped with palm-fronds, and borne by the naked maidens known as duchesses, sweating and whipped by guards on their bare shoulders. These females were extremely muscular, and no doubt chosen for strength, for when the drums came to their triumphant flourish, they did not lower the carriage but remained standing in pride of place overlooking the seated lords, who promptly shuffled to their feet, bowed extravagantly and sat down again to resume their various consumptions.

The guards bowed low, as did the slaves; Vimella whispered that the occupant of the carriage was the Queen of the Maroons. Through the gaps in the curtain of palm fronds, two bright eyes, sharp and menacing as diamonds, could be seen surveying the two captives, and in particular the white male. Floella stepped forward, carrying a ferocious whip, with a worn teak handle and nine fresh leather thongs, each three feet long, two inches wide and half an inch thick, and pierced with air-perforations to ensure maximum pain on chastised flesh. At the tip, each thong bore a cluster of seashells, which would add a further sting to the already cruel lash. Floella was stripped for action, wearing only her loincloth, her 'modesties'.

'Your majesty, Queen of the Maroons,' intoned Floella, 'my lords, and mistresses. I am privileged as mistress of guards to offer you the just spectacle of punishment: two slaves, detected at the wickedness of unlawful fornication and jig-jig unauthorised by the mistress of entertainment. It shall interest you that one of them, the male, is a new slave, brought to us by happy chance, and to remain until a ransom for his release has arrived from England. He is the new heir of the Mayfair Plantation, whose treachery has been so disgraceful, and we hope that his humbling by our generous hands and tongues will teach him to honour future accords. The bitch Vimella is well known as a slut, and her bum and back are no strangers to just tonguing. Therefore, I have decreed she will receive fifty lashes; the male, two hundred.'

There was a gasp of delighted awe, and vociferous cheering from the slaves and lords alike, none more enthusiastic than the mistresses of entertainment, who clapped and primped their hair as though going to a ball. Vimella's legs were now splayed apart, and her ankles fastened to a crossbar, so that her naked body was stretched in the shape of a starfish.

'The punishment will be given on both front and back of the body,' said Floella grimly. 'Do you wish for a bit to chew, slut? Or do you wish to cry shame, and leave the Maroons forever, to creep the jungle, alone and untongued?'

Vimella defiantly shook her head; Floella lifted her whip, and the tonguing of Vimella began. She applied her scourge first to the buttocks, with four rapid strokes; then the same, to the shoulders, the strokes more leisurely; there was excited murmuring among the watchers as Vimella's body flinched and began to shake harder and harder at each lash. Then Floella moved in front of the stretched girl, and lifted her whip over her breasts. There was a gasp, and then silence, as the cruel thongs lashed directly on to Vimella's nipples; this stroke made her head shake back and forward, and a low, despairing moan struggle from her throat. She took three more stern lashes to her breasts, and at each her body shook, but she was speechless.

This set over, Floella recommenced on the buttocks; then shoulders, then breasts again. Vimella's body purpled quite rapidly, and was lathered in sweat; after two dozen strokes, her head drooped over her breast, and she was revived with a bucket of water. She looked up, blinked as if seeing the crowd for the first time, and screamed. Then Peake shook his own bonds, and thumped the ground with his feet.

'Mistress Floella!' he cried. 'I beg you! Your . . . your majesty! Show mercy to this woman. Everything was my fault; I brought rum to the slaves and seduced the poor slut. I know little of your ways, but it seems to me her punishment has been sufficient. Let me take the rest of her punishment, mistress, and my own tonguing as well.'

Floella paused in her chastisement of the trembling maid, and looked round uncertainly. The House of Lords seemed to think this a good idea, or rather, the mistresses of entertainment did, communicating their desires with tickles, coos and shuddering little embraces. From the queen's carriage came a slight ripple of palm fronds, which Floella took to indicate approval.

'Very well,' she hissed. 'Cut the slut down, and bare the male. Your trousers off, Mr Smartbum, and then we'll see you wriggle, when your bottom really smarts.'

Vimella fell indecorously to the ground, but at once clasped Peake's ankles and kissed his bare feet.

'You shall never tongue him!' she cried. 'The white master must not remove his trousers. I warn you!'

The mistresses of entertainment murmured in irritation, and Floella scornfully ordered her guards to strip the victim. But Vimella reached up and did it, pulling Peake's garment fully from him so that his naked manhood gleamed proud in the morning sun. The gasps of awe became a tumult.

Vimella began to tickle and squeeze Peake's shaft until it stood ramrod stiff, to the great appoval of the mistresses of entertainment, although their lords seemed uneasy.

'He is fit to be a lord!' she cried proudly. 'Which of you can show as much? Which of you dares to whip him now?'

'Stand aside, slut!' roared Floella. 'He'll take the tongue, on front as well as back! That dangler will shrivel when his balls feel my whip!'

Floella's whole body shook, the nipple-rings jangling furiously from her wobbling breasts, and her face was contorted in a mixture of lust, anger and vengeful envy. The fronds of the queen's carriage parted and a cool, mellow female voice said 'Wait'.

Everyone's eyes turned to their sovereign, and as the fronds parted, she emerged from her reclining couch and stood framed by her doorway. Peake gasped. The queen was entirely naked, save that her whole body was studded with rubies, emeralds and pearls, with a diadem of sapphires on her head and a sparkling triangle of diamonds adorning the smooth shaven hillock of her fount.

From her pierced nipples and quim-lips hung large golden rings, and attached to these stretched a network of filigree gold chains that encased her sleek body like armour. Her lips too were pierced, each lip holding three tiny rings, and in addition she wore a vivid green tattoo which extended from her fount to her breasts, and represented the stem of a plant, its roots in her quim, its flowers her teats, and its buds the wide brown saucers of her areolae. Her hair was braided into woven strings or plaits, the tip of each carefully wound in gold thread, and they swung like willow fronds as she spoke.

'Vimella is right,' she said. 'We cannot tongue such a specimen. She may be refastened to take the rest of her own punishment. Meanwhile, the slave boy may be tied to my cortege.'

Floella seemed about to explode in rage.

'No!' she cried. 'He's mine! I want to flog him! I must! I've dreamt of nothing else . . .'

Her hand flew to her mouth.

'Bind Floella,' said the Queen with a pleasant smile. 'I cannot have impudence, so she shall be tongued for it. You, sir –' addressing Peake '– take the whip, give *her* the rest of Vimella's sentence, then fifty more for her own tonguing.'

188

Her calm, sultry tone suggested no more than giving out sweetmeats. Peake was released, and did as he was told. He made to pull up his garment, but the queen told him to stop.

'You will flog my impudent hussy as naked as she is, sir,' she said. 'Remove her modesties, and let her take it on the bare. Meanwhile you will work with one proviso – if I see you fail to stand in respect for me, even for a moment, then we shall resume your treatment.'

Floella was bound in the shape of the starfish, and Peake insisted on placing a teak chew-bit between her teeth, then commenced her lashing. The heavy-lidded glance of the Queen at his erect cock told him he was fulfilling his duty. He flogged Floella's squirming body very tightly, the strokes landing precisely, until her whole skin was a patchwork of purple. He applied the whip as she had done to Vimella, making her breasts shudder as he watched the tears well in her eyes impassively, and heard the strangled cries in her gorge as her teeth clenched the bit. When it was over, and she had taken the ordained seventy-six strokes, he waited until she was unbound before kneeling to kiss her feet, then handing back her whip to the sobbing female.

This obeisance made her smile faintly and bitterly, for Peake was immediately seized by the queen's duchesses and bundled towards the back of her carriage. Before they did so, Floella lightly brushed the tip of his cock with her trembling fingers and sighed. Peake was bound with a hempen rope that was tied tightly around his balls and fastened to the back of the carriage. His hands were tied behind him with the same rope and, thus yoked, he was obliged to stumble along as the queen's cortege proceeded away from the city square, past the grand houses of the city's elite, and along a cleared jungle pathway, where macaws fluttered noisily at their passage.

They came to a clearing, set with bright flowers,

hibiscus and bougainvillaea, in which stood a building like a warehouse, larger than the slaves' dungeon. The queen disembarked from her carriage, and was handed the rope that tethered Peake. Without looking at him, she led him by his balls into the cool of her palace. She nodded, and her guards threw Peake to the floor in front of a polished mahogany throne, which the queen ascended; after receiving the bows and curtseys of her females, she told them to depart to their stations, and Peake was alone with her. The walls of her chamber were decorated with rugs, stuffed pythons and heads of jaguars, and an array of whips made of leather, chain or strung seashells, canes of wood, metal and ivory, and everywhere sparkling jewels set in silver, gold or quartz. Peake stared up at the queen's impassive face, his own registering shock. She flicked her whip against the tip of his cock, which had begun to wilt.

'Tut tut, Mr Peake, you soften. I should flog you for that . . . or for your crime of looking at me directly in the eyes. What is so shocking about my face? Am I not pretty?'

'Your majesty, you are very beautiful,' murmured Peake. 'It is just that you remind me of someone I know. In no way as beautiful,' he added hastily.

She laughed, the sound of her voice like pearls in a crystal fountain. She flicked the rope that tied his balls; he grimaced, and she laughed again.

'Go to the desk,' she said. 'And remember to crawl in my presence, slave. Few males enter my house, and they must crawl in obeisance. Except when I . . . Well, take pen and paper, and write your telegram to England, requesting money. It shall be sent from Peake Town. You may seal the envelope. I trust you: since you surely wish to gain your own liberty.'

When he had completed his message, and handed her the envelope, she looked at the address and raised an eyebrow.

'Eulalia Preen? Can you be sure of that cow?'

'Shouldn't I be?' said Peake.

'Her address is not Rattan Hall, Kent, as I am sure you are aware, Mr Peake.'

Peake did not reply, and she smiled.

'You may demand the price of your liberty where you please. If it does not come, you submit as my slave for as long as I please. You have demanded it, I suppose?'

She purred as her whip brushed the tip of his cock.

'Still proud! I am complimented, sir. Eulalia Preen has no wish to do me favours – it was her that I had pursued to England by Lucinda Lalage, after she decamped with my best jewels. But Lucinda too has let me down! England must be a very seductive place, to corrupt maids thus.'

'What must be, must be,' said Peake, shrugging, as her whip gently stroked his penis and balls.

'And what must be is that you learn manners,' said the queen. 'You will be tethered at first. Whipped, of course. Dressed properly . . . Perhaps a pretty frock, to teach you humility, or a flower in your bumhole. And my tongue.'

The chamber rang with soft peals of laughter.

'You offered to take tongue for Vimella; the question is, can you wield it? Males are not normally permitted within my palace, simply because few are adequate. A real master is a man who knows how to be a slave himself. These strutting pretties of my tribe . . . Frankly, they are not big enough for me, Mr Peake. Nor big enough for the royal tattoo. My females can be more understanding of a queen's needs.'

She whipped him five times, very hard, on his bare buttocks, and he did not flinch, but stared at her, unblinking. Still his shaft stood stiff.

'My face reminds you of Eulalia, slave,' she murmured, 'because she is my sister. I wonder if I shall remind you of her in other ways?'

191

11

Slave Queen

At the end of a week, the queen permitted Peake to
stand upright in her presence, and go around with his
balls untethered. She also permitted him, when they
were entirely alone, to address her by her name, a
privilege rarely granted to males. He was to address her
as Mistress Orchid. Twice a day during that week, he
had received a beating on his naked bottom, in the
morning from one of the duchesses, in the evening from
Orchid herself. The beating was with cane or quirt, and
consisted of at least thirty strokes. At no time did Peake
betray any emotion other than a hissing of breath and
a clenching of his buttocks as his bare bum was stroked.
The queen said she found him amusing. He was not
allowed any clothing, not even modesties, as he
performed the servile tasks he was allotted. These were
to polish boots and whips and jewellery, to wait at table,
to wash clothing in the river, to cook simple dishes
under the supervision of a duchess, whose cane was
always at the ready to advise him of any culinary
transgression.

For kitchen duties, however, he was permitted to
wear a skimpy apron of palm-leaves, beneath which the
helmet of his dangler was visible, to the great mirth of
his supervisor. He slept on straw, in an outhouse with
the goats, and his balls were tethered to the same post
as their leashes. He was fed from a bucket, like the

goats, and bathed in the river; when he waited at table, his manners and service were expected to be smooth and impeccable, and he was given brilliantine for his hair and perfume for his body. The queen insisted on shaving him herself, with her own razor. She shaved his chin and pubis, and every inch of his skin besides. The queen took her luncheon alone, and here Peake was the only servant. When she was alone with him, she took pleasure in making him wear three heavy coconuts suspended from the helmet of his dangler. She said it was to stretch it and make him a proper male. Peake agreed it was uncomfortable but that he must submit to this curious indignity. The queen approved the notable progress (as she assured him) in his organ's size and girth, and the stretching of what she called his 'coconut bag'.

His appearance at table was as immaculate as a naked slave's could be, even when, for the sport of her lords and ladies, the queen made him join them for dinner: he had to kneel in the corner, his arms folded behind his back, and eat from a bowl on the floor. If he snuffled too much, or otherwise offended, his bottom would smart with a sage cane-stroke. The duchesses who served at table were attired as frilly maids, with black skirts and white blouses, stockings and aprons, except that they wore no modesties, and the short skirts allowed their quims to be plainly seen. Their minks were cleverly braided into little pillars of hair, each capped by a ribbon. They regarded Peake with some timidity, as his pubis was shaven like their queen's.

Whippings were administered not only to Peake, but to every member of the household. All were females; males, apart from dinner guests, appeared only briefly, in the guise of draymen or drudges. Matters were attended to with the great ceremony of a courtly society. A visitor to the Maroons, forced or otherwise, became aware that this society founded on plunder or extortion had little to do except entertain itself with elaborate rituals; correction was the most important ritual in itself, and the core of all others.

The only real 'task' for the fighting slaves of the Maroons was the defence of the kingdom against any incursion; and since anyone of fighting spirit on St Botolph endeavoured to join the Maroons, there seemed little threat from the twin inertias of the population and His Majesty's Government. The House of Lords included a minister of finance, a minister of external affairs, and the rest of the governmental charade, but the real power was in a flick of the queen's finger or the raising of her eyebrow. It was easy to understand why she dominated: it was because her manner was wry, unassuming and amused. She dominated by not being dominant: merely pitiless. To incur her wrath or scorn was a terrible fate, simply because she let it be known that it was terrible. She said to Peake when he was warming goat's milk for her bath that the sharpest sword is not the one you carry, but the one you are thought to carry.

The games played by the ladies of Orchid's palace were many and sensuous. Orchid made no secret of her pleasure in the company of young women, and her amusement at her power to bestow favours, with the accompanying rivalries between her duchesses. She told Peake she had read about the court of King Louis XIV of France, called the 'sun king', and renowned for the opulence of his court at Versailles, although he only took a bath once in his life, on doctor's orders. Orchid was a firm believer in twentieth-century cleanliness, with plenty of naked river bathing, but she had adapted Louis' policy of making his courtiers vie for small favours so that they would not vie for large ones.

She had her 'petty levy' which was her ceremony of rising in the morning, with a hierarchy of duchesses to attend her, each with specific tasks: one lady was there to hand her the silken bathrobe, another to draw her bath – the occasional ceremony of heating goat's milk was assigned, now, to Peake – another to serve her tea. Then there was a further hierarchy of robing, with a different duchess for each garment, from blouse to skirt to whip to underthings; the more intimate the garment the higher the status of the duchess. All garments must be presented, for Orchid to choose from or reject, right up to the silken panties, always presented to Her Majesty with triumphal reverence, even though she generally elected to wear none, and indeed generally preferred her splendid bejewelled nudity, or just the flimsiest and most teasing of garments.

The petty levy was a sort of game, as was the elaborate service of victuals. Any slight imperfection in the presentation of a dish, glass or garment might draw Orchid's eyebrow to rise a fraction of an inch, to the instant mortification of her luckless duchess. It was rare that imperfection was so gross as to merit a whipping, but when it did – a slopped teacup or creased camisole – the miscreant was punished there and then, with strokes to the bare before all her comrades. If serving at table or at the bedside, she was obliged to take her punishment still holding the articles of service, so that she had to strain to avoid any trembling which threatened her cargo and would incur further chastisement. Orchid did not order punishment: her raised eyebrow of displeasure was enough to make the miscreant female beg for her own correction.

Games proper varied from the innocuous, like hunt the thimble, blind man's buff or hide and seek, to more serious sports not dissimilar to those at Dothemaids Hall: including the 'egg and spoon' race, which here in the tropics became the 'mango race'. Everyday games had subtle variations, like binding the wrists or ankles of the contestants, hooding them, gagging them or tethering them with reins and bridles and making the girls trot like ponies. Most were played naked, except when the queen deemed it fit to have 'handicap' costumes in addition to the above restraints, and these might be a thick corset, chains or even leg-irons.

Wrestling was one of Orchid's favourites; though she remained a spectator, thrilling to the grapple and slither of oiled naked females, her lithe body suggested that she was an adept. In every case, failure was rewarded by lashing; victory by a kiss from Orchid, and the opportunity for the victor to administer the loser's formal punishment, the game itself often seeming as no more than an excuse or preamble for chastisement.

The chastisements were in fact even more subtle and intricate than the sports themselves. A favourite was the 'chastity belt', a sinister metal device which looked like a large upside-down umbrella-frame. It consisted of four long struts perched on the ground, rising to a waist cincher at the centre, with two-inch spikes on its inside. The cincher was fastened around the recipient, and she was obliged to remain standing, both by the four rigid struts and the pressure of the belt: any attempt to sit, ease her discomfort or even move unduly would cause obvious distress. Her legs would be splayed by a heavy steel 'stretch bar' cuffed to each ankle, and the wrists cuffed behind the back, or else the entire length of the arms restrained by a tight black leather sheath called 'the opera glove'. Restrained thus, naked duchesses were caned long and tightly on the bare buttocks, helpless to do anything more than quiver and sob.

If the queen was in carefree mood, such formality might be dispensed with, and a 'wet tongue' decreed, in which the girl to be corrected was plunged into the stream, tongued on the bare when still soaking – Orchid explained that a wet bum smarted more – and, after each set of seven strokes, was reimmersed to 'cool her off' for the next, but of course wetting her sore buttocks too. This chastisement always caused great mirth, as the victim's relief at the cooling water was mingled with apprehension of the next set on a newly-glistening wet bum. When Orchid felt slightly less carefree, the same procedure was applied, but whipping was delivered to the wet breasts too. Peake would watch, tethered on his leash and kneeling docilely by his mistress, his own bum already red from his day's first whipping, and Orchid would stroke his hair and say he was lucky to get off so lightly.

Sometimes Peake was beaten simply, bending over for punishment like a humble schoolboy. Sometimes his humiliation was more elaborate, and he was bound or trussed. That was when Orchid did not feel he deserved to get off lightly. On those occasions he would take it strapped to a flogging-horse, arms and legs bound, and often gagged as well, with a steel ball preventing him crying before the audience of giggling duchesses, who laughed as they spat papaya seeds at his lashed fesses. Two duchesses named Sweetbread and Blossom, both champion wrestlers, arrayed him in sumptuous tight leather, studded thongs for ankles and wrists, and a studded strap clenching his balls and cock, a hood with slits for eye, nose and mouth and heavy steel chains binding him and hanging from his body like willow fronds. Orchid whipped him with three canes bound together, and he took over three dozen with this flail. She flogged him very slowly, and very sternly, and taunted him that he was kitted as a beautiful master and must enjoy the variance of slavery.

'I hate it, mistress,' he spat. 'I hate the pain, hate my humiliation.'

At each stroke, the coconuts suspended from his cock's helmet banged together as he shuddered, and made the duchesses wide-eyed at the massive strength of his organ supporting the weights. She ordered Sweetbread to tighten Peake's cock-ring; she did so, and he groaned, then Orchid struck his erect organ lightly with the tips of her scourge.

'That doesn't stop your dangler from standing,' she said thoughtfully. 'I am most pleased, but nevertheless you will have to be taken down a peg.'

After they had removed the weights of the coconuts Blossom and Sweetbread removed their chemises, and knelt beneath Peake's helpless body. Both were superbly muscled, and Orchid favoured them as champions of the wrestling ring, where their ferocious couplings seemed to hover curiously between hatred and passion, and the fierce kicks, jabs and twists they inflicted on each other's founts and teats were more lust than torment. Now Sweetbread took Peake's balls in her mouth and began to chew and kiss them, while her comrade bared the ripe melons of her breasts and took Peake's helmet deftly between them, kneading and caressing it as the queen recommenced her flogging of his croup. Sweetbread opened her thighs to reveal the wet flesh of her slit, and allowed the coconuts to slap her stiff damsel, while opening her friend's slit-lips and rubbing her with nimble fingers. Orchid too was busy, frotting her own hard damsel as she caned the naked slave.

'We must make you spurt, Mr Peake,' she said. 'All over my duchesses' teats, like a wet little schoolboy. Is that what you are? Or perhaps a wet little schoolgirl . . .? We must find out who you are, Mr Peake, before your ransom comes.'

'I am master of Mayfair Plantation,' he groaned.

Sweetbread and Blossom changed places, and after squeezing his cock between her teats, Sweetbread now lowered her head and took his helmet full between her lips, right to the back of her throat. Her head bobbed up and down in time to the caning as she sucked him, her lips at the base of the shaft meeting Blossom's, whose mouth entirely cupped his balls. Orchid's frotting grew more intense, and she whispered that as his mistress she ordered Peake to spurt. His only answer was a moan of agony, yet still his cock was hard between Sweetbread's eager lips.

Orchid ordered a variant to his caresses; Sweetbread and Blossom disengaged, and now Sweetbread removed her skimpy skirt and bared her own buttocks, spreading her furrow wide against Peake's cock. Blossom took hold of the organ and guided it into her friend's furrow, not to the swollen quim-lips but to the wrinkled dark anal bud, where she pushed until Peake's cock had penetrated Sweetbread's anus to the full.

Sweetbread squeezed her bum-cheeks tight, and made a moan of pleasure as she began to milk Peake's cock with her bumhole, and at the same time Blossom cupped his balls with her hand, squeezing them gently and using them to steer his organ into her friend's bum. But Peake scarcely needed guidance, for at every stroke to his bare backside, his loins jumped in pain and his organ plunged of its own accord. Orchid paused, and thrust a long-stemmed orchid into Peake's own bumhole, to great mirth, as Blossom said the whorls of the orchid petals looked just like a lady's quim. At that, their frotting grew more passionate. Yet even when the queen panted in a spend, followed by the others' joyful squeals, Peake was not moved to make spurt.

Now, Orchid detailed Blossom and Sweetbread each to take canes, and flog him together; this time it was her own anus which writhed on Peake's stiff cock, thrusting deep in her elastic bumhole while she diddled herself quite openly, with fingers in her slit and thumb flicking her nubbin.

'Come on, sir,' she said. 'Give me your spunk, can't you feel how much my bumhole wants it? Spunk, sir, and your tonguing will stop, I promise. O, I'm so wet, damn you. Spunk in me, sir, I command.'

At length, when she herself and her duchesses had spent once more, Queen Orchid of the Maroons called for a pause. Slowly, she released Peake's cock from the squeeze of her bumhole, and picked up her canes, to tickle his balls.

'It seems your dangler is in need of correction,' she gasped. 'How would he like a flogging, just to himself? And those pretty balls . . . Tongued, sir, like your bum? How would you like that, sir? I am your queen! Your mistress! Spend for me now, or – or I shall have to think you have another.'

She rubbed his balls with her fingers.

'Such pretty orbs! Tell me, Mr Peake, why did you wrongly address Eulalia's telegram to this Rattan Hall?'

Her palm was rubbing the gleaming tip of his helmet. At those words Peake emitted a long moan of tormented ecstasy, and Orchid's palm was splashed with a fierce jet of hot cream from the bucking shaft of his cock.

'O . . . O . . .' he moaned as though in despair.

The queen laughed.

'I wonder if you have sent for money at all,' she mused. 'I wonder if you *do* want your liberty, sir: only a girl would wish to be a slave.'

Thereafter Peake was attired sumptuously, as a girl. His tonguings were still delivered; but now he had to fuss with stockings, garters and knickers, straps and corselets, before baring his flesh. Orchid said that she liked him as a girl, and he should be proud to be one. Peake replied defiantly that he was not a girl, and with a clacking of coconuts showed his cock, now lengthened considerably by the weight treatment. Orchid would laugh and put her hand on his organ to stroke it, and said that was what made his robing so exciting: that she knew all the while that beneath his girly front, there lurked this powerful manhood.

Orchid's love of her sisters was powerfully informed by her love of the silks, leathers and satins which touched and were perfumed by the female body. She liked her duchesses to have fashion parades which she called 'active displays', meaning that the females showed their fineries, then engaged in the sweetest and most

200

lustful practices in worship of their female garments. In her garden, scented by lush flowers and soothed by the twitter of parakeets, they stripped each other slowly and delicately, fingering and tasting knickers, stockings and shoes before showering each other's bare bodies in the softest kisses. There were playful spankings on knickers or bare skin; bellies were trodden by high boots, or the heels sucked between submissive lips; flowers and fruits were thrust with giggles into quim and anus. Orchid would bare her own quim and accept the homage of her duchesses on her open lips and her pert little damsel, or else lazily finger herself as she watched others at their girlish frottage. She said that Peake's eyes looked misty, and he said it reminded him of home.

Orchid now adopted Eulalia's system of dry rogering, and would make Peake spurt at the teats or lips of her duchesses, or sometimes frig him between her own teats, and afterwards, taking his priapic member into bum or quim, frotting herself to orgasm as she lazily thrust him in and out of her hole. She now seemed to treat him with greater intimacy, and they conversed as mistress to maid as they rogered. Because she knew her slave would not come to a spurt, Orchid could take her time, so that these couplings were long, leisurely and imbued with a certain deference on Peake's part; he was aware of his servile status as he was used as a tool for his mistress's pleasure. Orchid explained how she came about her magnificent tattoos, the design on her back representing the whirls of a lush orchid, whose stem was rooted between her buttocks, in her furrow.

When she had come to the Maroons, Orchid had been the object of much jealousy because of the excellence of her body. She said this simply, as a matter of fact. Her name, Orchid, was at first a contemptuous nickname, referring to the sumptuous petals of her quim, whose flaps did seem to resemble the whorls of an orchid. But she took the name in pride, even during the savage tonguings to which the other women's jealousy subjected her. Her beauty won her favours amongst the House of Lords, who were severally pleased by her lustful prowess and lack of inhibition. Orchid said she was uninhibited amongst males because, fond of the bodies and caresses of women, she regarded pleasuring the male, or submitting to him, as harmless fun. Her relations with females, however, were intense, and led to numerous contests in the wrestling arena, which she usually won.

It also led to her receiving numerous bitter tonguings, using every cruel refinement of restraint and punishment. Her very fortitude earned her more and harsher whippings, but she triumphed when Pegleg, the most virile and hence most authoritative of the House of Lords, suggested she should be Queen in place of Lucinda Lalage, who, to complicate matters, was her lover at the time. Lucinda picked on her for some trivial offence, and swore to flog her to the backbone: Orchid took two hundred and fifty lashes of the cat from her enraged lover, without crying, and then challenged her to wrestle. Orchid won; she had Lucinda pinioned between her thighs, and the company of Maroons bayed for her life, but Orchid was merciful, and instead appointed the defeated Lucinda as Duchess of the Petty Levy.

Their affair was over; Orchid selected Floella, briefly, as her paramour – she was Lucinda's cousin – but fell out with her when she discovered her in the embraces of Pegleg, who was spanking her bare bum most vigorously with his wooden leg while she sucked his cock. Orchid would not have minded, except that Floella had not asked permission, nor invited her to watch. Hence, she admitted, the harshness of her punishment of Floella upon Peake's capture: the girl was a man-eater, and had to have humility knocked into her.

The blossom of her flogging by Lucinda was

profound, and so she had it incorporated into her royal tattoo, on her belly, fesses and back. She took Peake's fingers and guided them across the soft morocco of her skin, and he said he understood now how beauty could come from pain.

Peake was assigned to fetch the goats' milk from the herd of the 'royal animals'. For this duty, he was dressed as a milkmaid, as were the duchesses who performed the milking. Then he would warm it for his mistress's bath, and one day he was invited to join her in the bath. He stripped his milkmaid's uniform, and lowered himself in beside her; Orchid promptly grasped his organ, and squeezed it.

'You shall be my goat,' she said with a sly smile, 'and I shall milk you.'

She said that the goat was the most useful of animals, since it would eat anything, you could milk it or use its hair, it was strong, and when you had finished with it, you could eat it.

'Just like a man,' she said impishly, 'except that a goat has more brains.'

'O . . . O . . .' said Peake, panting as the milk bubbled with his cream, spurting at her fingers.

She embraced him and continued to stroke his balls until he was once more erect. Now she began to feel his cock as though measuring it, and said that he was long enough – longer than Pegleg, the only other man to bear the royal tattoo. Then, for the first time, she kissed him long and hard on the lips, her tongue meeting his.

'Mmm,' she said, 'that was nice.'

Her hand cupped his balls and she began to frot him once more. As he moaned before his spurt, she murmured that the time of his ransom was up, and unless jewels or money came, he must himself take the privilege of tattoo, the very next day. Peake said that his whip-blossom, while painful, was not livid enough to warrant the adornment of a tattoo.

'O,' she said, 'the royal tattoo for you, sir, is not for your bum, nor your back. It is for here . . .'

She squeezed the tip of his cock as though to crack a walnut with her palm, and Peake cried out in his orgasm. Orchid brought him to stand once more and mounted him in the bath, giggling that it was not really a dry roger.

Peake said he did not understand why so many males and females submitted to the fierce discipline of the Maroons – particularly females. Orchid laughed derisively, and said the whip was the only language slaves understood.

'And we are all of us slaves, Mr Peake,' she said as the milk swirled around her writhing belly. 'The first king of the Maroons knew it, even as he torched the Mayfair Plantation, and led the people to freedom. Here, he created a mirror of the society they had burned, for he knew that people crave the certainty of discipline, the certainty of being cared for and wanted, the warm kiss of the lash as we huddle in the night's mystery. We are not captives like you, Mr Peake, we plead to be admitted to the Maroons, and even under the tongue, we may at any time cry "shame" and depart. None ever has.'

Peake asked what had happened to those earlier rulers of Mayfair, his own forebears.

'Times were cruel, and things were simple,' she said.

'I shall not remain a slave, mistress,' said Peake. 'My ransom will be paid soon, I am sure.'

She bent down, took his tongue for a moment between her teeth and bit it.

'When you take the tattoo, you shall be,' she whispered. 'You shall be my loyal slave girl, forever!'

After that, no further words were spoken; with the milk frothing around their naked bodies, their coupling lasted the whole morning, and there was a passionate despair to it, as though both knew it would be their last.

Orchid could not make him spurt, even when she ordered Blossom and Sweetbread to fetch a gnarled sweet potato and watch her bugger him with it. In the afternoon, after Peake had fetched the goats' milk, he waited for his mistress's sleep, and slipped into the city, where he found Spuzzy. He was arrayed in his milkmaid's smock, and placed a bandanna over his face to hide his pale skin, but he was nonetheless noticed and felt not a few hands, male and female, pinch his knickerless haunches and bum. Even Spuzzy grinned and made a half-hearted effort at flirtation, until Peake revealed himself; promised rum, Spuzzy went off to Peake Town on his errand.

The next day, Peake was not whipped, and in the late morning a crone came to adorn him with the tattoo. She cackled with delight as she saw his dangler, and began to stroke and squeeze it as though it were an amulet. When she pressed her dry lips to it as a sort of homage, Peake smiled and stroked her hair. She told him he must be brave, for the operation would hurt. Blossom, Sweetbread and Queen Orchid were at his side the whole time as the needle did its work, bringing him rum and water and towels. When it was over, after two hours of sobbing and moaning in unfeigned agony, Peake said he would rather take a thousand tongues than another tattoo. Herbs and balm from the jungle were applied, and his loins bandaged; for two days he was excused duties, while his pain subsided, and on the third day Orchid removed his pansements.

She threw her arms up in delight, and her duchesses brought a glass for his inspection. His cock was a symphony of glowing colours, and when the queen of the Maroons knelt and lovingly tickled his balls, and his organ rose to full stiffness, his cock was an orchid. He was hoisted naked on the females' shoulders, and placed beside his naked bejewelled mistress and borne in her carriage in triumphant cortege to the city, where he was displayed to the awed populace. They cheered and thronged to touch his erect cock. Orchid announced that her new slave was henceforth elevated to the House of Lords; the mistresses of entertainment simpered, and demanded a speech.

'Her Majesty's new slave will give no speech,' thundered Peake, 'for we are all of us slaves, are we not? And some of us may have forgotten the bitter joy of submission. Her Majesty, a slave to pleasure, shall now be given the ultimate pleasure she craves.'

Suddenly, Peake seized Orchid by her hair and pulled her roughly to the ground. She squealed, but his grip was iron. From Floella he seized a jewelled cat-o'-nine-tails, and began to flog his pinioned mistress, sparing no part of her naked flesh as he led her squirming and screeching by the hair, in a parade of chastisement through her city.

'See your queen, Maroons!' he cried, whipping her shuddering buttocks and breasts. 'See your slave!'

The whipping continued until Orchid was gasping and sobbing, too tired and hurt to scream, and her skin was deep purple. Peake taunted her that she should cry 'shame', but she shook her head in broken defiance.

'Then submit, mistress,' he said. 'You have only to kneel and kiss my feet, and submit.'

Still she took his whip, until her writhing had become a grim dance of pain to the hypnotic rhythm of his lashes. In the distance, a drum began to throb, and the Maroons chanted a strange song of celebration as their naked queen was flogged by her new slave, who was now their new lord.

Peake's arm rose and fell, his beating sombre, efficient and utterly merciless. At last, Orchid screamed in despair and sank to his feet, where she clutched his ankles and began to lick his toes like a puppy. Her scream turned to a high yelping moan, and her belly fluttered; a cascade of shining juice anointed the inside of her bare thighs.

'O, master, master,' she gasped. 'I submit . . . Take me.'

Peake raised her to her feet, his stiff organ caressing her still-trembling belly, and embraced her, kissing her deep on the mouth. His hand slid into the furrow of his buttocks, and emerged clutching a package of wax paper. He released Queen Orchid, opened the wax paper and threw it to the ground, leaving its contents in his palm.

'For you, mistress. My ransom has arrived. Now it is I who must cry "shame", for I can no longer be with you, and depart at once to claim my inheritance of Mayfair.'

On his palm sparkled five large diamonds.

'My jewels!' cried Orchid. 'The ones Eulalia stole! I never thought the bitch would return them.'

He gave her purpled buttocks a friendly pat and kissed her forehead; she trembled and beamed with pleasure.

'She didn't,' said Peake. 'I got them for services rendered. And how silly of me to forget, mistress – I have had them all the time.'

12

Mayfair

Peake's welcome at Mayfair was respectful, but cool: the eyes of the servants were suspicious. He was dressed once more in his white linen suit, and had equipped himself with a pearl-handled cane, as a badge of his authority, yet it seemed he needed none. By his face and composure, he was recognised as the successor of 'Mr Christopher'. The house was a sugar-white palace, still in reasonable repair, and dating from the burning of the original house by the Maroons. The Peakes had originally been pirates and buccaneers, and had built Mayfair to add a respectable veneer to their freebooting. One of their tricks had been to lure ships away from the safe little harbour, where the sugar boats would dock, on to the rocks, with the help of false harbour lights whose remnants could still be seen on the rocky beaches abutting the mansion.

Mrs Doofar, the housekeeper, told him with wistful pride that the Maroon revolt was at the same time the British burned the White House in Washington, D.C., and the new Mayfair had been built like the first, but with classical additions in deference to their continental neighbour. She was a handsome woman of about thirty, long-legged and ripe of figure, and her husband Alwyn worked on the estate as overseer. In the Caribbean tradition, Mrs Doofar was overseer and mistress in her own household.

Of one thing all were sure: Mr Christopher had become 'a bad master'. How and when, no one knew for certain, nor whether it was his addiction to drink or foolish speculations or 'small island fever', which often afflicted the white man. He was much addicted to beating his servants, too, with what Mrs Doofar called 'the rattan'. It seemed this meant simply a young sugar cane, the ripe plant being brittle, but when young as springy and painful as any whip.

'He even beat me,' cried Mrs Doofar indignantly, 'and on my bare backside, like the other wenches! Only Doofar is supposed to beat me, sir.'

Peake said that he proposed to be a humane master.

'Why no, sir!' exclaimed Mrs Doofar. 'You got to beat them, it is all they understand! I need a tanning once in a while, but it is Mr Doofar as should see to me. And it weren't the whuppings that hurt, it was the cruel look in his eye. A good master should be strict but not cruel.'

Peake soon installed himself in Master's Quarters, a palatial suite of rooms that looked out on to the flower gardens, lawns and the ocean. The humid air was enlivened by a salty breeze, and by electric fans which turned languidly on the ceiling. The establishment was eclectic: a mixture of the grandiose baroque – the dining room with its oak panels and rosewood furniture all the way from England, and the various salons in delicious pastel shades of pink, blue and lemon yellow – and the unpretentious dwellings of the staff, whose shacks seemed to have grown, or planted themselves with delightful insouciance amidst the manicured lawns and tended rose gardens, and even crept up to the white walls of the house itself.

There were about fifty staff, including the domestics and the field workers, but the actual number of bodies present seemed unfathomable, with every second person described as someone else's cousin, sister or pickney.

209

Even Mr Lyle, the estate's frock-coated bailiff, confessed that he had a separate register of 'unaccountable bodies'. Peake remarked that unaccountable or not, there did seem to be an air of swank or even foppery about his new charges, who bedecked themselves with flowers and nosegays, ribbons and cravats. Mr Lyle explained gravely that this explained the name 'Mayfair', and it stemmed from Black Jack Peake, known as 'Beau Peake' following his visit to England, where he had been presented to 'King Jarge the Third, before he went doolally' and had taken the waters at Bath.

Since the departure of Mr Christopher, the estate had continued its operations under the orders of Mr Lyle, and the household maintained by Mrs Doofar. There was uncertainty, though, and the sugar cane was piling up, uncollected by the small ships which were able to dock at Port Mayfair. A new master was needed.

It was morning when Peake arrived; he instructed Mr Lyle to keep the workers at their tasks until he had inspected the books, and in the evening he would address them. He settled down in his bright study, the French windows open to the ruffle of the sea breeze, and began to examine his property.

At lunchtime he was served rum and soda and a plate of sweet potato and lobster, with a bowl of fruit which the young maid carried on her head. She introduced herself as Pulchinella Tarnishe, and wore a frilly French maid's uniform which was quite congruous with the baronial splendour of her surroundings. It also hinted at Mr Christopher's tastes, for the short skirt and skimpy knickers over sheer white stockings were designed to please. She wore her hair in braids and Peake told her she was very pretty, and looked just like the queen of the Maroons. Pulchinella blushed and smiled hugely, and curtseyed before fleeing in a fit of happy giggles. Peake ate his food and, accompanied by rum and soda and a large cigar, settled back to his work. At five o'clock, Mr Lyle came to say the staff were lined up in the main courtyard to hear him.

'Well, Mr Lyle,' said Peake, 'there will be changes here, quite dramatic ones, from which all of us shall profit. We suffer from living in paradise, where there is always rum, sugar cane to eat, and a fish for supper. Successive bankers from London have been happy to mortgage the property, for they too are seduced by its perfume. In fact, since the days of Beau Peake, this estate has been barely struggling along. The island ports are simply not big enough for large freighters, so we have always underproduced and undersold our sugar. Even so, why should a freighter make a detour to our small island, when they can get all the sugar they want from Jamaica or Cuba? Also, sugar is never a stable investment: right now there is a world glut. Now, I have brought enough capital to pay off our estate's immediate debts. But the mortgage must be paid in full and prosperity established for the future. Therefore, we need another source of income. You look shocked, Mr Lyle – you equate sugar with hard work, and hard work with reward. But hard work and reward are not the same thing. That fine coat of yours, Mr Lyle – what is it worth?'

'I paid fifty dollars for it in Antigua,' said Mr Lyle proudly.

'Yet if no one wishes to buy it from you, it is worth nothing,' said Peake. 'Take gold or jewels – valuable only because rare, but of themselves useless. Like banknotes, they are only valuable because people think they are. This painting here – very pretty, and I can assure you very valuable, but were it not for Mr Gainsborough's signature, it would be worthless. The idea of value does not depend on work, or even quality of product. It is like our idea of beauty: elusive and inexplicable. People take sugar in their tea, when they

211

could just as well have honey. Ultimately, the only value is the *idea* of value.'

Mr Lyle asked how this would affect the fortunes and people of Mayfair. Peake laughed.

'Why, not at all! Mayfair will not change, except that it will have a different value, Mr Lyle! All the familiar things will stay. Consider the poor mariners lured to their doom by my ancestors' trickery: it was not the rocks that shipwrecked them, but their illusion of safety. My ancestors grew rich on an idea ...'

'But how can Mayfair be an idea, sir?' said Mr Lyle. 'All we know is real things: rum, sugar and the lash.'

Peake clapped his hands.

'Perfect, my dear Mr Lyle! Mayfair shall prosper not by real things, but by the idea of real things.'

Such were Peake's words to his new servants. Many heads were scratched, but agreement was ensured by a copious free issue of rum and permission for a dance and a 'jump-up', and Peake's insistence that the only thing they must accept was the need for complete obedience, under pain of discipline with which they were already quite familiar. To emphasise the point, he cracked his cane against his thigh. And for further discipline, everyone would be issued with a natty dress uniform, for smartness. This was greeted with glee, and heads nodded in approval: the new master was a man of understanding.

That night, Peake slipped naked between soft perfumed sheets, and fell promptly asleep by the light of stars and a crescent moon. His windows were open on to the balcony, beneath which the glistening waves crashed. Some time during the darkness, when all was still, he was awakened by the pressure of another naked body slipping beneath the sheets beside him. A braided head nuzzled his chest, bare breasts squeezed against his belly and warm thighs were pressed against his. He tried to sit up, but was pinned by velvet arms, one of which detached itself to take his hand and press it to a fount that was hot and already wet.

'It's me, master – your Pulchinella,' she whispered.

A hand slipped to his balls and cock, which stood in drowsy half-erection. She gasped, and rubbed the organ until it stood fully stiff. Her sighs were rapturous.

'You *are* the master,' she whispered. 'Don't you want to poke me with that glorious dangler of yours?'

Peake hugged her, and said she was awfully sweet, but that he was not accustomed to such directness.

'O, I always sleep with the master, when he wants,' said Pulchinella. 'And I thought you'd want, sir, being so far from home. I was the master's favourite, and he always spanked me most beautifully. Will you spank me, sir? On my bare bum? O, please, sir. I'm such a forward girl, aren't I, and I need a whupping for it!'

Peake said it sounded as if she actually liked being spanked, and she giggled, and licked his breast.

'Mmm . . .' she murmured. 'Yes I do, sir. I love the sound of it, the crack of a hand on my bare bum, and the lovely warm sting, smarting through me like a snakebite, and the glow afterwards. And I love to squirm about and rub myself on master's thigh, and get all wet . . . you know, down there. I'd really love to be spanked in public – isn't that wicked? Or whipped, strung up and tied, just like the old days.'

Peake put three of his fingers into her wet slit, and she fastened on them, writhing in pleasure, which increased to a sharp moan as he found her damsel, already stiff.

'O, you must spank me! Please, sir! How wicked I am!'

Peake sat up and placed her naked body across his thigh; without a word, he began to spank her. Her waist rubbed against his erect cock, and she grasped his balls, squeezing them as his palm rained blows upon her squirming bare bum. A moonbeam illuminated his tattooed cock, and she twisted her head to look, then cried out in awe and delight.

'An orchid! My master is an orchid. Please let me kiss it, sir.'

Peake said that she might do so after her spanking, and continued to slap her firm bare nates with his palm. In the starlight the buttocks began to glow a fiery dark blue, shading to purple. When he had given nearly two hundred slaps, he released her, and her head promptly fell on his erect cock, taking it all the way to her throat and sucking and tonguing furiously, with little gurgles of rapture. After a while, he pulled her by the hair and said she had not taken enough punishment, and that she must hand him his cane. She smiled and said he was a good master, and now she was warmed up for proper beating. He made her stand, then bend over and touch her toes, which was the way gentlemen took it. Then he gave her thirty strokes of the cane on her bare buttocks, which she took without a murmur, and only the slightest clenching.

Peake told her to keep position; he stroked her furrow with the helmet of his cock, then ordered her to turn around and kneel before him. She did so, her mouth open to receive his cock, but he grasped her big plum nipples and pulled them hard, so that she cried out in pleased surprise. Pressing his cock between her teats, he twisted and kneaded the nipples until they were stiff; she brought her hands up and pressed her breasts against his organ to massage him in turn. The tip of her tongue flickered on his peehole; when his first droplet of cream was apparent, she sighed and smiled, and bent to take him in her mouth, understanding his needs. But he delicately refused her caress, instead pressing her breasts more tightly against his shaft, so that his spurt jetted against her lips and chin. He continued to rub her teats until his cock was stiff again, and she purred.

Now she knelt on the bed, her bottom in the air, and Peake recommenced spanking, ordering her to spread her bum-cheeks. He plunged his erect organ into her quim and she squealed in delight; he thrust more, and then penetrated her to the hilt.

Still spanking, he thrust into her fifty times, without spurting, then withdrew, before he did the same with her anus, pushing his glistening cock into her tight little hole and thrusting fifty times. Her hand was busy frotting her distended clitoris; he withdrew, placed her on her back, positioned himself straddling her, and the tip of his cock met the throbbing little organ. With deft movements of his hips, he maintained a relentless tickling of her damsel until the flow of her love-oil was a torrent on her thighs, and at last her belly heaved and she cried out in spasm.

Peake agreed that she might spend the night with him; they dozed off, her hand cupping his still-mighty organ, and she purred herself to sleep in utter contentment. In the morning, Peake found himself alone, but not for long. As he roused himself, the door opened to admit Pulchinella in her frilly maid's uniform, with his hot breakfast.

'Hot eggs and sausage, and cold melon, master?' she said anxiously. 'Is that OK? I haven't been naughty?'

'Why,' said Peake, smiling into her sloe eyes, 'it is far too hot, you naughty girl.'

'I'm not wearing knickers,' she said happily.

When Peake had given Pulchinella the morning spank which she seemed to regard as her due, she watched him eat, kneeling docilely with her hands folded on her lap.

'That bum of yours must be made of teak, Pulchinella,' he said, and she glowed at the compliment. 'But tell me, have you ever spanked or caned others?'

'Why no, master,' she replied, as though the idea was the wildest fantasy.

'Would you like to?' he said.

'I never thought ... My cousin Floella does, I know, but she went to the Maroons, and they are scary. I could if they were naughty, I guess, but it doesn't seem right – it is I who am always naughty!'

'What about spanking other women, Pulchinella? English women who want to be spanked – or caned, and whipped very hard on their bare white bums.'

'Well, if they wanted it,' said Pulchinella doubtfully. 'I thought I was the only one . . . But English women. I guess it would be fun, and not like spanking normal people.'

Her hand flew to her mouth.

'O! I'm sorry, master! I didn't mean . . .'

Peake laughed and put his finger on her lips.

'A lady never apologises, Pulchinella. And you're quite right. It is not like spanking normal people . . .'

'O, how gorgeous!' cried the perspiring young woman as she carefully stepped down from the dinghy, brushing her chestnut curls from her brow. 'It's just like you said, Flossie! It's so British!'

She gazed at the splendour of Mayfair across the green sward and the blaze of roses and bougainvillaea. Her skirts and petticoats were in her hands, carefully bundled in protection against the lapping turquoise water. A group of young ladies stood beside her, all dressed in summer silks and all shivering a little in sultry anticipation. They clambered out of the water and on to the strip of white beach, then up to the edge of the lawn, where they stood drying their feet as three young black men approached at a military pace. They wore bright blue uniforms, with golden epaulettes and swords at their waist; their leader also carried a whip. Behind the women, their bags were deposited on the sand, and the boatman departed on his boat back to the distant ocean liner.

'Welcome to Mayfair, ladies,' said the group leader. 'Stand still to be counted.'

'Hi,' said the voluble young lady, in the accents of well-heeled New England. 'I'm Mimsy Croppett. Tell your boys to be careful with my bags, especially the green one.'

She pointed to the pile of cases on the sand.

'You address me as sir,' the leader said, unsmiling.

His followers went to Mimsy Croppett's luggage, kicked it over, then ripped the cases and rummaged through them, sniffing the luxurious silks and underthings with glee. Mimsy reddened, then paled with rage, and was about to open her mouth when the leader cracked his whip. He ordered them to take off their shoes, pick up their bags and follow him.

'One trip only,' he said. 'Those of you with too many things –' he leered at Mimsy '– will leave the rest on the beach, for the hawks to eat.'

Sobbing and almost speechless, Mimsy set herself to rescuing handfuls of her 'things' and stuffing them into one of her ripped suitcases.

'Flossie,' she hissed, 'what is the meaning of this? You said it would be the surprise of a lifetime – all my hidden dreams fulfilled! But these damn young bucks, their damn insolence, treating us as though we were slaves!'

Lady Flora de Cante smiled in strange, secret satisfaction.

'Yes,' she drawled. 'The thing about hidden dreams is they do tend to come as a bit of a surprise, Mimsy.'

'No talking, sluts!' cried the leader, cracking his whip once more.

This time, it cracked across Lady Flora de Cante's sundress, on her bare back. She smiled wanly, her eyes crinkling with sudden tears, and curtseyed to the young man.

'Yes, sir,' she murmured, and followed him.

They were shown into a gaunt chamber littered with straw palliasses, and told it was their dungeon – Mimsy shuddered! – and they would have it cleaned up before they got anything to eat. There were mops and buckets; the bathroom was an annexe, with tubs and basins and a pump, and a row of Turkish commodes in full view. Mimsy shrieked that something was horribly wrong, that she had been tricked, and demanded to see the manager or the American consul or both, and threatened to explode in tears until Edwina Cheshunt silenced her with a slap.

'You said it was the experience of a lifetime,' sobbed Mimsy. 'Look at it!'

'Well, it is,' said Edwina amiably. 'I bet you didn't have Turkish crappers at your boarding school, dear, or floors to mop on your hands and knees, and a big strong black man standing over you with a cane.'

Mimsy screamed that she would not stand for it; her scream disturbed a parrot in the rafters, which began squawking, 'Whack bum! Pretty polly! Whack bum!'

Edwina laughed, and said she would follow the parrot's advice. Mimsy had to be toughened and shown the rules, so that she would not spoil the experience for the rest of them. With Jane Reculver's help, she grasped Mimsy and squatted, pinioning the wriggling girl over her knee. She lifted Mimsy's skirt and tore off her pale pink knickers, then spanked her very hard at least thirty times on the bare bottom, until Mimsy's squeals and squirming had subsided into a low moan of despair. Panting, Edwina released her. There was polite applause from the other girls.

'Teach her what for!' cried Gwendoline Hedge.

'She mustn't spoil our holiday,' agreed Fleur Dovercourt.

'Except, girls, that it isn't really a holiday,' murmured Flora de Cante. 'Is it . . .?'

The terrified Mimsy at last agreed to behave, seeing she was in resolute company, and now the others began to comfort and caress her.

'It will seem hard at first,' soothed Joan Weimaran, 'but then, anything that's nice takes getting used to. We are all girls together, and must obey the master. How lucky we are that he summoned us! It is what we really want – even Edwina, who spanked you. She is a mistress, you know, and spanks and chastises all the time, beating the bottoms of her own slaves. But she knows her chastisement of others is a deep desire to be disciplined herself – daring a strong other to tame her. The master will do that. We know.'

There were sighs and laughter. Then it was decided that duties should be apportioned, so that they would please the master, and be rewarded with food. They stripped to underthings, carefully folding their dresses, and set to their tasks, and soon the door opened to admit Mrs Doofar, resplendent in her blue uniform of military jacket and short pleated skirt; she was armed with a whip, which without a word she proceeded to crack across the upturned backsides of the scrubbing girls.

She upset the folded silk dresses into heaps on the wet floor, barked that nothing was clean enough, and they must start again. Meanwhile a bare-chested male, wearing only his blue uniform trousers, laid a pile of rough clothing on the stone floor, and she said these were work dresses for their field labours. The girls looked at the servant male, their eyes full of imagining. Mimsy Croppett eyed his rippling dark muscles; she seemed to have taken heart both from the indignity of her spanking and the discipline of unfamiliar labour. She said cheerfully that she guessed it was a lark, and it would be something to tell the folks about, and it could be worse.

'And it can't last forever,' she said.

'That depends on how much you pay,' said Mrs Doofar.

'Cockeyed sort of holiday! You mean, the more you pay, the sooner you can go home? Ow!'

Mimsy jumped as Mrs Doofar's whip slashed her buttocks, tearing a hole in her pink panties.

'Quite the opposite, slut,' said Mrs Doofar.

The girls were ordered to dress in white smocks,

shapeless sun hats, and sandals. Then they were shackled with leg-irons, a long chain tethering them in a line, and marched to the sugar field, where they received a meal, a plate of nameless stew slopped from a bucket and eaten with fingers. Hunger overcame embarrassment and disgust, and they cleaned their plates, especially as the whip-wielding female overseer said that 'ninnies' would be punished. All agreed that they did not wish to be the first 'ninny', yet all eyed the shiny whip-thongs with cool, private interest.

Then they were put to work cutting the cane, with rather blunt machetes. They had to stoop and cut each stalk at the base, and add it to a pile, which at intervals was transferred to a cart. At intervals of twenty yards throughout the vast field were similar groups, some dark males, who worked wearing only loincloths, but the majority smocked English females – guests like themselves. The males worked at an easy rhythm, and it was only the females who seemed to strain themselves under the barks of their overseers. These wore blue uniforms, and were mostly female. All carried whips at their waist. One of them trundled a sort of dinner trolley, although it was empty.

The sun was hot, and their fimsy smocks were soon drenched with sweat, showing clearly the outline of their equally drenched underthings, their frills and flounces quite inappropriate to a tropical climate. Edwina was the first to cry that she was beastly hot, and was jolly well going to make herself comfortable. She stripped off her knickers, and wormed her way out of her camisole, followed by the faithful Jane Reculver. Then she looked for a place to store her clothing, and placed the garments neatly on the little trolley. At that, the female overseer noticed her, and flew into a rage, scattering the underthings into the mess of cane-clippings and dust. The work-party of males nearby at once stopped and turned to watch, grinning.

'Who gave you permission, slut?' roared the female.

'I'll be comfortable if I like,' said Edwina. 'I'm paying for this curious adventure, my girl.'

The men 'oohed' – the woman's rage was awesome.

'You call me "mistress", you slut!' she cried, cracking her whip. 'You –' she pointed at Jane Reculver '– go and cut a stout rattan. You know what that is – a young sapling cane. I ain't going to waste my good whip on your fat white arses. And you – bend over the horse and lift your smock.'

The trolley was in fact a portable correction frame, with fastenings for wrists, waist and ankles. Edwina began to protest, but in an instant, three of the male workers from nearby ran over, pinioned her and placed her squirming on to the frame. The overseer proceeded to cuff her by wrists and ankles. Jane Reculver, meanwhile, brought back a very thick 'rattan' and meekly handed it to her. Edwina was kicking and squealing, though not very hard; grimly, she stared at the gleaming rod which was to flog her. The overseer flexed the cane, and pronounced herself satisfied.

'It ain't a real rattan,' she said, 'but I'll hurt you just as hard, miss. Insolence is always punished here at Mayfair. You didn't come here to be at your ease, you sluts, you came to learn the manners of civilised folk.'

She removed her jacket, revealing her own tight white blouse soaked in sweat, and her bare breasts clearly outlined under the thin fabric. Her nipples stood up like pine-cones, as though in lustful excitement. Abruptly she lashed sharply across Edwina's stretched bare buttocks. The girl jumped with a squeal, more of astonishment than anything else, but at the second stroke her moan was of real pain, and her wriggling bottom attested to her distress. At each stroke, the overseer's breasts bounced prettily against the drenched cotton of her blouse, as a mute chorus to her exertion. The sweating males grinned as they watched the naked

Engish girl flogged; the pouches of their loincloths swelled.

One of them, whose pouch was quite vividly distended by his manhood, began an obscene dance, mimicking both the actions of the chastiser and the squirming of the bare victim. Without pausing or looking at him, the overseer suddenly slapped him on the tip of his erection, not to hurt him, but to make him squeal in embarrassment.

'You ninny, Larrabee,' she hissed. 'You interrupting your mistress. I'll deal with you, rude boy.'

She continued to cane Edwina on the bare until fifteen harsh strokes had been administered, and Edwina's buttocks were livid with the bloom of her correction. She was released and, on instructions, sullenly bowed to her tormentor, rubbing her crimson glowing nates.

'Gosh, mistress,' she panted through gritted teeth, 'that was damnably tight.'

The mistress grinned with pleasure.

'You asked for it, miss,' she said, 'didn't you?'

'I suppose I did,' said Edwina, grinning ruefully.

Now the mistress grabbed Larrabee by the ear and bent him over the whipping-frame.

'You asked for it too, you wicked ragamuffin,' she exclaimed. 'Off with those modesties, now. You going to get a rude boy's penance – the sugar stick where it hurts!'

The shamed male lowered his loincloth to reveal his huge dark cock, now wilting in his distress. It wilted fully when the mistress parted the cheeks of his buttocks and inserted the sugar stick deep into his bumhole where it hung, quivering, as he writhed in shame and discomfort. She lifted her whip and stroked its thongs across his naked buttocks. Far from subduing his fellow friends, her action increased their glee, and they watched enthusiastically as the mistress laid fifteen sharp strokes with her whip on his bare flesh. The girls too crowded to watch, not in glee, but in fascinated awe. When she had finished with the whip, she contemptuously pulled the sugar stick from his anus, and cracked it twice, contemptuously, across his nates, before dismissing him.

'Well, Larrabee?' she said. 'You liked that, didn't you?'

'How can you be so cruel, mistress!' he cried, wriggling in anguish.

'Because,' she said, 'you like it that way, boy. And now, sluts, back to work. You may all take off your modesties if you like. You just have to ask polite.'

The flogging, both of male and female, had induced a kind of defiant merriment amongst the girls. Gwendoline whispered it was like being back at school. The girls stripped to their smocks, aware of male stares at their discarded underthings, and then Joan Weimaran said nonchalantly it was still awfully hot, and would it be all right to work completely nude? In her request was mischief, and the girls' eyes were on the loins of the males. The overseer contemptuously approved, and said it would save time when it came to the next tonguing.

'Bad sluts got to be beaten, then work hard, then be beaten some more,' she said. 'That is life.'

Jane Reculver said timidly that she had not been beaten, although she too had removed her underclothes without asking.

The overseer yawned, and said she had forgotten. She told Jane to cut another cane, and when she had done so – it was even longer and thicker than Edwina's – the overseer told the girls that they must sort the matter out themselves. Joyously, the girls pinioned a far from unwilling Jane, stripped her completely and bent her over the flogging-frame. Then they passed the cane to each other and each gave her a swinging cut on the bare buttocks, Edwina cheating slightly by giving her two, right on her furrow, which was the only time Jane cried.

223

Naked, the girls set to their work, quickly developing a rhythm of bending low, cutting and stacking; so much so that they began to hum the Newton Abbot school song. Mimsy Croppett responded with 'The Star-Spangled Banner', to everyone's amusement, and the mechanical simplicity of naked, monotonous toil seemed to lift their spirits, as though their utter degradation were a comfort. All the while, the overseer prowled with whip at hand, to lash an idle bare bottom. She seemed to pick on Mimsy especially, and Mimsy's face gradually assumed a faraway brooding look. After one particularly vicious whip-crack, she gasped and began to pant heavily. She threw her machete down.

'Are you all right, Mimsy?' said Jane anxiously.

Mimsy did not answer, but looked at her with wide, almost frightened eyes, her breasts heaving. The teats were large and drooped beguilingly, and in her intense breathing, they slapped gently against her ribcage. She stared at their overseer and, with the tip of her tongue licking her lips, she hurled her machete down.

'Mutiny!' cried the overseer. 'Insolence and rudeness!'

Mimsy let her lips hang wide open, and ran her tongue over her teeth, mocking the woman. She did not resist as she was seized and pinioned to the whipping-frame, her naked thighs splayed. With a hiss of anger from the defied overseer, the sugar stick was thrust into her anus, and another into the opened flaps of her quim. The fierce punishment tools were thrust as far and hard as they would go – and still Mimsy emitted only a hoarse gasping, and no cry of protest. Her squirming buttocks and thighs seemed to be embracing the instruments of her torment. She writhed and shut her eyes in a fierce agony that was almost pride, and moaned in what seemed shivering pleasure as the overseer ran the splayed tip of a massive cane across her bare stretched buttocks. She had cut the cane's tip into three weals, four inches deep.

Mimsy took thirty strokes of the cane full on her bare bum, the firmness of her buttocks as proud at the last stroke as at the slashing first. During her punishment there was total silence. When she was unfastened, she walked coolly to her machete and picked it up, then bowed curtly. She did not even rub her inflamed bottom.

'Thank you, mistress,' she said in a clear strong voice, and resumed her work. The other girls took up their rhythm again, with Mimsy vigorously setting the pace.

'You English girls are so right,' Mimsy Croppett whispered to Lady Flora de Cante. 'I think it is going to be the experience of a lifetime, for all of us.'

There were three more tonguings before the sun sank low and they were shackled again to march back to their dungeon.

The routine of every day was henceforth exactly the same. Timepieces were forbidden at Mayfair, and only the rising or setting of the sun, the croak of toads, the call of cicadas and screechums and macaws, told what time of day or night it was. Every morning, at the crack of dawn, they were roused by a clanging bell. They had some minutes to perform their toilet and clean their dungeon for inspection, any imperfections being noted for future punishment at the end of the work shift. At first the girls were shy about performing their ablutions in public, but soon, in their numb spirit of slavery, they squatted quite happily on the Turkish commodes and chattered as they evacuated, anticipating the day's ordeal with a kind of rueful pride. Punishment, and such scraps of food or comfort as they could snatch in the burning sunlight, were their main conversation, apart from furtive and increasingly unashamed speculations about the muscular young black men who toiled half-naked alongside them.

They were shackled and taken outside to the court,

where they saw the master from a distance: the girls, or 'guests', were lined up for this morning assembly, about sixty or seventy of them, to witness the daily ceremonial punishment of a black girl named Pulchinella.

The purpose of this spectacle as to instil discipline and warn against imperfection, and it was a ritual willingly accepted or even, curiously, proposed by the young maid herself. She was tied tightly by wrists and ankles, and hoisted two or three feet into the air from a gibbet. She always approached her place of supplice quite gaily, and stripped off her frilly maid's uniform to be punished completely nude on the back and buttocks, with a cruel splayed whip which the master wielded with cold efficiency. At each stroke, her trussed body jerked and swung in the air, and the master carefully waited for her to be still before administering the next lash. Thus the ceremony could last upwards of half an hour. Always, after her punishment, she would kneel, her velvet skin glowing in the rising sun, and kiss her master's feet, before gathering her uniform and scampering away to her duties.

It was apparent that some of the girls were permitted to wear simple jewellery, ribbons or other adornments on their drab white smocks, as though some hierarchy existed amongst the guests. They carried themselves with hauteur, but the airs and graces of these girls seemed a world away from the back-breaking routine of work and punishment which was the girls' lot; just as distant as the cruise liner from which they had disembarked for their experience of a lifetime.

At first, Edwina and Flora de Cante had enthused about the piquancy of this 'holiday', and told of their experiences with the master in London, and the joys of both dominance and submission. Edwina insisted that all affection was about power, and that the kiss of the whip was the purest expression of power. It ultimately did not matter whether the body of a lady received or wielded lashes; all that mattered was her knowledge of her own puissance, to take pain or award it. And the knowledge of pain was that most beautiful and precious of things: self-knowledge.

But gradually even the idea of the master seemed distant, as their spirits and bodies submitted to the yoke of discipline and caprice of overseers, the females being more artful, and harsher, than the males. They amused themselves by giggling over the males' loincloths, and fantasising about the danglers beneath and what they could do with them. Their routine of fieldwork and flogging was illumined by the occasional punishment of one of the black males, usually naked and often with the cruel refinement of the 'sugar stick' to his caning. Sometimes, a miscreant – one of them, or one of the males – would be trussed naked, and 'flogged round the field'. A male was led on all fours by a leash strapped round his balls, with a sugar stick in anus; a female by a harness clamped to her nipples and quim-lips, with a short sugar stick thrust fully into both anus and quim, which pieces she was obliged to hold inside her for the duration of her punishment. The miscreant received ten lashes on the bare from every single overseer in the field. The girls came to regard the correction eagerly, as a great entertainment. Thus did they become true slaves.

13

Miss Rattan's Lesson

As time passed, even the most severe corrections were increasingly handed over to the girls themselves by a succession of mistresses, none of which they knew by name. It was as though their team spirit was being nurtured by the anonymity of their mistresses: only they, the girls of their dungeon, had real existence. Sometimes the mistresses were English, wearing decoration on their blue uniforms: these were slaves who had been soundly broken in, and promoted to break others. They recognised the slave girl Pulchinella, now proud in her blue uniform; she still took her ritual flogging at morning gathering, but in the field she was the hardest of mistresses, and even said openly how much she relished the squirming of a white bum under her cane.

It scarcely came as a surprise when some of the girls recognised Katie Mann. She was splendid in her fine uniform, and was the most vicious of all the mistresses. She gave no hint of knowing them, except by a particularly sneering way of pronouncing their names and telling them repeatedly what filthy English sluts they were. Mimsy once protested that she was a filthy American slut, and got thirty on the bare for her trouble. Miss Mann liked to be nude herself as she caned the naked slaves, saying it made her arms freer and her strokes harder. No one argued.

The master was a shadowy figure, a god almost,

whom they saw flog the dangling Pulchinella at morning assembly, or morning sacrifice as Mimsy tartly called it. Their spirits hardened with their bodies; their skins became leathery with the sun and the lash, their muscles taut with constant exercise. There was no modesty; they worked nude, and in their dungeon lived nude for most of the time, squatting at their intimate ablutions without care or interest. Their precious frocks and fripperies were stored under their mattresses, but even these were forgotten, as belonging to another world, until Joan Weimaran idly inspected her kit one day and discovered it gnawed by rats.

The others found the same: mild amusement was the only reaction. The days were gone where a misplaced curl, the wrong shade of lipstick or a dress that was a whole month out of fashion would cause social banishment. Here, appetite was satisfied by the meanest achievement, and palates jaded by riches and fashion were honed by utter degradation to take pleasure in scraps. Gradually, each of the girls in turn admitted that she relished her submission, and the sting of the lash made her feel alive. Even Edwina said that humility was more joyful than dominance.

Their squabbles were not over social niceties, but over scraps of food; their vanities not from frippery, but from bravery and toughness under the lash. An errant maid was entrusted to her comrades for flogging, and by the by, the overseer did not even trouble to witness chastisement, merely taking the dungeon's word that correction had been imposed, and the number of strokes noted. If food was scarce, whips were not. It was only on the caprice of a particularly cruel mistress that a girl would be removed to the 'cells', sometimes for a day, and return pale and subdued. It was with difficulty that she could speak of her punishment, but in whispers, stories were exchanged of floggings in truss, with chains, hoods, leather or rubber corsets, and artful tools to painfully fill each and every orifice of a girl's body and remind her mercilessly of her enslaved state.

To these corrections too they became hardened, and acquired a kind of pride that, utterly broken, they could be broken no further. Relatonships were formed that were sapphic in nature, and pursued without shame. Caresses and masturbation took place between two girls, or even three or four, along with playful spanking and much tribadic licking of breasts, toes and quims. Those girls not in the group of onanists looked on blankly, or frotted themselves as they watched – or just slept.

'Daddy used to warn us against ending up on Skid Row,' said Mimsy cheerfully. 'He thought that the worst hell imaginable – alone, friendless, hungry and brutalised. Yet here we are, on Skid Row, and it's OK! It's what we want . . .'

'It is – *us*,' said Jane Reculver in wonder.

'I am hungry for more than food,' said Flora one day. 'I think we all are.'

She sat in a circle with four of the others; each squatted cross-legged, with her fingers idly exploring the spread quim-petals of her neighbour. In the centre of the circle, Jane squatted with her fesses up and received languid slaps on the bare from each of the tribadists, while she diddled herself, on Edwina's orders.

At Flora's words, their faces said the same thing.

'I bet we all dream the same,' said Minty Astor. 'We all frig ourselves thinking of those young bucks and their muscles, and what's under their modesties. Diddling is all very well, but a girl needs cock, and male cream in her slit.'

They continued with their diddling; their slaps to Jane's buttocks grew fiercer as their eyes closed and each came to spasm in her private imagined delights.

Fulfilment was not difficult, and there was no planning at all. Submission leads to its own casual

230

brazenness; Mimsy dropped her machete – an imperfection – and cried 'O, shit!', and unladylike language was a fearful imperfection. She was strapped to the frame for a very long flogging, and the young bucks clustered to watch. Quite coolly, Flora de Cante grasped one full on the bulge of his cock, and led the astonished male into the sugar cane. When she returned with her flushed and still surprised buck, she wore a faint smile. Edwina and Joan followed her example, and Mimsy's flogging was only just complete when they too returned.

The next day, Joan was taking a beating, and two of the other girls did the same. The young males now got the idea, and only a wink was needed for them to obey the hungry and implacable maids. Thereafter, a flogging was the sign for dalliance, and an unspoken system of honour grew, that each girl was to 'volunteer' for punishment, by deliberately offending, to allow the others their pleasure. The males would stand preening and showing off, hoping to be chosen. Jane Reculver surprised everyone by taking four of them at once, saying afterwards that it was only fair. The next day, Minty Astor took five at once, lording it over her comrades until Edwina ordered her thrashed for 'side'; but afterwards it was the custom for a maid to hold up the fingers of one hand – or even two! – to indicate the number of cocks she wished to pleasure, while her comrades watched.

It had to be done quickly, before the distraction of punishment was finished, and the girl would simply kneel like a dog with her buttocks spread to take a rapid succession of cocks in her quim. Edwina decided she wanted to be poked in her bumhole too, so another finger-code was devised for that. Then Flora wished to suck cocks and swallow the cream, or rub it on her breasts, which she insisted was good for skin tone, so she instituted a code for that too. They called their signals 'the menu' and joked to the males that they

231

could have their pleasure *à la carte* although the boys did not quite understand.

They did understand, however, that slavery had made the females insatiable for pleasure and sensation; a girl whose day was enlivened by finding an extra scrap of goat meat in her stew bowl could not fail to appreciate an inexhaustible supply of stiff cocks. The risks they took were greater and greater; they did not care. What punishment could be greater than their incarceration at Mayfair? Mimsy reminded them that they could always go if they wanted; Peake Town was only a day's march, and it would be easy to hide in the bushes beside the road, if they really wanted to escape. But she was greeted with blank looks, as though such an idea were meaningless and unthinkable.

'Escape, Mimsy?' said Jane. 'What would be the point?'

'Well, I don't know,' said Mimsy. 'I really don't know.'

The day came when Flora was caught by the overseer. Edwina had to take her flogging rapidly, although she had tried to draw it out with much squealing and wriggling, in the hope of extra lashes; nevertheless it was done, and the overseer heard grunting coming from the sugar cane. She smashed her way through the stalks, and in the little clearing, or 'dining room', she found the naked form of Flora de Cante, stained with dirt and shining with sweat and spurt, kneeling on the trampled cane floor. Beneath her was a black male, his cock in her quim; behind her straddled another, his organ pumping in her anus; a third male had his cock plunged to the hilt in Flora's eager throat and she was tonguing him as the others vigorously poked her. And there were seven naked males, their modesties in their hands and their cocks throbbing, waiting to take their turn.

For a moment, the overseer was speechless. Then she stammered that this was a monstrous disgrace, that they were all for the cells, for the worst whipping they could

232

ever imagine, that the master himself had to be told at once . . .

'All for the cells, mistress?' said Edwina sweetly.

'Yes, all of you! You are all in this together. And the cells will be the least of it!'

'Then,' said Edwina, 'we haven't much to lose, girls. Might as well be flogged for a dozen sheep as one lamb.'

'Stop!' cried the overseer, cracking her whip – but too late. She retreated, wailing in distress as the other overseers seemed too cautious to come and help her.

The throng of naked maidens pressed in uncanny silence towards their male comrades. The males came running, and the girls efficiently seized their bulging cocks. Joan and Minty simply lay down on the crushed sugar cane and opened their thighs, to be pleasured immediately by one thrusting buck after another. Mimsy sucked cock after cock before joining the two and opening her own thighs, playing with her clit and nipples to entice admirers, as if enticement were necessary. Soon, all the girls had found their satisfaction, and the cane field became a lustful spectacle that Minty cried was sugar indeed. The passionate energies of the contestants in this joyous wrestling had in no way dissipated when the overseer returned with reinforcements, consisting of bulky young men in full uniform, all with sticks and whips with which they lashed out at the writhing bare bodies. Even that did not quell their ardour; Edwina and Flora and the others moaned in ecstasy as the whips lashed their bare skin, making this cruelty part of their pleasure.

At last, the entire work gang was chained once more, and marched to the cells, where the master would decide their fate. They were obliged to travel naked, without shoes, hats or smocks, all left in heaps on the cane field. Their progress, nude and in shackles, was the object of derisive attention from the girls whose smocks were adorned with trinkets and fancies.

233

'Such a shame!' sneered the mistress, flicking her whip over the backs of her chain gang, whose flushed joyous faces were not dimmed by the awfulness of what awaited. 'To think you were on the verge of being promoted. You have almost done your basic time, and become good docile girls. And now this – giving way to wicked lustful temptation! You'll have to start all over again, if the master doesn't –' She paused, and shuddered. 'No, he is too kind to do that.'

'Doesn't what, mistress?' said Jane meekly, ignoring the automatic slash to her buttocks which rewarded her speaking without permission.

'Doesn't send you away from Mayfair!' replied the mistress, horrified.

The males and females were led to the cells, a dark building some way from the main house, and taken below into the foul passages. Each girl was locked in her own cell. Mrs Doofar was there to supervise the females, while Miss Mann, simpering, looked after the males. Mrs Doofar tut-tutted with disapproval as she passed from one cell to the next, accompanied by burly young men, to determine the restraint each maid would suffer as she awaited the master's visit, and his verdict as to their ultimate punishment. After each cell visit, she looked through the spyhole at the trussed girl and pronounced herself satisfied. Then she approached the master, and told him the errant maids were ready for his inspection.

Peake was in conference with Pulchinella, who had just finished clearing away his luncheon things. She was in her frilly maid's uniform, and told him brightly that she loved going to the fields to oversee the slaves.

'It seems right, master,' she said. 'You punish me in the morning for my naughtiness at night – how lovely it is to be so helpless while you thrash me in public – and then I go to flog others in my turn, for their naughtiness. Just being subdued and treated like slaves makes them naughty, don't it? But master – you always sleep with me, and I worry. Other masters have plenty of gash, as they say. Wouldn't you like me to find you a nice one amongst the ladies?'

Peake laughed, and said he would think about it. He had to go to the cells and inspect some very errant girls – ones on the brink of leaving their dungeon, but who had given way to indiscipline. Pulchinella said she knew them well, at least their backsides, and said they were the baddest girls she had ever seen at Mayfair.

'I know them, too,' said Peake thoughtfully.

He proceeded to the cells, wrinkling his nose at the stench. All around him the passages echoed to sobs and muffled grunts and moans of the males and females in bondage. He inspected the males first: their bondage was a simple plugged harness for cock, balls and anus. The females had received more thoughtful treatment, and each was held moaning in a different and artful restraint. Peake entered the cell where Jane Reculver was held, and stroked her hair, smiling at her fondly.

'Well, Jane, you've been naughty,' he said. 'It'll be a public flogging for you all, you know.'

'And loss of privileges,' snapped Mrs Doofar, without a hint of irony.

Jane was unable to answer, but moaned softly and piteously behind her gag. She was bound in a 'hangball', her wrists and ankles strapped together in front of her, then her body hoisted up on a pulley so that she hung from the ceiling in the shape of a triangle. Her waist was squeezed in a tight corset of black rubber and her legs were sheathed in thigh boots of the same fabric, the garments obviously much too small and most uncomfortable. Her breasts, croup and quim were bare, and added to her suspension were clamps to nipples and quim-lips, fastened to the ceiling by tight chains, so that further discomfort would be caused if she tried to move or struggle.

She was gagged with a black strip of leather that forced a silver flap against her tongue, and a twin-pronged 'pacifier' was thrust deep into both quim and anus, secured to her waist by a silver chain that pressed uncomfortably across her furrow and left a thin red mark on her downy belly. She moaned and shook her head, widening her eyes as if to ask the master what was to happen. Her reward was a sharp stroke to the bare buttocks from Mrs Doofar's cane, which made her shudder and squeal as the clamps pinched her nipples and quim.

'No howling, slut,' said Mrs Doofar. 'You've had the hangball before, when I found you with dirty fingernails.'

Peake nodded his approval of Mrs Doofar's efficiency, and told Jane that all of her 'gang', and the male offenders too, would be chastised most severely.

'Whipped in public, and in bondage,' he said pleasantly.

Jane was silent.

'Of course, when you see the instruments, you may always cry shame and depart. You may even do it now, with a squeal for your freedom. You know that, Jane.'

She nodded.

'But you won't, will you?'

Jane stared at her master with moist eyes, then emitted a low broken sob that was sorrow and desire and passion and longing. Slowly, she shook her head. She would not squeal for her freedom.

Peake visited every cell, and inspected every girl, trussed and gagged with all the arts of a mistress, and using every instrument bequeathed from the long, merciless history of Mayfair Plantation: shackles, sheaths, ropes, stocks and pillories, and pinioning devices for the most intimate crevices of the female body. To every girl he put the same question, and every girl answered the same. Peake decreed that they should

236

remain bound in the cells until sundown, when males and females would be taken to the yard and beaten. The manner of their fustigation was to be the 'flagpole'; the males first, with the females having the fearful pleasure of watching their chastisement while still in bondage. Then they would be unbound and would mount the flagpole, which would be pleasantly warm from their paramours' squirming bodies.

The flagpole was really two flagpoles, laid end to end on a series of trestles, about four feet from the ground. All of Mayfair was there to watch; it was dusk, and the stars and moon were faintly showing in the velvety, scented air. The naked males were led out first, and were invited to bend over the poles at regular intervals, so that their toes and fingers were just touching the ground. Then their ankles and wrists were bound together, and a heavy chain snaked all along the pole, to which each pair of bound extremities was fastened. Thus weighted, their bodies were balanced uncomfortably on their bellies, and in addition to enduring the force of the rods on their bare croups, they must constantly squirm to remain in an upright position.

Peake, in a dark crimson uniform, supervised the two correctors: Mrs Doofar and Miss Mann. Each held a heavy cane of three bound teak rods about four feet long, and positioned herself at one end of the array of naked male croups. Both women removed their jackets, and their bare upper bodies were clearly visible through the sweat-drenched cloth of their blouses. Their nipples stood firm, as if in high excitement at their task of flogging male bottoms.

They started their work on Peake's signal: each bottom recived four strokes of the cane, before its chastiser proceeded to the next. The two females met in the centre, bowed, and continued to the other end of the pole, so that the luckless occupants of the centre had the shortest time to recover from their first smarting until the second fell. This procedure was followed four times, until each croup glowed with thirty-two cane-strokes, and the pole was a mass of squirming, moaning male bodies. The crowd cheered wildly.

The males were escorted back to their dungeon, naked but, in their sobbing submission, unchained. The watching females were released from their gags and bonds; they moved to exercise their bodies, but in a moment they too were stretched and trussed across the pole. Their naked bottoms gleamed in the starlight as Peake took the heavy cane from Mrs Doofar.

'The master tongues alone . . .' whispered the crowd.

Peake raised his instrument and whipped Jane Reculver's bare bottom with four hard strokes. She wriggled, and moaned softly; he touched her flamed skin gently before moving to the next trussed slave.

'Thank you, master,' whispered Jane.

Peake flogged each female bottom with four of the tightest strokes, and each female murmured her grateful thanks. Then he repeated the set in the reverse direction. When each pair of naked fesses glowed the deepest sullen purple, he stopped, having counted twelve passes in a full two hours; the moon was high; each naked, helpless English girl had taken forty-eight strokes of the cane on her helpless bare bum, without a single cry.

Peake clapped his hands.

'You have learned your lesson,' he cried. 'You have tasted freedom, but chosen the beauty of submission instead. You have become slaves: you have become ladies! And now your party may start.'

'I don't believe it!' cried Mimsy Croppett. 'Half an hour ago, we were strapped to that horrid flagpole and having our tushies laced by the master, and now we are the belles of the ball, in our glad rags.'

She emptied her champagne glass and was promptly served another by a uniformd male.

'They aren't very glad,' said Edwina, 'seeing as they are all eaten by rats and things. But they do seem to have a certain slut chic: all these rips, my stockings and knickers are rags – and I can see your bare left teat, Mimsy.'

'The master is so wonderful,' murmured Jane Reculver.

All around them in the scented Antillean night, ladies flounced in silks and frills, or else in charming little black numbers skimpily fashioned from scraps of rubber or leather, with little attempt to conceal knickerless quims or unsupported breasts; gentlemen strutted in blue uniforms, or else in top hats and evening dress – sometimes in patent leather shoes, sometimes in bare feet. Overseers carried 'dress whips' or 'party canes' gaily adorned with flowers or ribbons. A cream-suited band played, which Edwina said was known as The Food of Love, and wove threads of lust and pleasure with sweetly decadent music. Teasing, Edwina approached the leader and kissed him on the cheek, then on the swelling of his manhood. Then she lifted her flimsy dress and squatted knickerless on the mouth of his giant horn, which rested on the ground. The pressure of her body muffled the sound to a braying like an elephant, and Edwina cried out shrilly at her vibratory pleasure.

'You have acquitted yourself well, sluts,' purred a cool, familiar voice.

Beside them, splendid in a meshed dress of thin leather strips that showed her ripe breasts with beguiling clarity, was Miss Mann, the stern headmistress, and now the equally stern overseer of Mayfair Plantation. Her face smiled, but the jewelled cane-handle at her belt gleamed.

'Miss Mann!' cried Minty Astor. 'Why, mistress, you have been awfully hard on us. I have never been flogged so tightly, so often and so . . . so wonderfully! Except, of course, just now. The master . . . O, he is superb.'

The girls' faces glowed.

'I know,' said Miss Mann. 'I dare say you will not want to leave Mayfair, now that you have proven yourselves worthy. The real Mayfair would seem thin after this: we have lords and ladies and swells, but ours are more real.'

'I feel so gay!' cried Lady Flora de Cante. 'It is just like a do in Berkeley Square. I wonder who *she* is?'

She gestured at the throng of beaux and ladies in finery, and smiled at one virile gentleman with an eyepatch and a wooden leg, much surrounded by females. Near him stood a female glistening with gold chains, jewels and ornaments, her costume a wondrous depiction of flowers and orchids, who, on second glance, was entirely nude under her adornments: the orchids were tattoos.

'She is Orchid, queen of the Maroons,' said Miss Mann. 'I believe the master has some business with her.'

Edwina returned, breathless with pleasure and making no attempt to hide the rivulets of oil on her bare thighs. She said that dear Ragamuffin was the absolute best.

'I guess this is our farewell bash,' said Mimsy. 'Gee, I feel it! Does my bum smart, girls, or am I just imagining things? Back home the boys will call me rawhide. They'll have to . . . I just couldn't do without it now – without correction. But we'll have to go, won't we? We've paid for the joy of our submission – it is so damn blissful! – but for how long will the master want us as slaves?'

Jane pointed to the lights of a ship on the the horizon, and said it was perhaps the ship even now approaching to take them home, wherever home really was. The girls mused.

'I should correct you for bad language, Mimsy,' said Miss Mann cheerfully. 'I am still an overseer, you know.'

'Sure you should, mistress!' cried Mimsy defiantly. 'You go ahead, it might be the last spanking I get for a while.'

She bent down and threw up her skirt, to show her naked bottom glowing purple from her lacing by the master.

'Are you sure you can take it, miss?' said Miss Mann, as she prepared to spank the sullenly glowing skin.

'Not at all, mistress,' murmured Mimsy, ruefully rubbing her bare bum. 'That's what makes it so thrilling.'

Miss Mann gave her a strong fifty slaps on the bare, after which Mimsy rubbed her bottom some more. Her wriggling under the spanks seemed to cause a ripple of excitement, and soon the girls of the dungeon were playfully spanking each other on the bare, to the amusement of the throng. The merriment was infectious; champagne flowed, and reserve dissolved, until the company was lustful, encouraged by Ragamuffin's sly rhythms. Mrs Doofar paraded past them, with Mr Doofar proudly in tow, and said it was a splendid jump-up and her sluts did her credit. She glanced at a pair who had begun openly coupling, standing up and pretending to dance, but with the mistress's ankles draped around her slave's shoulders as his loins pumped into her. Mrs Doofar smiled and said that a good jig-jig was part of jump-up.

Champagne trays circulated, with a difference: certain of the male servants were now naked, carrying their silver trays balanced snugly on their erect manhood. This caused much mirth, and of course very rapid consumption of champagne, and Miss Mann declared that the girl who took the last glass got a 'tickle' from the cocks whose attentions had so recently caused their chastisement. By chance, it was her; the tray fell, revealing a superbly stiff black cock, and her mouth fell open, her eyes hooded in sudden desire. It had not been clear what she meant by a 'tickle' – now, as she unconsciously rubbed the moistening crotch of her dress, it was. Flustered, she excused herself, saying she must ask the master. Peake was in conversation with the naked tattooed woman, the queen of the Maroons. Miss Mann whispered to him, and he took something from his pocket. She lifted her tight leather dress, and he reached down and fumbled at her fount; then she bowed and scampered back.

'Yes!' she cried. 'I can't wait, tickle me now, my buck.'

She plumped herself on the ground, on her back, and lifted her dress to spread her naked thighs, her quim and inner thighs already well-moistened with her love-oil. The girls stared; attached to her quim-lips was a gold padlock, its thin tongue inserted through piercings in the wall of her flaps themselves. Triumphantly she snapped the padlock open, and said the master had been gracious enough to unlock her; in a moment, the giant black cock was buried to the hilt in her wet quim, and the man's buttocks thrust and slapped like muscled ebony pistons.

A servant slid amongst them, bearing champagne, and spoke in a humble voice. Edwina started in recognition.

'Why, Juliet!' she cried. 'I haven't seen you since that wonderful production of *The Drudges* at Oxford, and here you are – a perfect drudge yourself!'

'Not a drudge, mistress,' said Juliet Haize modestly. 'A queen – and the master's, here, forever! I bear his lock.'

She was attired only in a severe rubber corset which forced her breasts up tight and high, so that her nipples were almost at the level of her chin, and the squeezed breasts formed a little platform. To the nipples was clamped a chain which passed around the neck and supported them, and on the platform of her breasts she balanced the champagne tray. Her hands were bound behind her back in an 'opera glove' and her ankles were tied to a short stretch bar, so that on her perilously high heels, she could only hobble. She nodded down to her naked shaven quim: between the full pink lips of her quim hung a golden padlock.

'This is realism, mistresses,' she said proudly. 'I may call you mistresses, now that you have passed your tests and become true slaves. I dare say that, like me, you have felt homesick from time to time. But what is home but an idea of home? Mayfair is home, for it is real. And now, mistresses, please punish my insolence in addressing you uninvited.'

Miss Mann, without pausing in her submission to her lustful partner, unfastened her jewelled cane, which she handed up to an astonished Jane Reculver. Juliet twitched her bare bottom expectantly and, with a straight face, not spilling a drop of champagne, she took nine strokes very tight across her bare buttocks, making no sound except a deep sigh of satisfaction and little murmurs of 'Yes, O yes . . .' As her punishment was completed, the writhing body of Miss Mann burst into a spasm, as though the caning of another's fesses had triggered her own ecstasy.

Juliet smiled and said that great things were afoot; there was to be an alliance between Mayfair Plantation and the kingdom of the Maroons. Mimsy pointed to the great ship as it drew nearer, and wailed that she never wanted to leave and that she was sure the ship was coming to drag her away – from her true home!

'It's all dollars and cents,' she said bitterly. 'I don't think I can afford to stay!'

Edwina comforted her, and said that money should not be a problem; against Mimsy's virtuous protests, she said the English ladies should club together to help their colonial cousin. But that was not the problem; there was no point in paying to be slaves if the master spurned their enslavement.

Miss Mann rose, and said she was sure the master did want them as his slaves, else why should he have honoured them by personally flogging them on the flagpole? There were other ways of paying for enslavement than money or jewels, and was not a woman's body the finest jewel she could offer? As sluts, they had tasted their animal freedom and jigged freely in the field with any cock they desired. As true slaves, their locked quims would belong to the master alone.

'He may poke for hours, in slit and bum too, and bring a girl to spend after spend, but he will never grace you with his own spend,' she said breathlessly. 'You are used, like an empty vessel of your own pleasure. It is so contemptuous, so humiliating – so wonderful. Now I must return, and be locked again in his possession.'

They watched her address the master, who sealed her quim once more with his key. Then he approached them, accompanied by the tattooed beauty of Queen Orchid, attended by her duchesses Sweetbread, Blossom and Floella Tarnishe, all dainty in their frilly maid's uniforms, with Floella proudly sporting a maroon ribbon of seniority. They surveyed the girls, who had unconsciously formed a line and stood demurely with heads bowed.

'You see, mistress,' said Peake, 'they are a fine crop of English sluts. I think they should make a good dowry for the marriage of our two kingdoms.'

The girls raised eyebrows: their master had addressed a female as mistress! Now he addressed them.

'You sluts have performed well. You have been broken to submission by the just regime of my plantation; you have been trained to endless, severe and unremitting punishment, and have learned to inflict it without mercy on each other's bodies, in the manner of a true slave, for whom the body is merely a vessel of its master's appetite. You have submitted to the drudgery of the field, but have freely taken the cocks of every

244

male, proving there is joyful lustful freedom even amid hardship. But a slave must belong only to her master. I am prepared to deem you true slaves and offer you sojourn here: when you accept to be locked in submission.'

Mrs Doofar's expertise pierced their quim-lips in brief time and not too painfully, and an hour later the girls lined up nervously to receive their locks. Mrs Doofar carried a tray of golden padlocks, from which each slave girl selected one, and threaded it through the new perforations of her quim, then snapped it shut. The company was still at jump-up, and the revelry was too lively to be interrupted, but amid the writhing bare bodies, all faces were turned to witness the spectacle of the new slaves' supreme obeisance. Eyes were also turned to the jewelled lights of the ship at anchor now, and a small boat which seemed to be heading for the beach.

Peake stripped off his uniform and made himself naked, handing his raiment to Pulchinella. When he stood nude before his new slaves, he bowed courteously, and his cock rose smoothly to its full erection. All females gasped as the bright orchid flowered on his manhood. Then he passed along the line of raised skirts, holding two keys. He gave the first key to each girl, allowing her to lock herself in submission, then took it back. When each girl was locked, she was permitted to make obeisance, kneel and kiss the tip of her master's erect cock. When the ceremony was complete, he took his clothes back from Pulchinella and, dressed once more, handed Orchid the second key.

'My slaves are your slaves, Mistress Orchid,' he said.

The orgiasts now interrupted their jump-up to cheer loudly, and the girls of the dungeon smiled in utter bliss as they touched their shiny new emblems of enslavement. But the cheers died in puzzlement as the company parted to allow the passage of a stranger: a tall young woman with flowing russet hair, cocooned in a sumptuous white leather cape, accompanied by a second female with long blonde hair and a fetching party frock of lemon-yellow.

'Not so fast,' said a cool English voice, with a slight American lilt. 'I believe that is the correct phrasing. Well, well, what a merry rabble I have inherited.'

The reaction of Peake was astonishing. His mouth gaped, he trembled, and his face blushed fiery red.

'Miss . . . Miss Rattan!' he gasped.

With imperious nonchalance, she divested her cape and flung it at him.

'Make yourself useful, boy,' she said. 'I came dressed for the party . . . My, you *are* a confusion! I guess you haven't been properly attended to.'

She flexed a coiled horsewhip, also of white leather, which nestled at her belt. Under the cape, she wore a dazzling white satin corset, like a skimpy swimsuit; it clung to her body's curves like paint, revealing every detail of her ripe fesses and fount, while her breasts were pushed forward by a conical, pointed brassière built into the corselage, above a waist thinned impossibly by the invisible armour of her costume. The narrowness of her wasp-waist threw the full peaches of her croup into magnificent relief.

There were three apertures visible in her wasp-costume; at her fount and at the tips of each thrust-out breast, so that nipples and quim-lips were exposed. Her own quim was pierced. From it a golden chain snaked through piercings on the big purple plums of each nipple, formed a golden necklace and then married the wide orbs of her earrings.'As you can see, ladies,' she said, 'I am my own slave.'

Orchid glowered at the intruder.

Miss Rattan addressed Peake.

'To business, you scruffy little boy,' she said briskly but not without kindness. 'In a nutshell, all this belongs to me. Mr Harold F. Parkhurst tragically passed away, in a hunting accident – although what there is to hunt in the South Bronx escapes me – and left me a rather wealthy widow. I never realised how much whisky people could drink. Such a lot of money, and in so many places! Bermuda, the Bahamas, London . . . Well, I am quite tuckered out from globetrotting, and figured I just needed a little bolthole where Mr Harold F. Parkhurst's business associates would not come around with their tiresome affections. And in Foulkes's Bank in London, I met dear Jasmine here, who told me all about you, Peake. I paid the mortgage, lock, stock and barrel, the very moment of foreclosure. You *have* been a lazy boy! And an impudent one . . . But I'm sure it's nothing that can't be whipped out of you.'

Orchid reached out a restraining hand; Miss Rattan jerked it aside furiously.

'Not so fast, *you*,' sneered Orchid. 'I am queen of the Maroons, and my kingdom is married to Mayfair.'

'Well, you can get divorced straightaway,' snapped Miss Rattan, 'if you don't want to feel good cowhide on that bare arse of yours. My maid Jasmine has the documents, and you will find I am in complete legality.'

Orchid's handmaidens looked venomously at the quivering Jasmine and Miss Rattan, who had regained her haughtiness.

'On the island of St Botolph, it is the Maroons who are legality,' hissed Orchid. 'And our way is to fight.'

Miss Rattan opened her eyes in mock astonishment, and said that she supposed the lady wished to wrestle for supremacy. Orchid said that was so.

'How quaint,' said Miss Rattan. 'Well, if it will humour you, miss. I suppose we should fight naked, just the two of us. My gold chain is too valuable to break, and the nearest decent jeweller is in Miami. You will undoubtedly beat me, but it will be instructive, I'm sure, for my future as mistress. We should keep our whips, to add spice.'

She spoke the last sentence with deadly seriousness, and as the women stripped, Orchid retorted that she would have no future on the island, for she would be whipped back to her damn boat, and her documents shoved where they belonged.

'Dear me,' said Miss Rattan mildly, her nude body glimmering in the starlight.

Suddenly her leg flashed up and Orchid groaned from a savage kick to her belly, which was followed immediately by a chop to her breasts. She staggered, and Miss Rattan got her in a headlock, holding her bent double while she kicked her fount and teats with lightning blows.

'You are familiar with South Chicago rules?' said Miss Rattan pleasantly. 'Good. I thought so.'

The combat did not last long, and after five minutes of frenzied kicking, grappling, twisting and pinching, Miss Rattan had Orchid firmly pinioned face-down on the dirt, with her legs kicking helplessly and her arms pinned behind her. Miss Rattan invited her to submit, and was refused.

'Well, I have no choice,' she sighed, unhooking her coiled whip from her waist. It was too long for deft use at close quarters, so she folded it in half and began to whip Orchid's naked buttocks. Orchid hissed and spat as the tongues of the whip empurpled her bare skin, but she was helpless. Time after time, she was called on to submit, each time answering a contemptuous, 'Never!' The flogging continued, Miss Rattan's arm untiring and her breasts bouncing like metronomes at each lash, until the whole company was watching this wondrous display of power. The Englishwoman *must* be the new mistress, went the murmurs.

Orchid's bottom was a living dance of pain, her skin deep purple and even black where Miss Rattan had flogged her most cruelly in her cleft and on the soft inner thighs. At length, Orchid's quiverings grew lifeless, her bottom jumping as though she were no more than a rag doll being chastised, and she sobbed that she submitted. But Miss Rattan, caught in the hypnotic rhythm of her whipping, continued to flog the naked victim, calm of mien but with real fury in her eyes.

'Mistress, desist, I beg you,' said Peake. 'The woman has submitted.'

'The slut must be taught a lesson,' said Miss Rattan evenly, and continued her beating. The crowd grew uneasy as Orchid's inert body continued to jerk under her cruel beating. Yet a pool of shining liquid was clearly visible, flowing from her naked fount! Suddenly, Orchid's head rose and she howled, not in anguish, but in a deep spasm of tormented submission and joy. Miss Rattan rose and faced Peake, who suddenly surprised her, grasping her waist and bringing her to the ground, where he pressed her face to the dirt, and kept his foot on her neck. She had time for only one squeal before he spoke.

'You have won, Miss Rattan, and you're to be my mistress, and the mistress of Mayfair – but you said yourself that sluts must be taught a lesson. You continued to flog Orchid after she had submitted, and that was jolly unfair.'

'I asked for it,' said Orchid, panting.

'Never mind. It was improper. You are not yet mistress of Mayfair, Miss Rattan. You have not formally taken possession from me. I know that, when you do, you will be vengeful to me a hundredfold. But, for the moment, I must chastise you. A lady must not be improper.'

Miss Rattan twisted her head and stopped squirming. Her eyes opened wide, as if awaking.

'You are right,' she whispered. 'I was improper. Flog me, master. Make my bare bum dance.'

Peake delivered fifty whip-strokes to Miss Rattan's naked fesses. At each stroke she moaned softly, as though in love, and the waves of her russet hair flowed in time to her croup's dance. When it was over, he helped her rise, and said the new mistress of Mayfair must now take possession. Miss Rattan smiled and rubbed her crimson bottom.

'My, she said, 'you flog hard for such an inky little squirt. Right, sir! Let us have that ridiculous uniform off, and get you into something more tasteful.'

Her eyes lighted on Floella.

'You, miss! You would look good in his uniform, as he would in yours. Be so good as to swap.'

Peake was arrayed in the full panoply of a French maid and led to the flagpole, where Miss Rattan said breezily that he knew the drill. He bent over and lifted his skirt to bare his bum. She let him wait, shivering, while she donned her white satin corsetry.

'You were right, boy,' she said, stroking his bare buttocks with her palm. 'I do feel vengeful, and something else, too. It is a long time since I had such a lovely bum to chastise. I suppose you have been spurting in all these girls, and that too deserves chastisement.'

Peake protested fiercely that he had waited.

'Surely not for me, you insolent boy?' said Miss Rattan softly, lifting her whip.

In total silence, Peake took one hundred and twenty lashes over the period of an hour. When his buttocks were aflame, and tears streaming down his cheeks, Miss Rattan took hold of his throbbing, stiff cock and proudly displayed him.

'People,' cried Peake, 'I bid you welcome the new mistress of Mayfair, who shall henceforth wield the whip and hold the key to all slaves, of which I am first.'

As cheers rang out, the new mistress received her first supplicant. It was Orchid, queen of the Maroons, who begged to make obeisance, and take the lock at her own fount.

'Mayfair and Maroons must still be married,' she murmured, 'but in the marriage of mistress and maid.'

Edwina led the new slaves in offering obeisance to the new mistress, while Ragamuffin, with a naked girl happily squirming on his horn, boomed 'Here Comes the Bride'.

'Susie, why did you take Peake's flogging?' said Edwina.

'Peake was right. I should have asked Orchid's permission before continuing her chastisement. Women alone can be broody and imbalanced, and I . . . I have been too long without a male. A mistress needs the male cock to serve her, to tame her: small matter whether the male acts as slave or master. It is the balance of nature, dear Edwina.'

She cupped Peake's balls and squeezed them, then pulled him towards her by his stiff cock and kissed his cheek.

'And to balance *my* nature, this beastly, wicked, smutty schoolboy shall henceforth be my slave.'

'Your *adoring* slave, mistress,' Peake interrupted. 'Ouch! That hurt!'

Envoi

Binky Bevercon wiped the sweat from his brow as he dropped his suitcase and rang the doorbell at Mayfair. The door was opened by a svelte young maid in a black frilly uniform. A fine gold chain trailed curiously from between her thighs.

'I'm looking for a chum of mind, Thomas Peake,' he began. 'I was just in the neighbourhood, and –' He stopped in embarrassment.

'In the neighbourhood! That's a bit thick, Binky, but you are welcome.'

'Peake!' cried Binky. 'Well I never! You do look well. Quite a sparkle in your eye, old boy.'

Binky was admitted, bathed, fed and, to his delight, encouraged to change into 'proper clothes'. He described his adventures in coming to St Botolph in a roundabout way: a series of 'misunderstandings' with horse-racing gentlemen which made it appropriate to seek sunnier climes.

'Biarritz – some shady characters there; Monte – too hot in every way. Europe quite on the blink, old boy. Then lovely Leslie suggested I might meet some like-minded spirits *chez* Peake in the West Indies, where they wouldn't mind me dressing up, as it were. It's rather fun, isn't it? I say, I met this awfully nice cove in Peake Town, name of Spuzzy, and it seems he has a telegraph link to the racetrack in Antigua, and, well, there's this dead cert – you couldn't see your way to lending me ten dollars? Rest assured I haven't given away any secrets, old boy.'

'There are quite a lot of us here in proper dress, Binky,' Peake said with a smile, 'and few secrets. It comes of being slaves of such a stern mistress. Miss Susan Rattan, of Newton Abbot School for Young Ladies.'

'Does she whack a lot?' said Binky.

'Every day. More.'

'Gosh.'

Binky's eyes shone. He remarked that there seemed to be quite a lot of 'spiffing totty' with not many clothes on.

'They too are slaves. And they too are lashed on the bare. It is a privilege. We are all slaves in truth, Binky. All padlocked or chained by something, even as prisoners of our own desires. The trick is to find our most fruitful enslavement! That perhaps explains the sparkle in my eye. For too long I fancied myself a master, chastising the naked flesh of willing, even adoring females, and handsomely rewarded for it. But I know that all the time I was seeking to recapture the blissful moment when Miss Susan Rattan first whipped me, and placed me forever in her power.'

Peake paused, then said shyly, 'I am no longer a virgin, Binky. I belong to Miss Rattan in every way. She even has a special name to mock me and teach me my place. She calls me "Eulalia". And forever I shall be chastised for bearing the tattoo of another.'

He lifted his skirts and showed Binky his naked, tattooed cock, which had a gold ring pierced right through the helmet. To the gold ring was attached the little chain.

'That is called an "Albert", he said, 'and is very fashionable in certain London sets. Miss Rattan attaches me so that when indoors I am always at her service.'

'Women!' said Binky, drawing heavily on his cigarette. 'You know, Peake, I've had some fun, but I'm still no nearer to understanding them. What *do* they want?'

'There is no point in trying to understand what women want, Binky,' Peake said. 'The only important thing is to give it to them. Here is ten dollars for you. Don't worry – submitting to Miss Rattan's lesson, you'll earn it!'

There was a twitch on the golden chain that bound Peake's cock-ring to Miss Rattan's chamber. The master selected a stout cane, and went contentedly to attend his mistress.

NEW BOOKS

Coming up from Nexus and Black Lace

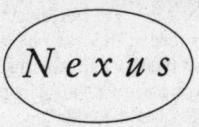

There are three Nexus titles published in September

The Black Garter by Lisette Ashton

September 1998   Price £5.99   ISBN: 0 352 33283 2

The cruel Hera leads the Black Garter with a merciless hand. Her elite group of prefects secretly patrols Hera's finishing school, helping her to administer cruel and degrading punishments whenever Hera deems it necessary. New recruits are subjected to humiliating initiations, but the prize of acceptance makes it a sacrifice worth enduring. When a spate of scandals hits the school, private investigator Jo Valentine is called in to find the source of the incidents. She soon discovers that the finishing school is no place for a lady.

New Erotica 4 Various

September 1998   Price £5.99   ISBN: 0 352 33290 5

In this, the long-awaited fourth volume of a best-selling series, we have collected together the best extracts from the finest and most erotic Nexus titles from the last two years. Here naughty girls are chastised by whip-wielding mistresses, young innocents are trained in the art of giving pleasure, and masters and slaves act out their darkest and deepest fantasies. In its variety of settings and styles, this unmissable collection features a fantasy to arouse every reader.

Susie in Servitude by Arabella Knight

September 1998   Price £5.99   ISBN: 0 352 33146 1

Under the stern tutelage of Madame Savage, Susie, a trainee corsetière, soon discovers that discipline is always in vogue, regardless of whether she is measuring clients intimately for a basque, or providing special other services at the Rookery, madame's private establishment. Forced to deal with jealous rivalries and intrigue, Susie nevertheless comes to appreciate the strict enforcement of madame's cardinal rule – that the customer must always come first. This is a new edition of one of Nexus's most popular tales of correction.

'S' – *A Journey into Servitude* by Philippa Masters
October 1998   Price £5.99   ISBN: 0 352 33286 7

S's descent into total submission continues with this, the second volume in an exciting new series. Here she is taken to her master's palace and displayed as his plaything. As her disciplined training continues, she becomes more and more skilled at pleasuring her master and his friends, taking a perverse pleasure in having her sexuality rigidly controlled. But she yearns for a sign of affection from him – will he ever be able to admit his attachment to her?

Darline Dominant by Tania d'Alanis
October 1998   Price £5.99   ISBN: 0 352 33287 5

When Darline Pomeroy engages the submissive young Patrick to be her boy-maid, he is made to serve her in many humiliating ways. He must wear women's clothes, paint Darline's nails and perform household chores; if he makes any mistakes he is whipped or caned. Darline introduces him to a number of her dominatrix friends, who delight in teaching him the rules of good and ladylike comportment.

BLACK *lace*

There are three Black Lace titles published in September

Darker than Love by Kristina Lloyd
September 1998   Price £5.99   ISBN: 0 352 33279 4

1875. The morality of Queen Victoria means nothing to London's wayward and debauched elite. Clarissa Longleigh is young, beautiful and unworldly and is visiting London for the first time. She is eager to meet Lord Marldon, the man to whom she is promised, knowing only that he is handsome, dark and sophisticated. He is, in fact, depraved and louche and has a taste for sexual cruelty. In a summer of decadent parties he resolves to rouse Clarissa's innermost desires and satisfy her in a way no other man can.

Risky Business by Lisette Allen
September 1998   Price £5.99   ISBN: 0 352 33280 8

Liam is a working-class journalist fighting a battle against environmental injustices. Rebecca is a spoilt rich girl used to having whatever and whoever she wants. Their lives collide passionately when Liam, on the run from a furious enemy, hijacks Rebecca's car. They are forced into a dangerous intimacy with each other and she finds it difficult to resist Liam's charms and dark desires – will she ever admit how strong her lust for him really is?

Dark Obsession by Fredrica Alleyn
September 1998   Price £7.99   ISBN: 0 352 33281 6

Interior designer Annabel Moss is commissioned to revamp the luxury home of Lord and Lady Corbett-Wynne. Lord James, Lady Marina, their family and their subservient staff maintain a veneer of respectability over some highly esoteric sexual practices. No one who stays with them can avoid becoming embroiled in their high-class games of debauchery – least of all someone as kinky as Annabel. This is a new edition of one of the most popular Black Lace books.

Undercover Secrets by Zoe le Verdier

October 1998   Price £5.99   ISBN: 0 352 33285 9

Anna Caplin is a twenty-seven-year-old television researcher working on *Undercover* – an investigative current affairs programme. She is ambitious and determined to use whatever means she can to crack a story. When her boss offers her the chance to infiltrate a secret medical research laboratory, she grabs the opportunity, not realising the dangers she is letting herself in for. The institute's director has sinister sexual motives and it isn't too long before Anna is being subjected to some highly unorthodox tests.

Searching for Venus by Ella Broussard

October 1998   Price £5.99   ISBN: 0 352 33284 0

Spirited and naughty Louise is in the final year of her art history degree. She intends to track down a lost painting for her dissertation, and soon finds herself involved in a series of highly-charged erotic liaisons as she searches around rural France. From the earthily lustful rustic to the debauched sophisticate, she encounters lascivious partners who introduce her to ever darker and more unusual pleasures.

Nexus

NEXUS BACKLIST

All books are priced £4.99 unless another price is given. If a date is supplied, the book in question will not be available until that month in 1998.

CONTEMPORARY EROTICA

THE ACADEMY	Arabella Knight		
AGONY AUNT	G. C. Scott		
ALLISON'S AWAKENING	Lauren King		
AMAZON SLAVE	Lisette Ashton	£5.99	
THE BLACK GARTER	Lisette Ashton	£5.99	Sept
THE BLACK ROOM	Lisette Ashton		
BOUND TO OBEY	Amanda Ware	£5.99	Dec
BOUND TO SUBMIT	Amanda Ware		
CANDIDA IN PARIS	Virginia Lasalle		
CHAINS OF SHAME	Brigitte Markham	£5.99	July
A CHAMBER OF DELIGHTS	Katrina Young		
DARK DELIGHTS	Maria del Rey	£5.99	Aug
DARLINE DOMINANT	Tania d'Alanis	£5.99	Oct
A DEGREE OF DISCIPLINE	Zoe Templeton		
THE DISCIPLINE OF NURSE RIDING	Yolanda Celbridge	£5.99	Nov
THE DOMINO TATTOO	Cyrian Amberlake		
THE DOMINO QUEEN	Cyrian Amberlake		
EDEN UNVEILED	Maria del Rey		
EDUCATING ELLA	Stephen Ferris		
EMMA'S SECRET DOMINATION	Hilary James		
FAIRGROUND ATTRACTIONS	Lisette Ashton	£5.99	Dec
THE TRAINING OF FALLEN ANGELS	Kendal Grahame		
HEART OF DESIRE	Maria del Rey		

ANCIENT & FANTASY SETTINGS

THE CLOAK OF APHRODITE	Kendal Grahame		
DEMONIA	Kendal Grahame		
THE DUNGEONS OF LIDIR	Aran Ashe		
THE FOREST OF BONDAGE	Aran Ashe		
NYMPHS OF DIONYSUS	Susan Tinoff		
THE WARRIOR QUEEN	Kendal Grahame	£5.99	Dec

EDWARDIAN, VICTORIAN & OLDER EROTICA

ANNIE	Evelyn Culber	£5.99	
ANNIE AND THE COUNTESS	Evelyn Culber	£5.99	
BEATRICE	Anonymous		
THE CORRECTION OF AN ESSEX MAID	Yolanda Celbridge	£5.99	
DEAR FANNY	Michelle Clare		
LYDIA IN THE HAREM	Philippa Masters		
LURE OF THE MANOR	Barbra Baron		
MAN WITH A MAID 3	Anonymous		
MEMOIRS OF A CORNISH GOVERNESS	Yolanda Celbridge		
THE GOVERNESS AT ST AGATHA'S	Yolanda Celbridge		
MISS RATTAN'S LESSON	Yolanda Celbridge	£5.99	Aug
PRIVATE MEMOIRS OF A KENTISH HEADMISTRESS	Yolanda Celbridge		
SISTERS OF SEVERCY	Jean Aveline		

SAMPLERS & COLLECTIONS

EROTICON 3	Various		
EROTICON 4	Various	£5.99	July
THE FIESTA LETTERS	ed. Chris Lloyd		
NEW EROTICA 2	ed. Esme Ombreux		
NEW EROTICA 3	ed. Esme Ombreux		
NEW EROTICA 4	ed. Esme Ombreux	£5.99	Sept

NON-FICTION

Please send me the books I have ticked above.

Name ....

Address ....

....

....

.... Post code.......................

Send to: **Cash Sales, Nexus Books, Thames Wharf Studios, Rainville Road, London W6 9HT**

Please enclose a cheque or postal order, made payable to **Nexus Books**, to the value of the books you have ordered plus postage and packing costs as follows:

UK and BFPO – £1.00 for the first book, 50p for the second book and 30p for each subsequent book to a maximum of £3.00;

Overseas (including Republic of Ireland) – £2.00 for the first book, £1.00 for the second book and 50p for each subsequent book.

If you would prefer to pay by VISA or ACCESS/MASTER-CARD, please write your card number and expiry date here:

....

Please allow up to 28 days for delivery.

Signature ....